BACK FROM THE DEAD RED

also by
Sara Harris

House of Madness
Katie's Plain Regret
As it Pleases the King

BACK FROM THE DEAD RED

Mistress of the Sea
Book 1

SARA HARRIS

WordCrafts Press

Although a work of fiction, ***Back from the Dead Red*** is based on actual events. The author has endeavored to be respectful to all persons, places, and events presented in this novel, and attempted to be as accurate as possible. Still, this is a novel, and all references to persons, places and events are fictitious or used fictitiously.

Back from the Dead Red
Copyright © 2021
Sara Harris

ISBN: 978-1-952474-90-3

Cover concept and design by Mike Parker.

Published by WordCrafts Press
Cody, Wyoming 82414
www.wordcrafts.net

*To those gypsy souls who always look to the past before
stepping into the future—this book is for you.
You are my people.*

Chapter One

1717, Swansea, Wales

Murmurs from the crowd, all gathered into the stuffy Welsh church to witness my wedding to the fat, hairy-eared copper baron Charles Hoolihan, quieted as I stepped onto the plush carpet that had been laid out especially for this day.

Nothing too good for my Drucilla. Charles' words, trembly with age, echoed in my mind. A hint of nausea burned the back of my throat at the prospect as to what awaited me tonight. I would finally be alone with my suitor-turned-husband, who was easily twice my age. And I wasn't exactly a young maid myself.

The blood red carpet stretched before me, down the length of the aisle, before ending abruptly beneath the pale cross that hung on the far wall. Sea-inspired tapestries, specially commissioned and hung for today, covered the church walls and gave the room a foamy blue feel. The colormen Charles had brought in from England had certainly delivered on their job.

I tugged at the waist of my simple dress, smoothing imaginary wrinkles. Charles had suggested I wear a billowy dress, in accordance with his opulent social standing here in Swansea's society. We had even gone to the dressmaker and chosen a fluffy pattern. But in the end, I'd opted for this clamshell white frock, something like a schoolmarm might wear, that hung straight down to the floor. It accented none of my feminine features and promised the same. Charles had grinned through tight lips and patted my shoulder when I made my choice, but I still walked out with the dress I picked.

I swallowed hard. My clammy palms tightened around the spray of flowers I clutched. Already, they were beginning to wilt. The long lace veil that couldn't be adjusted to cover the blade scar on my cheek may well have been a veil of iron fitted over my hair. All around the edges, my coal black mane insisted on peeking out wherever it could, clamoring for freedom.

Bright sunshine broke through the dismal clouds that had masked the day and shone through the balcony doors that were graciously left open. Just below, white capped swells of the north Atlantic crashed over the rocky bank in tune with my pounding heart. A sudden breeze swept over the balcony and through the open doors. I sucked in the air, heavy with salt, as a seagull cried in the distance. If I was still of a crying sort, I would have let go a tear or two now. But all my tears dried up long ago.

I surveyed the room with a wary eye. No family, since I had none. No friends, since I had none of those left, either. The faces of women whose names I didn't know beamed from the church pews.

Fat aristocrats, all of them.

None of them would have offered me a penny when I was down and out in the poorhouse of Swansea. Not a good morrow nor even a smile. At least, not until Charles Hoolihan, the richest man in Wales, took a shine to me. Now, here they sat, grinning at me as though an invitation to tea was about to fly off each of their pursed, wrinkled lips. They knew as well as I that once the vows were said, I would be a richer woman than the entire lot of them put together.

I kept my face stoic and stared back at them.

Beneath the pale cross that dominated the far wall, Charles hobbled out and took his place next to the minister. His jagged, stumpy teeth peeked out from under his uneven moustache, even when he wasn't smiling, and his chubby hands were clasped at his middle. A golden-handled sword hung at his side and he kept shifting his hefty weight, like a man uncomfortable wearing a blade.

I'd known men like him before. They were the easiest to kill. But those days were behind me, a memory so distant, that at times, I wasn't certain the memories belonged to me. The blade scars on my face and neck reminded me that they were in fact mine to cherish.

You'll make new memories. The tiny voice inside me sounded positive and certain. *Finally, you'll be a woman of wealth and stature. A respectable woman.*

On a signal I obviously missed, a handful of the wedding-goers stood in unison. My eyes widened as one woman, wrapped in a pink shawl, strode over to the large harp that sat indiscriminately in the corner and eased herself down on the seat. She strummed an eloquent series of notes before the rest of the standing women began to sing.

Is that The Song of the White Piper?

A gnarled grandmotherly woman appeared at my side. "Go ahead dear, it's time."

I didn't look at the old woman as I exhaled the breath I'd unwittingly been holding. Steeling my backbone, I began the slow steps down the red carpet. Alone.

Three more steps. You can do this.

He's a good man, I'm sure.

He'll never do me wrong and I'll want for nothing the rest of my days.

Charles, who I more often than not mistakenly called Mr. Hoolihan, grinned from beneath the cross. I couldn't look in his rheumy, hopeful eyes and focused just over his shoulder as thoughts swirled in my mind. The tapestry on which I focused featured a large wooden ship amid the frothy swells of the sea. Towering masts, billowing sails, and a jungle of ratlines made this tapestry my favorite. I searched the image for a Jolly Roger, or even that of a heavy bodied and bare-breasted woman, but found none. Still, my lips refused to turn up into a smile on what should be the happiest day of my life.

The harpist silenced, and the women took their seats as I stepped to Charles' side. So quiet was the church that I wasn't entirely sure I was breathing. I forced a swallow as the minister opened his mouth to speak.

The back door of the church met the wall with a crash and made me jump. Color heated my cheeks and I spun on my heel, my bouquet all but crushed in my grasp. There, in the outline of the doorway, stood a man clad in black.

His tall boots folded over just below his knees and his matching black waistcoat and britches took my breath. I blinked, then blinked again.

A ghost? A gasp hitched in my throat. His *ghost*.

Chapter Two

Seventeen Years Earlier, London, England

ntry fee, sir." The large, muscular man that looked as though he threw heavy loads since the day he was born stared down at me from beneath his furrowed brow. He extended his hand. "Now."

I stuck my hand in my pocket and fingered the tattered wanted poster that filled it. "You see," I began, trying to hide my Russian accent by clearing my eighteen-year-old throat. "I was unaware of the requirement of an entry fee."

"Then off with you, you unlicked cub," he growled. "You can't pay, you can't come into White's Chocolate House."

I ignored the insult and stepped aside, my heart thumping in my chest. "I understand your job here is important," I stammered. *Mikhail,* I thought to myself, *you haven't come this far for nothing.*

The large man didn't pay me any mind as he extended his hand to a gentlemanly sort of fellow in a tricorne beaver hat. The man slipped a pound into the large man's hand and strode inside the elite establishment.

"It costs a pound just to set foot in the door?" My eyes widened. "All chocolate drinks included, I pray."

"'Course not, them's extra," the doorman grumbled. "Now pay up or clear off."

Another patron paid the man and walked inside. I chewed my lip and stared after him. My entire reason for making the journey from Russia to London seemed further away now than it had on the icy Moscow street. I wet my dry lips and cleared my throat again. "Sir," I began, stepping nearer to the brutish doorman, "I cobbled streets in Moscow for a year to save up enough to buy myself passage here to London. Didn't count on having to pay extra fees once I arrived."

The man shifted his uncaring gaze to me, spurring me on.

"I have business with a man inside, I'll only be a moment."

He sighed loudly. "If you are entering the chocolate house, the entry fee is one pound." His gaze hardened. "Except for you. For you, the fee is *two* pounds."

"Pardon?"

His stare turned frosty. "One pound for the establishment. One pound for me. For having to listen to your sad tale and look upon you, you tatterdemalion."

I glanced down at my shirt and breeches, each made by my mother's own hand before her death. Patchwork, they were, consisting of pieced together squares of wayward calico. The man was right. I was a disheveled sight to look upon.

A man, dressed in shiny black silk and a large white wig, sporting golden rings in a rainbow of colors on his fingers, strode up. He and his entourage, all sporting golden earrings, stopped short and stared.

"I don't have two pounds, I don't even have one pound—" I began.

A sharp slap from the man stung my face. "Then be gone with you!"

I set my throbbing jaw. "My business inside will take but a moment—"

The man drew back his hand again, but this time I was ready. I ducked his open-handed slap and readied myself into a fighting stance, eliciting a whistle and whoop from the group of ogling men.

"Two pounds on the blond boy," one of the men yelled.

Another answered, "Five on the lobcock—er, the money-taker!"

The group of rapscallions, headed by the man in black, burst into a drunken cacophony of laughter. The burly doorman's face went scarlet as the men waiting to gain entrance made sport of our predicament.

I swallowed back the hot fear that burned my throat and tried to figure a way out of this mess. The man in black, thankfully, stepped to my side.

"Good heavens," he began. "For a sprout the likes of you having the gall to take on an oaf the likes of him—" He turned and gave a stony glance to the money-taker. "Your business must be quite important inside. It will be quite a sport just to see what becomes of you on the other side of these walls."

The man in black slid his arm around my shoulder and nodded to one of the men behind him, who paid the money-taker for the lot of us. He guided me inside, my heart still pounding.

"My name is Teach, Charles Teach." He gestured to the men who flanked us. "And these are my men. We are, how would you put it politely, regulators of goods that traverse the seas."

One of the men with next to no teeth leaned down near me with a grin. "We be pirates, we be."

I tried not to look afraid. All the way from Moscow to London, I'd heard of bands of sea-roving pirates who'd cut your throat as soon as look at you. Teach's name was one I'd heard of most. Night after night, I'd imagined what would happen when I finally arrived in London. Never had I figured I'd manage to fall into favor with Teach and his nest of pirates.

"I much appreciate your paying my entrance fee," I began, but Teach cut me off.

"I do not have a habit of loaning money to strangers without exacting something in return." His eyes glistened. "Tell me, what is your business here? If I am amused, consider your debt paid. If I am otherwise—" He shook his head and drew his finger across his neck.

I gulped as the other men laughed. My mother, despite her many flaws, had raised an honest son. "I am here to seek out my father."

Teach looked bored. "For what purpose?"

"After my mother died, it was my job to go through her things. I discovered a bundle of letters. And this." I withdrew the wanted poster from my pocket and held it out to Teach, who accepted it with renewed interest.

"I read the letters, all of which were to my father. They began as love letters, then turned to angry letters. Threatening, even. Stating if he ever came back to see us, she'd kill him. After reading more, I discovered that my father left her maimed after a night of beatings, during which his goal was to kill me. Now that I'm bigger and my mother is dead—"

I accepted the poster back from a speechless Teach. "I figured I'd give him the chance to try again."

"You say that your father is depicted here, on this poster?"

"I do."

"So your father is Stenka Razin, the most infamous Russian pirate in the world?"

"He is."

"Young man, I have sailed with your father many times, taken many ships. He is as cunning and ruthless—and deadly—as they come." A chorus of aye's rang out in harmonious tandem from Teach's men. "You won't kill him."

I blinked.

"He'll kill you."

I breathed in the scent of the chocolate house. It smelled as rich as its patrons. "Perhaps. Not much left for me to live for, aside from to kill him."

"Are you armed?" Teach asked. "With steel, I mean?"

"I plan to kill him with his own blade." I studied the ground, realizing how green my romantic plan, concocted under the stars amid vodka and smoke, sounded. I hoped I wasn't flushed schoolgirl red, as I had a tendency to do when embarrassed. "He deserves the humiliation," I mumbled.

"No doubt he does." Teach drew a thin blade from the sash about his middle. "Here, take this. I want to see entertainment, not a bloodbath. Now, at least you have a fighting chance."

I nodded and accepted the blade.

"I tell you what. I'll find your father for you. Who shall I tell him is calling?"

"His son, of course."

Teach's thin lips drew back over his teeth in a snarl. "I'm not an ignorant fool. Tell me your name."

"Mikhail Nemirovsky," I stammered to the tune of cackling pirates, "sir," I added in a whisper.

"That name will never do, especially in an outfit as *memorable* as yours." Teach crossed his arms and studied me through slitted eyes. "What was your mother's name?"

"Molly. Molly Nemirovsky Rackham."

"I see." Teach snapped his fingers loudly. At once, a waiter appeared with a platter of spicy-smelling chocolate drinks. Teach paid them no mind, the snap was for me. "From now until the day you die, which may well be today, you are to be known as Russian Jack Rackham."

Chapter Three

1717, Swansea, Wales

A silver, curved cutlass hung easily at his side as though it was simply another appendage he bore, and the tell-tale fur cap, complete with ear flaps, sat atop his head. His face was smooth, save the shadow of a beard, and his piercing green eyes threatened to burn clean through me.

A collective sigh rose from the women who filled the pews, and a few began to fan themselves.

The man's commanding presence ensured that the room's silence. Then, like a bursting storm cloud, the chatter arose from the women in the pews and filled the room.

"It's Russian Jack Rackham, dread pirate of the Atlantic!"

"It can't be. He's dead. Hanged in chains in London."

"No, not chains. Russian Jack was hanged in the gibbet in Derbyshire."

"The late Queen was known to favor certain pirates. Perhaps some in authority still do."

The black-clad pirate's full lips twitched as the murmurs swirled about the room like flies over a rotting corpse.

Lord above, that's no ghost.

I tore my gaze from his and glanced at Charles, who swallowed audibly. He returned my glance and drew his sword from its scabbard with shaky hands, probably for the first time. I closed my eyes at his ineptitude as Russian Jack's stare sizzled almost tangibly on my skin.

Charles fumbled with the handle of his sword before turning his attention to the unwelcome guest. "Wh-what do you want—sir?"

Russian Jack dragged his burning stare from me to Charles. Achingly slow, Jack drew his glittering cutlass from his scabbard and held it by the jewel encrusted handle for all to see.

The legendary life-taking cutlass that supposedly never left the hand of Russian Jack was as rich in jewels as rumors promised. It was widely whispered that the gems that adorned the handle of the sword, which had taken over a thousand lives, came from not only England, but also the Orient, and even the new world.

"I've no quarrel with you, sir." Jack's thick Russian accent rolled out over the aristocratic crowd like a hypnotic curse. A cutlass could be pillaged or stolen. An accent couldn't. There was no doubt that it was truly Russian Jack who stood before us.

A few women swooned.

Charles forced another swallow. A look of relief swept across his pale face.

The tall pirate tilted his chin and let his fabled cutlass fall with a clatter at his feet. "I have no quarrel with you, nor any here. I simply beg a word with Back from the Dead Red."

More gasps threatened to suck all the air from the room as Russian Jack touched his hat in true gentleman fashion. Slowly, he retreated onto the balcony, just out of sight.

Heat burned in my cheeks as all eyes in the room shifted to the girl who moments before was destined to become the copper king's blushing bride. Me. I glanced at Charles. He held his sword as though it was a crying infant.

So much for a fresh start.

I let out a huff and threw down the sad bouquet. Gathering my dress into my fists, I stomped back down the aisle.

Mouths mostly hung agape as I passed, but a few mutters still met my ears.

"I thought her name was Drucilla. Didn't Charles say her name was Drucilla?"

"Yes, and she is the daughter of a late English preacher—is she not?"

"Back from the Dead Red? Where have I heard that name before?"

I hesitated at the end of the plush aisle. Careful not to make eye contact with anyone, I stuck my toe under Jack's cutlass and flipped it expertly into my hand.

"I thought she looked familiar—that young woman has a wanted poster of her own!"

Ignoring them, I continued onto the balcony and slammed the doors behind me.

There, within the confines of the balcony with only the sounds of the sea lapping at the rocks below, I drank in the appearance of the notorious pirate. Leaned leisurely against the railing, Jack stared out to sea as though he didn't possess a care in the world. I cleared my throat and tried to ignore the odd sensation that tightened in my belly.

Russian Jack straightened his back and shifted his easy glance to me. "A woman with a blade. What a deadly combination."

I held out the cutlass to him, which he accepted almost gently. The corners of his full lips pulled up into a soft smile. "Hello, Red."

The tears I thought were forever dry returned with a vengeance as I flung myself into Russian Jack's waiting arms.

"Oh Jacky." I breathed in his exotic scent and felt my long-tight muscles relax for the first time in recent memory. "I thought you were dead."

"Dead? It was close—" Russian Jack's arms circled me as a gull cried in the distance. "But dead or not, I could not let my wife marry another man, now could I?"

Jack's breath was gentle on my hair as he took off my elegant veil. It was the only opulent piece of my wedding ensemble. Charles wouldn't be swayed in matters of the veil. Spanish lace to commemorate his late mother's heritage.

Jack admired it a moment then draped it gently over the balcony and took me back into his arms.

"Redella," he began with words as strong and commanding as ever, "do you remember how we met?"

The salty air was sweeter on the balcony in the arms of the man I loved and I allowed my lips to stretch into a wide smile. "How could I forget?"

He traced the scar on my cheek with his thumb, strumming it like the harpist had done the strings inside. "Seems you were about to marry the wrong man then, too. What were you, but seventeen?"

I let my mind drift back to those innocent days that seemed to have played out so many lifetimes ago—

Sullivan O'Brien, or Doctor O'Brien as he preferred to be called, checked the compass and turned the massive wooden wheel aboard *The Scarlet Rose*. His schooner skipped over the gentle waves as he turned us toward the open sea. "How do you feel about becoming Mrs. Doctor O'Brien once we reach Jamaica, Redella?"

My black hair tumbled down my back in twin plaits, well past my waist. Still, the little pieces that managed to escape flew this way and that, catching in my eyelashes and the corner of my mouth.

I didn't bother to ask why we couldn't wed in London. The first time I did, Sully reminded me with harsh words not to question a man's decision. Hours later, when his voice had returned to the velvety tones he used with everyone he considered beneath him, he'd explained that all his family would be in attendance in Jamaica—at least what was left of his family. The memory as to what had come next was fiercely fresh.

"Isn't your only living blood relative your brother? And he's sailing with us, is he not?"

Sully raised his hand as though he meant to slap into me the sense I obviously lacked.

I squeaked and raised my arms to shield my face. When I

dared open my eyes, Sully stood before me, hand still raised. He didn't strike, however, and simply walked away. I was lucky then, and I knew better than to mention it again now. I let my mind drift back to the present.

"Yes, of course." I batted at my wayward strands of hair and squinted against the full brightness of the midday sun before adding the last part. "Darling."

Sully's curly red hair billowed in the salty wind and he checked the compass again. "Darling. Ah, how I love when you say that." He offered me a wink. "If only your mother could see us now. It'd be her dream come true."

I chewed my lip. *Why did he have to say that?*

A pod of dolphins danced at the bow of the schooner and caught my attention. I stared at them as I thought about my beautiful mother Drucilla, taken all too soon.

"A tumor," Sully diagnosed shortly before she passed. "Which spread like a lamp oil fire, burning away healthy tissues and leaving many more tumors in its wake."

Her dying wish was that he would take care of me. I read it myself, scrawled on a piece of paper from her bedside table. Because, according to her, "the streets of London are no place for a young lady so sweet as Redella, my precious jewel of a girl."

And take care of me Sully intended to do.

The day of my mother's funeral, Sully presented me with a golden band and promised me forever. I'd never felt love before, so perhaps this feeling of security—though a bit pushy—was it.

As soon as the bags were packed and loaded onto *The Scarlet Rose*, it was settled. I was to be his wife. We would wed on an island beach. And I would live out my life pretending that my husband being closer to my mother's age than mine didn't bother me.

"Perhaps you would like a schooner of your very own as a wedding gift, hmm?"

His kind offer pulled me out of my dreary state, if only momentarily. I shifted my attention from the dolphins to my fiancé.

"You could even name it after your mother. The Drucilla Jerningham."

"Thank you." I forced a smile. "Darling."

He didn't return it.

I turned back to the water, an odd sensation in my stomach. Sea sickness? Perhaps. The sudden heaviness of the ocean air made breathing difficult, like sucking my breath through a damp cloth. I tried to ignore the worried feeling that clenched my gut and searched the water for any sign of the playful dolphins. One leapt, then the lot of the dolphin pod disappeared beneath the surf and didn't resurface.

"Take care now," Sully warned. "We're sailing into a fog."

"Why should I take care?" The words were out of my mouth before I could stop them.

Sully turned his full attention to me, as though I was a child in need of admonishing. Heat crept into my cheeks and I dropped my gaze to the deck.

"Oh," I stammered under his direct glare. "Forgive me, I simply meant what is there about a fog that's worrisome?" My heart thundered in my chest. Whether it was due to Sully or the thick air, I wasn't entirely sure.

Sully didn't answer but continued to stare at me until I met his eyes. Even then, he remained silent. It felt like an eternity.

"Good that you corrected yourself," he finally said. "No woman of mine will talk in such a brash manner to her betters. Ever. Understood?"

I nodded, though I would much rather have melted into a puddle on the deck and seeped between the boards, out from under his penetrating eyes. "I understand."

"You understand—what?"

I wracked my brain as a glint of sunlight flashed off the sword hanging at his side. I shivered and took slow, shallow breaths. "I understand. Darling."

Sully turned his attention back to the billowing gray fog that lay just before us, covering the water as far as the eye could see.

"The trouble with fog, my dear, is different for both of us. You see for me, there is the ever-present trouble of pirates. Scalawags who prefer to skulk about in the shadows and take that which is not theirs. For you—" He let go a throaty chuckle. "A silly girl like you may be in danger of falling overboard and drowning."

Sully's chuckle at my expense transformed into a deep, bellowing laugh as the soupy fog curled across the deck in fuzzy, beckoning fingers.

"Pirates?" I'd seen wanted posters in London, offering handsome sums for the lifeless bodies of such sea raiders as China Joe, Russian Jack, a fellow named Bluebeard and the infamous cutthroat Blackbeard himself. "Between England and Jamaica?"

"Yes. These are Blackbeard's waters, the same waters that transport Spanish riches between the Caribbean, Europe, and the New World." Sully studied the fog. "And everyone who's anyone knows that Blackbeard is a fiendish hound from hell who does the devil's work on earth. Or, should I say, on the water."

Redella placed her hands over her mouth and willed the burning swells of sea sickness to subside. "Do tell me more." *Anything to keep my mind occupied and off this infernal nausea.*

Sully looked thoughtful. "Well, there's China Joe, who prefers to keep the captain of overtaken vessels alive."

I hiccupped. "Alive? Why ever for?"

Sully looked sternly at me . "So as to torture them, of course."

I gulped.

A strange grin twisted his mouth into an odd, smiling shape. "Silly girl. Do you know nothing of the real world? Some men are rumored to have lingered alive for two agonizing weeks at the skilled hand of China Joe."

Sully had the capability of making me feel only inches tall, and stupid, when he spoke in such a manner. Whether he realized it or not, he seemed to become emboldened by the sound of his own voice.

"And don't let us forget Russian Jack Rackham, son of a filthy English whore and the godless Siberian pirate Vladimir

Nemirovsky." Sully spat into the thick fog that engulfed the deck. "Took his mother's last name. Still has a penchant for the whoring faction, like that mucky Bonney Anne of Ireland."

I rested my head on the side of *The Scarlet Rose* and closed my eyes. "I've heard of Irish Bon. Same woman?" I hiccupped again. It burned.

"Yes, that's right. Sailed beneath Russian Jack."

"He allowed a woman on board? Not bad luck?"

Sully shrugged. "She behaves like a man and is said to look like a man. So, he signed her on like a man. They had a falling out over a game of cards, I believe. Then Bon took to manning a whoring ship that caters to pirates." Sully squinted into the fog. "Enough talk of those cursed sea gypsies. Come here, Redella," he commanded. "Come near to my side where you're sure to be safe."

I prefer to be called Red. Not Redella, I thought. Thankfully, the thick grayness descended over *The Scarlet Rose* before I could push myself up from my seat. The world I'd known moments before disappeared.

"Redella?"

I thought briefly about hurling myself overboard. Perhaps the dolphins would be kind to me and take me back to shore. Or, the more likely scenario, perhaps I would get eaten by a shark.

"Redella!"

I imagined his freckled hand flying through the thick fog to strike me. I lifted my head and wrinkled my nose in what I figured to be his direction.

"Ignorant whelp you are! Answer me now!"

My thoughts turned back to the sharks that may or may not be circling *The Scarlet Rose*. I'd never been a strong swimmer, especially not stronger than a shark.

No, I won't make it. This, such as it is, is destined to be my life, so I may as well make the best of it.

"I'm here. *Darling*. I'm safe."

"Stay away from the railing," he growled.

I reached my arm over what I figured was the railing and wiggled my fingers. "Yes, Darling. I won't fall over."

"No," a foreign voice growled. "She won't be going anywhere."

Pirates.

My blood turned to ice within my very veins and my fingers froze in mid-wiggle as I tried to place the accent.

Not English pirates. Not Welsh—

The Scarlet Rose tipped and lurched as the anchor was hoisted over the side by unseen hands and splashed into the water below. My stomach lurched, too, and I vomited over the side. As the fog gave way to a gauzy mist, like when you're waking from a dream and you aren't sure what is real and what isn't, I realized the seasickness subsided a bit. The profile of a man, a burly, big man, filled my vision. I jerked my hand behind my back, lest Sully see that I'd been defiant about the railing.

Notorious pirates have taken The Scarlet Rose and you're more worried about Sully admonishing you? I tried to shush the small voice in my mind.

"You in command of this sloop?"

That accent is Russian.

Clad in black, the pirate towered over Sully and his words were like Russian hammers on an anvil. Hard. Unforgiving. Unrelenting. "By the sound of it, you wouldn't be the kind of man who would allow a mere slip of a girl like this one here—"

The pirate whipped his jeweled cutlass from its scabbard and pointed it toward me. Our eyes met. His, piercing green and mine, widened by the sight of him. I paid no attention whatsoever to the blade.

His physique was one of a man who hefted heavy loads for a living. Strong arms, a wide chest. An angular jaw gave the appearance of a man in charge, no matter the company he was in, be it governors—or pirates. A tall fur hat, like something sent back from the New World, sat on his head and looked as natural as the nose on his face. Wisps of blond hair that peeked out from beneath the gray fur were sun-bleached almost white.

A deep tan colored his face and his wide, full lips flickered into a smile.

Staring at me, he spoke to Sully. "No, you wouldn't let a *woman* like this command anything."

Something twisted in my stomach.

Not seasickness.

Fear perhaps?

No, I'd known fear. This wasn't it.

Before I could rationalize it further, he spoke again in his commanding tone.

Turning his full attention back to Sully, he slid his cutlass back into its sheath. The jeweled handle sparkled in the pinprick rays of light that shone through the fog. I exhaled the breath I didn't know I'd been holding.

"Give her no tasks, eh? For fear she'd do it better than you?"

Sully's pale face colored. "I'll thank you not to speak of my fiancée."

"Your *fiancée*?" He didn't look back at me though I continued to stare at him. Something in me wished he would meet my gaze again.

"Yes, my fiancé, you, you—" Sully stammered. "You—you brute!"

A chorus of rum-roughened laughter rang out from everywhere and joined that belonging to the man in the fur hat. There was no denying it, we'd been overrun.

"A brute?" The man in black grinned and clicked his tongue. His tan skin, weathered by salt and sea, cracked into almost friendly planes.

I flickered a smile and tossed my braided hair over my shoulder. Still, he didn't look at me.

Appearing almost friendly, he spoke again. "I prefer to be called Russian Jack. Not a brute."

My breath caught in my throat and a rabid murmur escaped Sully's lips but formed no words. He didn't have to. Tales of Russian Jack and his sea-faring brutality, not unlike the one's Sully was telling only moments before, were so prominent along the London streets I'd almost figured him to be a man of fiction than one of flesh and blood.

"I see my reputation has preceded me."

He showed innocent ships on the high seas no mercy. Russian Jack never left captives alive and he took no prisoners. His ways were ruthless and his soul long since damned. I should be scared.

Why aren't you shaking, Red?

A flash of movement caught my eye. *Sully's brother Johann!*

I tried not to stare as Johann crept up behind Russian Jack, his sword drawn. Just a step or two closer and he would be in the killing zone.

Without warning, the deadliest pirate to sail the Atlantic let out a roar. Spinning on his booted heel, he drew his cutlass. As Johann raised his blade above his head to strike, Russian Jack slashed him across the middle.

I watched as Johann's eyes widened and his hands flew to his gaping gut. Before he could make a sound, Johann's body fell with a sick thunk at Russian Jack's feet.

"By God's Blood man." Sully's voice was a croak as he fumbled with the gold knots of his blade's handle, which was still securely tucked at his side. "You've cut down me brother!"

Finally, Sully freed his sword and brought it aloft. I couldn't read his eyes, but surely he meant to avenge his brother's death. Before his blade reached its deadly arc, he hesitated.

Sully was no killer and he knew it. His hesitation proved to be a fatal mistake.

Russian Jack slashed my fiancé through the heart as easily as he would slice a crust of bread from the loaf.

The light, like a flickering candle down to its final moments, faded from Sully's brown eyes as he turned to me. Ever slow, he sank to his knees. Behind him, Russian Jack flicked Johann's blade with the tip of his boot. It flew expertly into his outstretched hand.

Sully clutched his sword in one hand and the hem my skirt in the other. His eyes locked onto mine. Pleading. Afraid.

I looked for any sign of apology in his deep brown eyes, any hint of regret for leaving me at the mercy of a notorious killer. I found none. He wasn't afraid *for* me. He was simply afraid to die.

I stumbled backward. Sully collapsed on the deck at my feet. His scarlet lifeblood pooled around the russet haired body that would move no more.

Russian Jack studied Johann's sword briefly before tossing it to a potbellied pirate. A snicker rippled over the lot of them as the short man plucked it from the air like an apple from a tree.

An angry breath slapped my lips in a huff. Without thinking of anything aside from Russian Jack's lifeblood spilling alongside my fiancé's, I bent and snatched Sully's sword from the deck with both hands. I may be just a young slip of a girl in the eyes of a ruthless sea gypsy, but as a London debutante, I had one thing they didn't. Honor.

The snickering stopped.

Despite the sudden silence, Russian Jack paid me no mind.

I lifted the tip of the blade until it pointed squarely at his back. *No need anybody know this is my first time to handle a cutting instrument of any sort.*

"Russian Jack." I was powerless to quell the tremble in my voice or the tremble in my hand. "Today, you've breathed your last. Let it be known that woman named Redella Jerningham took your life to avenge the murder of her fiancé."

Finally, the green-eyed buccaneer cast a hollow glance in my direction. I hoisted the blade in a wide arc above my head. From the corner of my eye, I saw the hairy pirate beside me draw Johann's blade, but my realization was too late. He thrust it toward my neck with a deadly growl.

Like the striking of a snake, Russian Jack drew his cutlass and deflected the blow that could have easily relieved me of my head. I flinched as someone's sword met my cheek and opened the skin of my once-flawless face, gifting me with an angry, gaping gash.

My eye twitched, but I didn't cry out. Blood ran down my face and neck in a sticky ooze, like holy tears from a virgin statue. Fresh rage fueled my hands and brought Sully's sword down with a whistle.

It missed its mark.

Quicker than my eye could follow, Russian Jack's blade was held at ready. He nodded at me as though to invite me to tea.

I jabbed.

Our blades met midair with a clang.

"I could teach you how to do that, Redella Jerningham."

Spatters of blood dotted the white, wrist-length gloves I'd slipped on this morning, when the world still made sense. I raised the blade like an axe and brought it down with all the force I could muster.

Russian Jack stepped slightly to the side and my silver met the deck in a purposeful crack. Splinters scattered like birds from a gunshot. "With proper form, you'd be deadly."

I thrust the blade again, feeling full well the weight of the steel in my burning muscles. Russian Jack didn't have to move much to dodge my attempted blows, but dodge them he did. Expertly. It was as though we were embroiled in a masquerade dance, and the night was coming to an end.

My chest heaved and my face throbbed as I stumbled forward. The probing eyes of the men who'd overtaken *The Scarlet Rose*, those who had stood idly by as Sully was murdered, followed my every move.

I willed my sword to rise for just one more blow. With quivering arms, I managed to heft the blade over my shoulder. My breath came faster and none of us aboard knew what would come next.

"You killed my love," I managed through clenched teeth.

Russian Jack leveled his blade at my exposed middle. I didn't look away from his direct stare, even though the tip of his sword met my breast. "My dear girl, you have yet to discover what love truly is."

I sucked in a deep breath and arced the blade in what should have been a death blow. My heart slapped wildly inside my chest, like a bird's flailing attempts to escape a creeping housecat. Russian Jack's handsome face never changed expression. Before I could end his life, he flicked his wrist in a movement so subtle, it would have gone unseen should I have averted my glance. Sully's blade flew from my sweaty palm and tumbled overboard, through the remnants of the fog and into the frothing sea that lapped at the hull of *The Scarlet Rose*.

I stared at my empty hands to the tune of quiet laughter from the pirates as Russian Jack sheathed his cutlass. The weight of his stare was heavy on my face and I lifted my chin to meet it. The sails creaked and slapped as *The Scarlet Rose* rode the waves and a passing shadow of pelicans, hunting for a meal, clouded us momentarily.

Russian Jack, unlike his crew, wasn't laughing. Those green eyes burned with an intensity that turned them from their saltwater shade to almost black.

I shivered helplessly as he closed the space between us. Before I could move, he took me into his arms.

"Love," he growled. "By God's Blood I'll show you love."

Chapter Four

Swansea, Wales

And you did, Jacky," I whispered into his shoulder. "That time with you was—"

He growled in response. That low, soft growl that not just anyone got to hear. I'd come to know it well. "Aye, it was."

The chilled ocean breeze kissed my skin and sent a shiver up my spine. Or maybe it was being in Jack's arms again that did it. "I thought I would never feel you again. I still can't believe you're here."

"Where else would I be? My wife was set to marry another man. I couldn't stand idly by."

"You were sentenced to death? Were you not?"

"Aye, I was."

"How did you escape death's clutches?"

Jack stroked my arm with long fingers. "Come now, where were we in our reminiscence? I believe I was just about to win your heart—"

He held me in his arms on the deck of *The Scarlet Rose*, the notorious pirate Russian Jack. My fiancé's body lay at our feet, devoid of any life. And I wasn't sad.

"Marry me."

My insides turned to mush and my knees threatened to give way. Jack held me at arm's length. "Say you'll marry me, Redella. But I shan't call you Redella. You'll be Red. My Red."

He even knows what I like to be called. I tried to stifle the brewing feelings of attraction and see the man for what he was. A brutal killer. I steeled my jaw. "You're a murdering savage, Russian Jack. I won't marry you."

A thick course of laughter rose from the pirates as they unloaded our goods onto the black-masted ship that materialized in the mist next to us. A Jolly Roger fluttered in the thick, salty air. Jack paid them no mind.

"You have guts the like of which I've never seen. I can't teach that. But I can teach you the rest." The ocean stopped lapping as Russian Jack erased the space between us. With one strong hand, he cupped the side of my face. My eyes shut on their own as our lips met.

Like a quilt on a winter's day, Jack's kiss brought an immediate warmth to my body against a cold I'd not known was there. My hands were drawn to his muscular chest as we stood together, frozen in that moment. He stroked my cheek with his thumb and sent spasms through my core, something I'd never felt before. Jack broke from our kiss but kept his face close. So close that his breath warmed my cheeks.

"Marry me, Red. Command my fleet as my equal. My partner in every way." He brushed the tip of my nose with a kiss. "You'll want for nothing. Together, we'll be rich beyond our wildest dreams."

My thoughts were a tempest. This morning, I'd had nothing more to look forward to than being touched by an arrogant ass of a man who thought he was entitled to my heart. And my bed.

But this man—this *pirate*—

He stared at me with those eyes that threatened to look straight through me. Something told me that Russian Jack was at my mercy, just as much as I was at his. And we both knew it. Spasms quaked through my core again and left me aching. Wanting. Craving something I'd never had—something Russian Jack could give.

Dried blood cracked on my cheek and the slash mark, though

not too terribly deep, stung. However, it was something else that lit my veins on fire.

An entire new world, never anything I had before considered, unfolded before me. Jack's words sent my insides aflutter.

Rich beyond our wildest dreams.

Command a pirate fleet as the captain's equal.

These things alone were enough to entice a debutante to piracy. However, it was the smoldering look behind Jack's piercing eyes that almost made the decision for me. I nodded.

"Is that a yes?"

The old Redella, who nursed her dying mother and allowed herself to be swept along in life, never making decisions, melted away as I wrapped my arms around his neck and knocked his signature fur hat to the deck in the process. "Aye, it's a yes."

His bleached blond hair stuck this way and that and gave him the look of a schoolboy who'd skipped his lessons in favor of playing at the beach. The old Redella was gone, the new Red—the fiancée of a pirate captain, was here to stay.

I buried my fingers deep in those thick yellow waves and a smile that made no sense spread my lips wide. "Yes, I'll marry you, Russian Jack."

And I meant it.

After Jack and I climbed aboard *The Black Otter*, I discovered that I wasn't sad over Sully. A handful of Jack's pirates were still aboard *The Scarlet Rose*, which had just become the newest vessel in Russian Jack's fleet, as evidenced by the fluttering Jolly Roger that was hoisted in place of the English flag. I glanced at the schooner that had hours before been my prison, destined to carry me to a life of inadequacy and misery, and another new feeling churned in my gut. I felt liberated.

It made no sense, but I didn't care.

"Here here," Jack called.

The scurrying, stowing, and general movement stilled to a stop until all eyes were on Jack. None had seemed to notice my boarding with him until this moment.

"We plundered a ripe maiden when we boarded *The Scarlet Rose*," he announced. "A crate of Spanish coins, freshly minted. And bolts of *golden* cloth."

The pirate crew, most of which had stayed aboard *The Black Otter*, mumbled a collective, knowing mumble.

Jack nodded. "Yes, we know what that means, don't we men?"

"Aye aye," a few men grunted.

"What was your final destination, Red? Let me guess—the islands no doubt?"

"He said we were going to get married in Jamaica," I whispered, my voice muted.

He looked down at me. "Your pig fiancé was trading the golden cloth for men. Women and children, too."

"You don't mean—"

"He had business to conduct on the side, Red," Jack whispered back, so that only I could hear. "Slaves from the islands to bring back to England. In bondage."

Jack turned and addressed his crew again. "The Scarlet Rose. No doubt the man who captained her was a headhunter."

My eyebrows knitted together above my eyes. All the doctors in London had dark-skinned servants bustling about their homes, didn't they? Doing the cooking, minding the cleaning. Answering the door. Scrubbing everything. Dull eyed, never smiling.

A rogue memory leapt to the forefront of my mind. I'd been searching Sully's home for him as my mother's breath grew weak. Her final moments were near and he needed to be there by her side. And by mine, if the words of love and devotion he often whispered to me were true.

I'd peeked into his washroom only to discover Sully, naked in a tub. His back to me. A young female servant, younger than me by a mint, poured a bucket of steaming water over him.

"Too hot, witch," he barked. His arm shot out from the tub and disappeared in her skirts. His muscles tightened as he grabbed her between the legs. Hard.

She yelped in pain as I eased the door shut, unsure of what

I'd just seen. A burning bile rose into my throat as her dark, hopeless eyes met mine through the closing crack of the door.

Jack's booming voice drew me from my unwelcome reverie. "The headhunter also had a most precious jewel aboard."

Without warning, he hefted me onto his shoulders. My face ached from the slash, but a sudden grin spread my lips wide despite the pain. "Now this jewel is mine!"

A raucous whoop went up from the crew.

"We'll be married today!"

I laughed. Here I was, amid plunderers and murderers, beneath the infamous Jolly Roger, and I was laughing.

The whoops turned to good-natured jeering as Jack sat me down. Pirates stepped forward, one after the other, to offer good-natured congratulations.

As I watched Jack, everything I thought I knew about life and the world where I lived melted away. His comfortable stance as he stood aboard the rocking ship as though he was made for life at sea, and his wide smile ensured his friends and shipmates stayed at welcome ease. He wouldn't care if I failed to fold my napkin properly at high tea, he wouldn't chastise me or raise a hand to me if an unladylike word passed my lips in his presence. In fact, he planned to teach me to be a version of myself I never dreamt of being. That thought alone brought a sizzle to my veins.

However, the longer I watched Jack speak to his crew, the more my eyes traced his masculine frame. From his hard jawline, to his rolling Russian accent, tight-fitting britches, and the way his muscled arms flexed as he moved and spoke, parts of me that had just this morning been content to be used at whim by a blaggard of a man also sparked to life with a foreign want. I fought the urge to wrap my arms about his waist and draw him close. To feel his body enveloped in mine, to have his warmth near again. I licked my lips and swallowed hard.

Never had I figured on coming into a predicament such as this. Polite society certainly hadn't prepared me for it. However, when I looked up at his smiling, ruggedly handsome face only to be rewarded with an intoxicating wink, I didn't hesitate any longer. I wrapped my arm around his waist and pulled my body close to his until I could feel his heat through his waistcoat and britches.

Surprised, Jack squelched the conversation he'd been enthralled in with another large man and focused all his attentions on me. "Well now," he cooed. "What have we here?"

I pushed onto my tiptoes and pressed my lips to his. He didn't pull away. Instead, his tongue caressed my lips, further stoking the growing flame within me that I was beginning to like.

The crew let out another whoop.

"She be a saucy one, Jack!"

"Finally found a woman to match your blade, eh oh Jacky?"

As the laughter came to a natural end, Jack spoke again. "She'll be my second in command. As much your captain as I."

The light and airy mood on deck transformed to weighted as crooked smiles turned to downcast frowns. Russian Jack sensed it, too. He rested one hand gently on the jeweled grip of his cutlass. "I know it's been said bad luck follows ships with women on board." He looked down at me. "But I disagree. Aboard *The Black Otter*, we make our own luck."

A few men began to growl. Apparently, they figured I'd marry Jack and stay in port.

"If any has a problem with this, best tell me now."

He studied each face. My flickering smile faded.

Jack's face transformed from ruggedly handsome to that of a stony killer. Something inside me lurched.

"*Niet*. If you don't speak up now, I'll show no quarter when you do."

The silence, punctuated with salt water slaps against the hull, was deafening. I stared at Jack as fear crashed against itself in the deepest part of my stomach.

After what felt like an eternity, his face softened. "That's what I figured. Now that I don't have to kill anyone, let's have a round of introductions."

I exhaled hard and looked at the crew.

My crew.

There were six of them. Each would easily blend in to the poorest of the poorhouses in London. It must have shown on my face.

Russian Jack laughed. "They may look bedraggled and hopeless in the eyes of a woman such as yourself. But be warned. These men are the most fierce and cunning, and *loyal*, upon the sea."

I nodded. Jack rested one hand on my back and pointed to a large, unsmiling black man with the other.

"Red, this is The Poison Lightning. We took a slave ship off the Ivory Coast. All the Africans headed for slavery were eager to get off *The Black Otter* when we got them back to the coast of Africa. All except him."

Manners a distant memory, I stared into the deep, glittering eyes of the bald African. For a fleeting instant, I thought I saw lightning flash there. I blinked, then it was gone.

Unsure of proper protocol, I extended my hand like a man. "It's a pleasure, Mister—Lightning?"

His dark, flawless face didn't change expression. He simply stared at me. *Through* me. With my hand still outstretched, I shivered and glanced at Jack, who chuckled.

"No mister needed. He has no name, just The Poison Lightning. Some who sail the seas believe that if they touch a woman, they lose their ability to do magic or tell the future. The Poison Lightning here is one such man."

I lowered my hand in awkward jerks. Still, the man with skin like milk and coffee stared at me as though he meant to pluck my very soul from between my bones.

There are no rules here. At least none that I know. I'll make my own.

I stared back, just as hard as he stared at me, and studied his eyes. There were no more flashes, but glittered they did with what some might take to be pure hatred. The longer I stared, the more I figured hate to be as foreign to The Poison Lightning as this entire pirating empire was to me.

"Poison Lightning," I whispered, effectively breaking the tense silence. "How did you get your name?"

He didn't speak, but Jack did. "The night we took the slave ship, a storm whipped up from nowhere, without warning. Lightning seemed to be centered over us on the slave ship. Once everyone was loaded onto *The Black Otter*, a coward of a headhunter tried to charge me. He'd been hiding, you see, and waiting. A bolt of lightning took his life before he could take mine and sunk the ship."

Jack pulled up his black, billowy shirt and revealed his muscled stomach. A scar peeked out from under the shirt and disappeared into his trousers. "Lightning was close."

My mouth fell open.

"The Poison Lightning claims to have sent the storm."

I looked back at the man who would never be a slave.

He nodded an infinitesimal nod.

"To meet you today, is truly a pleasure."

Finally, his dark face cracked into a series of planes as his lips tilted into a makeshift smile. He shifted his glance to Russian Jack and nodded again, almost imperceptibly. Almost.

Never having spoken a word, The Poison Lightning turned and swaggered to the main mast and began to climb the rigging as easily as I might climb a set of stairs.

"Tommy, meet Redella. But we get to call her Red," Jack said as the next man stepped up to us.

I stared at the short, squat man that had appeared before me and recognized him at once.

"I appreciate you not relieving me of my head back there." I touched my cheek and forced a smile.

"No hard feelings, me hopes."

His voice was high pitched and musical. I stifled a smile. "None at all."

Hair curled from over the top of his torn shirt, which had been stitched together from various pieces of fabric. He smoothed at his black hair that had thinned in several places on his head.

His chubby belly peeked out from under the too-short shirt, or perhaps his britches simply weren't pulled up as far as they should be. "Tommy Tew, Miss, the son of *Thomas* Tew. Perhaps ye recognize the name?"

Before I could tell him that yes, I had in fact seen wanted posters of a buccaneer by the name of Thomas Tew along the streets of London, he continued.

"Me father was the fiercest bucko to sail the seas, he was," he boasted. "His blood runs in me very veins, it does. He discovered the island of Madagascar, he did, and the curious people who call it home." Tommy paused to take a breath. "He did," he whispered.

As much as The Poison Lightning didn't speak, Tommy made up for it. I nodded politely. "You are a man proud of your lineage, I see—"

Tommy paid me no mind. "Me father was killed when his ship was overtaken by a Muslim vessel, ten-thousand strong they was, damn them." He spat dramatically onto the deck. "Lest I'd be sailing alongside him now."

My head bobbed on its own. "A man who loves his family so much, I must ask. Do you have a wife, Tommy? Or siblings?"

"Uh-oh," Jack muttered. A few pirates behind Tommy exchanged tired glances.

Tommy's face flushed from an olive hue to almost purple. "Me half-brudder. Prince Ratsimilaho. Lives on me fadder's island. Someday—"Tommy drew his sword and slashed a coil of rope that had, until that moment, been lying innocently on the deck.

"Someday," he repeated through clenched teeth. Tommy sheathed his sword and stalked across the deck, muttering to himself.

I glanced at Jack. He offered me a wink. "This here is our resident royalty." He paid Tommy's odd change in behavior no mind and pointed to a tall, slender man with a pleasant face. "Red, meet Prince Solomon of Poland."

My eyes widened as the prince bent at the middle and placed a polite kiss atop my outstretched hand.

"No prince necessary anymore," he explained, "but Cap here refuses to drop the troublesome title." He smiled a wide, white smile. "I much prefer to be called Solo, Miss Red."

Something inside me softened in Solo's company, like we were old friends instead of new acquaintances. "Solo, tell me, what brings you to *The Black Otter*?"

Golden rays lit his sun-kissed face as he tilted his face skyward. "My father's shipping business is one of the largest and richest in Poland. One night, I was scouring his books and learned that, like your former fiancé, my father had dealings in the slave trade. I investigated my findings."

My eyes were wide, as though I was back in my childhood nursery in London, listening to a fairy tale being read by my old governess as the gentle dusk cloaked us in an easy dark. "I had no idea the slave trade was as expansive as you gentlemen have described."

A few snarky snarls roiled at my use of the word gentlemen.

I ignored them. "What did you do?"

Solo smiled. "The only thing I could. I snuck down to the docks under the cover of night to see for myself what went on while the world slept."

"And what did you see?"

"What I saw—" Solo's smile faded, and his eyes turned stormy. "My father was there with a whip. Roughly ushering men, broken men, and women from one of his merchant ships to the shore. Children too." He shook his head as though to clear the thoughts from his mind. His blond hair had several shades of gold hidden within its strands. "I vowed then and there to do something about it."

Solo shared a warm, knowing glance with Russian Jack. "I heard tale that some pirate ships overtook slave ships such as these and granted those poor unfortunates aboard their freedom."

Sully's venomous words from earlier echoed in my ears. Sea gypsies. Savages. Brutes. *Granting stolen souls their freedom. Nothing like what I heard about pirates.*

"Just so happens I ran into a few from *The Black Otter* fleet down at the pub not long after. That's when I struck a deal."

"What kind of a deal?"

Solo smiled that bright smile. Despite being clad in salt-stained rags, he would never be able to hide his high birth. "Well, I agreed to give sustenance and shelter to pirates by way of Father's shipping business."

Solo turned his full attention to me and winked. "After all my dear Red, revenge served through doing good is the best kind of revenge there is."

Jack clapped him on the shoulder. "When Solo was exiled by his father, the King of Poland, we at *The Black Otter* fleet were all too eager to welcome him aboard. And his use of oratory is a welcome respite from the silence when we're days at sea."

The pair shared a laugh as though they were old family members instead of strangers-turned-shipmates. I offered a smile. "Truly, it's a pleasure Solo."

"The pleasure is all mine, Miss Red." Solo jerked his head in a quick nod and pointed to the other pirates aboard. They had grown weary of introductions and gone back to their storing, piling, and grumbling. "If you'll excuse me, I've work to attend to."

I nodded again, flabbergasted by Solo's charm and manners.

"Second order of business." Jack appeared beside me and slid his arm around my waist. "I believe you'll be requiring a wedding gown." Something deep within me, something I couldn't place, churned at his touch and willed him to do more than simply hold me in one arm.

"Have you known a man, Red?" Jack's voice was heavy with want. He stepped into the cabin that was, until today, his and his alone. He pushed the wooden door back with his foot and it slammed shut with a solemn thunk of finality.

I sat on the straw-stuffed mattress and fidgeted with the blankets. I'd been sliding the sleeve of my makeshift wedding gown up and down my arm in an attempt to look alluring, should my new husband enter our bedroom. Now, here he was.

I swallowed hard.

The moonlight streamed in from the port window behind me, illuminating Jack with an otherworldly glow as he stepped toward me in heavy, purposeful steps. My stomach turned up in knots.

Before I could utter a response, Jack was in front of me. The aroma of the strong Spanish ale they'd been passing around deck after our crude wedding ceremony was almost tangible as he fingered my hair. A shiver danced over my naked shoulder.

His voice was a throaty whisper as his hand fell heavy on my knee. "Did that ginger blaggard know you, Red?"

I uncrossed my legs and tried to remember to breathe. "No. No one has ever known me."

Jack's breath came quicker as his fingers curled into my hair. "Then with your permission—"

His lips met my exposed throat in a hungry kiss. A flash of sensations flooded my body in unexpected places and I allowed him to spread my knees wide.

"Permission granted."

Chapter Five

Aboard The Black Otter on the high seas

Reflections of the waves through our porthole window danced across the far wall. I stretched and rolled over into Jack's arms. We'd been married over a month and my secret muscles still ached with a divine throb after a night of passion spent with the man who'd stolen my heart and overtaken my body time and again. I stared at him as he slept.

Jack's sun-bleached hair, where I'd wrested my fingers as he deeply explored my body and brought those elusive sparks to light, stuck out this way and that. The tanned and strong-jawed face of the notorious pirate was soft, boyish, and strangely defenseless in the early morning light. I let my fingers dance across his chest and down the lightning scar on his stomach.

A wanting, deep within my core, urged me closer to him. The lightning scar traveled down into the area that would normally be hidden by his trademark black britches and continued on across the top of his thigh. As my fingers meandered along, Jack's full lips flickered into a sleepy smile. "Good morning to you, too, Mrs. Rackham," he murmured without opening his eyes.

I squeezed his thigh and groaned a quiet groan in the back of my throat. At once, his manhood began to swell.

"You're like to get me spoiled, waking up to such things each morning."

"Good."

His lips found my neck in a ravenous kiss. Jack nibbled here and there as his muscled arms wrested me atop him. In a fluid movement, he had my filmy night dress hiked up so that our wet skin met in familiar places.

Finally, Jack opened his eyes. He cupped my face in his hand and slid his thumb across the blade scar on my cheek. "You're beautiful, Red."

Before I could answer or even lean to kiss him, someone banged the door in sharp succession. Tommy's voice chimed from the other side. "A fog be comin', it is."

"A fog, or ships Tommy?"

"Aye, Cap."

Jack covered his face with his hands in exasperation. "Tommy, have you seen ships?"

"Of course me has, Cap. Ole Tommy wouldn't have come down otherwise, me wouldn't."

I stifled a giggle.

"We're due to meet up with the rest of *The Black Otter* fleet in the next day or so, are you certain it isn't our own men's ships you see?"

"You know me, Cap. Ole Tommy can smell the gold, he can." Tommy paused. "And I smell it, Cap."

Jack was out from under me and on his feet in a moment. My aching muscles would just have to wait. "We'll be right up, Tommy."

I sucked in my lower lip and tried not to pout.

"If you're going to run this ship as my equal, it's high time I teach you how." He wrenched his britches into place and plucked up his fur hat from his desk. "You'll learn by doing, Red. Watch and do as I do. Me and the other men."

I squirmed on the mattress and tried to name the odd emotion that soured in the back of my throat. "Watch Charles Swan and Dark Water William?"

"They're cunning. You will learn much from them."

I shifted my weight on the bed. I wanted to tell Jack that I wasn't comfortable around those two, but I had no reason to back up my feelings.

"You'll do fine, Red." Jack winked. "I have a gift for you."

I arched an eyebrow and slid my legs over the side of the bed. "Better than the one you were about to give me before Tommy interrupted?"

"Far better."

I pulled on one of Jack's black blouses and stepped into the billowy skirt I'd constructed from a torn sail.

Jack pointed to the far wall where two swords hung crossed above the door. He strode over and plucked one down as though he was plucking a peach from a tree. "Be a dear and slide my cutlass from under the pillow."

Confused, I did as I was told. "Why do you need your cutlass when you have a sword in your hand?"

"This little beauty was my first fencing sword," Jack explained as he accepted his cutlass and jabbed it into his belt. "This blade here has shed the lifeblood of many men in its day. Taken many lives."

I hugged my arms to my chest and shivered.

"But for every life it has taken, it has saved mine doubly. It's priceless."

My hands twisted in my lap. "What does it feel like. To—" My words trailed off as the fog clouded the porthole window. "To take someone's life for the first time?"

Jack let the silence that filled the room be for only a moment before he eased himself onto our bed. "There are no words to describe emotions that you feel in battle, regardless of which way the battle goes." He twisted the blade in the dim light. "You become someone else and you will never be the same."

I sucked in a breath and let it out slow. "Never the same?"

"You become the self that God intended you to be." Jack stood. "Or you die."

A thunderous charge of feet down the stairs interrupted Jack's reverie. "We've come to a ship!" Tommy's voice was sharp. "Come on, Cap!"

Jack ignored him. "This blade made me into Commodore of The Black Otter fleet, affectionately called Captain Russian Jack

Rackham. No longer Mikhail Nemirovsky, worthless pick-pocket son of a consumptive English whore. Today," he continued in his even tone, "this blade is yours. And you shall use it."

My heart panged as I accepted it. "Who was your first kill?"

"A pirate who aimed to kill me first." Jack opened the door and paused but didn't look back. "My father."

The Black Otter was already alongside the unsuspecting ship when I crept onto the foggy deck. It has only taken me a moment to find the scabbard for my new sword, but it was in that moment that I lost sight of my husband.

"Jack," I whispered into the silence. "Jack? Where are you?"

I stood there, ignorant of how to proceed and feeling strangely lost. From the fog came a sudden sense terror turned my blood to ice. My breath hitched in my throat.

Something was happening. But what? Where? And to whom? I shook off the cloak of chilly fear and opened my mouth to call out to my husband.

An ironlike hand fell onto my shoulder and my words died on my tongue.

Jack.

I closed my eyes and exhaled in a huff as I reached to grasp the hand that had found me. "Thank G—" My eyes flew open, hard and fast. This skin was much too rough. I swiveled my head slightly and squinted into the fog.

The Poison Lightning's face appeared before mine like an apparition. His grip tightened on my shoulder as he placed a finger over his lips. Eyes, black like boiled coffee, stared into mine as his tell-tale finger melted away from his taut lips and disappeared into the fog that surrounded us.

I started to nod, to show him that I understood his message of utter silence. Before I could, the hand that disappeared exploded forth and met my stomach. Palm open, The Poison Lightning's sinewy hand patted and grabbed across my stomach in awkward pats until it reached my hip. The fingers that gripped my shoulder tightened.

Oh God. Words swirled in my mind and crashed together like gulls in a gale. *This man is going to have his way with me.*

My fingers tightened around the grip of Jack's sword as I prepared for my first kill.

The Poison Lightning's experienced hand brushed my fingers aside as easily as one would brush flies from a pie. Quicker than I could comprehend, he yanked my new sword free of its scabbard and pushed me down. Hard.

My knees met the boat deck with a crack and The Poison Lightning let go of my throbbing shoulder.

My sword glinted in the dim light. I made a dive for it, but The Poison Lightning lifted it high.

"Arggh," a voice shouted from above.

The metallic clang of swords tolled above me.

"Umph," someone grunted. A gush of warm rain wet my face as a lifeless body fell to the deck beside me.

I swiped at my cheek. Blood.

Curls of fog wisped away from the dead man. With wide eyes, I searched his face. A long black beard elongated his golden-brown face, and the white turban that curled around his head was dotted with red. I glanced up.

The Poison Lightning extended his hand to me. I took it.

When I was safely to my feet, he pressed the handle of my blade into my trembling fist.

"You saved my life." The words were a whisper on my lips. *Did he know that I thought he was going to rape me?* I thought briefly about apologizing but decided against it. If I was going to lead these men, I couldn't be weak. At least not in their eyes. I gripped the sword's handle but didn't sheath it. "Thank you."

The Poison Lightning didn't acknowledge my thanks. Instead, he made a *V* with his fingers and pointed to his eyes. Then, he swiveled his hand to all the area around us.

Yes, I understand, I wanted to say. *Keep a sharp eye, because danger is near.* But I knew better than to talk.

The sun's rays breached the cool fog as I crept along behind

The Poison Lightning with my blade held at ready. I thought about all I'd been taught over the last month. Between Jack's teachings and Solo's helpful tricks, I'd learned much. Apparently not enough yet to keep my sword in my own sheath. If the situation had been less sinister, I would have shaken my head, but be it as it was, I didn't. An odd feeling washed over me from nowhere. I furrowed my brows. The top of my head was beginning to burn when I felt it.

I stopped. The tiny hairs on the back of my neck rose like hackles on a cur. For a moment, I strained to see into the fog, but it was useless. The sun hadn't been out long enough to burn it off yet. I closed my eyes.

Solo had described this very thing to me. The none-too-distant memory of his harshly-accented Polish words sang in my head.

"It's called the sixth sense, Red," he offered as he clanged his sword against mine. I lifted my blade and attacked again as Jack looked on, offering pointers on footwork and posture from where he sat on an overturned box.

"Mrs. Rackham, remember your balance. Hold your arm like I showed you." Jack demonstrated by curling his arm behind him at shoulder level.

"Like a masquerade dance," I agreed without looking directly at him. Still, I lifted my arm as he did.

Solo's piercing stare never left my face. "When a man—or woman—means to kill you or do you harm, something in your body senses it before they even make their first move."

I drew my breath in slowly through my nose as my sword flew on its own. "Is that so?"

"Be aware of your surroundings. Know what is what and what is where—" Solo jabbed at me. I stepped to the side, behind a curtain of rigging. Solo's lips tilted into some semblance of a smile. "So that everything around you, boxes, rigging, masts, cannons—they become your ally."

I tilted my chin.

"But never forget to feel for your sixth sense."

I froze as the icy steel of Jack's blade pressed into my neck from behind.

My recent memory fizzled as I took in my environment. This was real, this was now. I tuned out the fear and the heat and let the creaking boards and slapping of the sea water against the helm soak into my senses. Then, there it was.

The sound of someone's baited breath.

The infinitesimal scuff of a boot, creeping along the deck.

The sound of someone's thundering heartbeat.

Or is that mine?

Still as a marble statue, I listened.

Jack's voice, far away, exploded like a cannon. "Intruders! They're on *The Black Otter!*"

Like the clap of thunder before a downpour, Jack's booming voice unleashed a cacophony of clanging steel, cursing, growling that filled the sky over the sea.

I spun on my heel and let go a roar as I drove my sword into the gut of the breather behind me. The fog began to melt away like frosting from a cake, revealing a gruesome scene that played out like a bloody stage play.

Our eyes met and I tried to ignore the blade of his own that was arched to deliver a death blow and perhaps split my skull in two, had I not delivered mine first.

I yanked on the handle as I'd seen Jack do, but it didn't budge. Instead, the man gripped the blade with his hands and whimpered. I yanked again. His turban fell off and rolled across the deck.

"Lodged in the backbone." Solo's voice was a welcome respite from the howls around me. "Like this."

He pressed his booted foot next to my stuck blade and pushed hard against the man. My first kill slunk to the deck with a groan.

The blond former-prince only smiled. "Your first kill."

I nodded. *Now I've done murder.*

"They boarded us." He held my sword lightly in his hand and

swept the bloody blade across his britches. "If you didn't kill him, he would have killed you. And thought nothing more of it."

"Solo! Behind you!"

The Polish prince-turned-pirate whirled and slashed the approaching pirate across the throat with my blade. He turned back to me, tossed my sword, and offered a gleaming grin before sprinting back into the melee. "Remember to slide your feet if you engage an opponent," he called.

I spotted Jack locked in combat with a pirate near the rigging. Holding my sword before me, I made haste to my husband.

The buccaneer's hand circled Jack's throat, but he couldn't seem to tighten it to a death grip. Jack appeared oblivious to the fingers that clawed at his neck as he held his rival at bay with the jeweled cutlass pressed beneath his chin. They danced beneath the rigging, each trying to gain an ounce of ground against his opponent to finish him off.

I must help Jack, but how?

With wild eyes, I glanced about.

I remembered my first training scenario with Jack and Solo aboard *The Black Otter*. Each were fighting each other, demonstrating proper dueling technique, before they turned and charged at me. Unsure of what to do, I had started up the rigging. The splintery ropes bit into my hands at once and my muscles burned. No London debutante's hands were meant for climbing salty, worn rigging.

Solo and Jack both stopped cold. "Darling, you never go up."

I let my husband pluck me from the ropes. "Why not?"

Solo laughed a throaty laugh. "Well, we can go up. But not you, Red."

That comment hit me hard. *Who are these men to say that I am part captain but unable to climb my own rigging?* So when the sun went down, each night without fail, I went up. Up the rigging, more and more each night. My palms blistered and slowly callused and the climbing got easier.

The Arab pirate and Jack danced beneath the rigging in what

looked to become a dance to the death. I studied the environment. The only place to go was up.

I clenched the bloody blade between my teeth and began to climb the ratlines. The coppery taste of enemy blood turned my stomach, but I fought back the swells of nausea. The ship pitched and rolled as a monstrous wave built just off the starboard side of *The Black Otter*. I ground my teeth onto the metal and held on to the rough rope so tightly that my fingers went numb.

The wave rose over the gory mess of pirates and crashed down like a divine hammer. My body snapped this way and that, like a water drop shaken from a dog's fur. Finally, I opened my eyes and looked down. The force of the wave had torn Jack and his nemesis from the other's grasp, and each lay on the deck. Jack's jeweled cutlass lay between them.

The brown pirate moved first.

I pulled the blade from my teeth. All sense of fear had taken permanent leave. Jack was in trouble.

The rogue wave appeared to have sapped the will to fight from all the deck as his long fingers fumbled with Jack's sword. I stared at my target and pointed my blade toward the deck.

Three—two—

The brown pirate rose from the deck and coughed as he hefted Jack's cutlass into his grasp.

One.

"No!" The word ripped from my throat hard and fast.

My fingers unfurled from around the rope. My body cut through the salty, humid air and I landed on my mark. The blade that saved Jack's life so many times before did its duty by my hand as it ground through the flesh of the rival pirate captain and took his life—before he could take that of my husband's. I'd taken two lives in one day, yet I felt more like myself than ever before. My conscience, strangely enough, had been more deeply plagued when I was engaged to Sully.

She was crouched behind the wheelhouse when I saw her. The fog that had burned away during the fight left in its wake heavy, humid air. We'd come out on top against the Muslim pirates, though as I looked around at the piles of robed bodies, I wasn't sure how.

"Jack," I called.

A splash sounded as another body fell to its watery grave. A moment later, Jack appeared. "A fine opponent he was. He didn't even have a sword. Almost bested me with just his hands."

"Do you suppose the crew still think I'm bad luck to have aboard?"

His piercing seafoam eyes were brighter than before. "You're my guardian angel, sent from Heaven. No matter what anyone says. Or believes."

I stared at him a moment, intoxicated, before I remembered why I called him over. I shook my head. "Oh, um, we have a stowaway."

Jack crouched down. "Welcome aboard, Miss. I'm the captain of this ship, and I'm truly sorry that you had to witness that horrific display."

He extended his hand to her. She clutched a brown robe about her thin shoulders and glanced first at his hand, then at me. "I'm still tied. Got the rope off my ankles and made it up the stairs. Thought I could jump overboard in the chaos."

"Oh." I forced a smile and went to work on her bounds. "Wouldn't you have drowned?"

She rubbed her wrists as the too-tight rope fell to the deck. "Didn't matter. Just as long as they couldn't touch me anymore."

My forced smile melted before I found my voice again. "That's over now. No harm will come to a woman on board *The Black Otter* as long as Russian Jack is in charge."

She exhaled and stood up without the aid of Jack's hand. He rose with her. "What's your name Miss?"

"Monica. Monica Joan from Wales."

My smile transformed from forced to full. "'Ello Monica Joan. I'm Red, Captain's wife."

Monica Joan didn't return my smile. "They took my ship overnight. Just trying to reach the mainland. That's all."

Jack turned to me. "Thank you, my darling, for wielding your blade well. Did I not tell you that you'd be deadly?" He leaned in and pressed his lips to mine. Muscles I didn't know I had relaxed with his kiss.

"Now," he whispered, "take care of the lass. God Almighty himself knows what happened to her aboard that ship from hell. Let her know she's safe and that she'll reach the mainland safely."

After another quick kiss, Jack turned and trotted off across deck. Probably to finish looting the other vessel.

I glanced at the only other woman aboard. "Well, Monica Joan. Let's get you out of those clothes and into something a bit fresher, shall we?"

Finally, a flash of trust brightened her dirt-streaked face. "Your husband you say? Aye, you make a handsome couple."

A rabid blush heated my neck.

"Seems you and your handsome husband are my saving grace."

Somehow, in some world, we could be friends. "Come along. Let's get you changed."

"I will," Monica Joan agreed. "But please. Wipe the blood from your face. You look—" She studied me a moment through her clear, green eyes. "Like a bloodthirsty pirate."

Chapter Six

Aboard The Black Otter on the high seas

I made Monica Joan a pallet in the cargo hold. Poor thing." I took my place next to Jack at the railing of *The Black Otter*. With one booted foot propped on the railing and the sun setting over the sea behind him, I couldn't help but slide my arm around his waist and give a squeeze.

Jack smiled down at me. A dark bruise ringed his neck. "You two were fast friends."

"She was just in the wrong place at the wrong time, I suppose."

"Unlike my Red. Who always finds herself in the right place at the right time." He took my hands in his and turned them over. "Should be raw from the ratlines. Alas, my Red has been practicing. I've seen lots of things out here on the high seas, but I've never seen a move like that."

I ducked my head. A lock of black hair caught in my eyelashes. "I've never dreamed that I could do anything like that. But, you were in trouble."

Jack raised each of my palms to his lips and brushed them with a kiss. "I love you, Red."

"I love you, Jack."

He stared into my eyes for a moment and said more than a lifetime of words. Ever slow, he tucked the wayward tendril behind my ear. "Are you okay, Red? That was a ruthless fight. If I were new to pirating, it may have even shaken me up a bit."

I shifted my weight.

"Talk to me."

Sparkles from the setting sun spangled the glassy face of the ocean. "Some of the men, our men."

Jack waited in silence.

We stared over the railing together. "I expected the carnage, and nothing came across as surprising. Except that they snuck onto our ship. However—"

These men were my crew as much as Jack's, he'd said so himself. Not wanting to be critical of something I didn't fully understand, I chose my words carefully. Still, I couldn't look at my husband.

"The one you call Dark Water William." I glanced over my shoulder. Sure enough, the unsmiling African with a face like thunder and his greasy English companion, Charles Swan, stared at Jack and me from the wheelhouse.

Jack followed my glance and offered a nod to the pair.

"Chow's waitin' in the galley, Cap," Charles called. He possessed a voice like a sick, whiny child. I winced.

"We'll be down shortly, men."

I watched as they slunk across the deck like a pair of thieves who wished to be unnoticed in a room filled with fine things. Jack kept his voice low. "He must have sensed us talking about him."

"Charles Swan was the other one, actually."

Jack raised an eyebrow. "That doesn't surprise me. Where one is, you can usually find the other. Tell me, what was it they did that perturbed you?"

I studied the railing as though there would be a test. "They seemed to—*enjoy* the macabre. In fact, I believe it excited them."

"Excited them?"

"Yes. Charles laughed that hideous laugh of his as he took a man's head off, and Dark Water—"

I felt like a schoolgirl tattling to her governess. "He licked the blood of the men I saw him kill."

"I see." Jack placed his booted foot back onto the railing and exhaled. "Dark Water came off another slave ship liberated by *The Black Otter* fleet, just like The Poison Lightning. But the damage was already done to Dark Water, from a young age I figure."

The memory of the way the tall African with skin like coal stilled his movements before turning to glare at me when I first came aboard *The Black Otter* gave me pause. A shiver gripped my backbone when his scintillating eyes met mine that day and didn't disappoint today.

"He'll not harm you," Jack assured me. "But take care round him. Same as you'd take care round a caged tiger at a menagerie of animals."

I slid my tongue across my teeth. *He'll not harm me?* Before she went to sleep, Monica Joan caught my hand in hers and whispered to me her fears about Dark Water and Charles. They'd circled her in the heat of the battle, the lust in their eyes and the bulges in the front of their britches weren't unnoticed. Thankfully, the battle turned bloody and they seemed to forget her. I bit my tongue and decided not to share Monica Joan's fears with Jack.

"And Dark Water's friend? Charles Swan?"

"A rootless Englishman, slippery in his morals, but seems to dote on Dark Water. One of the hardest workers you're likely to meet. He would outwork me—if I'd let him."

I decided Swan was not to be trusted. He carried himself in a way that disturbed me, but not so much that I could aptly describe it to Jack. His shifty eyes always darted between Dark Water and Jack, as though he was unsure of who to follow.

Or perhaps afraid of showing Jack where his loyalty truly lies.

Truth be told, his pencil-thin moustache and pointy nose, coupled with the stringy hair that hung sadly over his too-large forehead, gave the skinny man the look of an outcast orphan. Perhaps in some life, he had been.

Jack's voice interrupted my thoughts. "You killed two men today."

"Not only have I stolen. But now, I've done murder." The reality of what I'd done hit the pit of my stomach like a stone that would stay there always. How could sins such as these ever be forgiven? My Catholic upbringing told of all sins being forgiven when confessed and the penance given by the priest was performed. If no penance was performed, I would pay fiery, eternal consequences, should an enemy relieve me of my head. Or my life. "Oh Jack, what have I done?"

"You've stayed alive in the life you're living. And you protected that of your husband."

"Do you believe we will atone for our sins at judgement?"

Jack's smile faded. "I do."

"Then how do you justify this life? How can I?"

Jack sucked in a deep breath. "God gave us commandments, did he not? Those commandments are for the landlubbers. Upon the sea, we have our own commandments."

"What are they?"

Jack draped his arm over my shoulder. "Let your conscience be at rest, Red. You've done nothing against God or your captain. We'll go over the articles of our ship in due time."

My heart thundered in my chest, but began to slow with Jack's words.

He pointed out to sea. "See that there?"

A dark shadow appeared on the water.

Another ship.

My knees turned to water and I gripped the railing. The adrenaline from the Arabian pirates had just begun to ebb. The thought of having to do it all again—

It hadn't taken me a terribly long while to find my sea legs, but sometimes, when the ship pitched just right, the nausea would win. The world pitched around me but had nothing to do the waves on the sea.

Jack caught my elbow before I could slink to the deck. "See the flag, Red?"

A Jolly Roger fluttered from the mast.

"That's *The Spanish Rose*, another ship in our Black Otter fleet. My ship, *your* ship." Jack slid his finger along the blade scar on my cheek. "Tonight, you'll meet men who work aboard her."

"Then, the captain grabbed my neck but my cutlass was under his throat!" Jack demonstrated with loose movements. Several jugs of rum passed around the circle of men who spent most of the night regaling the stories of their bloody, high-seas adventures. The pirates cackled and cat-called as Jack demonstrated, badly, how he and the captain danced across the deck, each only an inch from death. Despite the darting glances from the strange men, I smiled, too.

The heavy-bearded pirate Jack called Red Legs Roberts sat off to the side and watched the goings on with a gallon of rum tucked between his knees.

"Another one to treat carefully," Jack had warned when the men from *The Spanish Rose* boarded *The Black Otter*. "He possesses a temper that has left pubs aflame and has a fiery personality to match. An angry lad, hungry for revenge. You see, not all slaves are Africans." Jack's look softened a bit. "I picked up Red Legs in Barbados, where he was bound as a slave. He was the whipping boy."

I'd heard of whipping boys. Whenever the children of the master of the house misbehaved, they themselves were not punished. Instead, a slave was chosen to endure the punishment for him. "Please, say no more."

"Bloodthirsty for headhunters he is. As we all are, I'm sure. And the loot we take helps, too."

I'd nodded and studied the face of the angry pirate. Something about him, though obviously roughened and hard, struck me as vulnerable. Right behind the eyes, perhaps. "Red Legs," I said where only Jack could hear. "I believe he has potential."

Jack let go a belly laugh. "Ah, my dear girl. A good captain rules his, or her, ship with an iron fist. Not with emotions."

I blinked as the fresh memories fizzled. I didn't realize I had been staring at Red Legs until he met my gaze.

Jack's voice broke the silence and made me jump. "It was all lost, I thought. Then, an angel from above rained down upon that captain like hell's fire."

All the pirates turned their heavy stares to me. Some were missing an eye, others were cut up and scarred. Some were missing teeth, and others, their hands. I shifted in the straw.

"My angel," Jack said. "My partner in every way. Redella."

An uneasy silence fell upon us. Red Legs drew a long swill from his jug and spat. Without fanfare, he stood up and strode out of the galley. Thankfully, the uneasiness that had filled the cabin went with him.

A *Spanish Rose* pirate, sporting one eye and a scarred, bald head, reached behind him and produced another brown jug. A low laugh rolled over his thin lips. Chills danced down my backbone as they drew back over his teeth like a rabid dog. Soon, all the drunken men joined in. I stood up. "Gentlemen, I leave you to your much-deserved rest."

Jack caught my arm. "I'll walk you down. Men—" He faced his crew with rosy cheeks. "Save me some of that rum."

By the time we crossed the deck, rum-slurred sea shanties chorused from the galley. My smile mirrored my husband's. "They're really something, Jacky."

"Some of the most bloodthirsty—and *loyal*—upon the seas." He slipped his arm around my waist as we stepped down the tumbledown stairs together. "Red?"

"Yes?"

Jack looked down at me with such intensity, I feared he may hoist up my skirt and have his way with me, right there on the stairs that led down to our cabin. I shifted my weight. Under the bulk of his stare, I realized then and there that I may be the one to immodestly hike my skirt for his pleasure, without any worry as to who might wander onto the stairs to the captain's quarters and bear witness. A blush warmed my cheeks, but something else flamed hot between my thighs.

What is this side of you, Red?

Jack paid my obvious bewilderment no mind. "Not all pirates

are princes, Red. And not all pirates are seers and guardians like The Poison Lightning. And not all pirates are simple like Tommy. You're keen witted and brave. Trust those wits."

I nodded as the flash of want for my pirate husband drained from my face and body and a chilled fear replaced it.

He smiled again and wrinkled his nose at me. "I'll be down later. Keep the bed warm for me."

Our thick wooden door scratched slowly across the floor. I struggled to open my sleep-heavy eyes. "It's about time," I attempted to tease. "I was beginning to think you'd rather spend the night with your ship's mates than with your wife."

Jack didn't answer. Instead, he stepped inside and pushed the door shut, hard. His steps were heavy and offbeat.

"Sounds like you're tipsy, Jacky." I sat up and rubbed my eyes. The darkness was too thick to make out anything other than his shape. "Come on now and lay down."

Jack's heavy steps stopped at the side of our bed. Still, he had not spoken a word.

I shifted on the mattress. "Was the rum good?"

He grunted as I heard his britches slide down to the floor.

I sucked in a breath.

He's certainly acting odd.

"Jacky?"

"*Jacky*, bleh."

I froze. The blood in my veins went icy.

That is not Jack's voice.

"Is that what you call the fearless leader of *The Black Otter* Fleet? Jacky?" The voice's owner coughed deeply and spit on the floor. "Before you think about doing something stupid and opening your fool mouth, you ought to know I have a blade at your neck right now. Move or cry out—and you'll feel it."

All the new faces from *The Spanish Rose*, and even the old ones from *The Black Otter*, flashed through my mind. I kept my mouth shut and tried to visualize the room I shared with my husband. Surely daggers were stashed about, here and there.

Like the cutlass under the mattress. The swords over the door. But that was too far to grab in a pinch like this.

Jack had his cutlass on him, as he always did, and the only other blade I knew for sure was hanging over the door, with mine. If the mysterious intruder truly had a blade to my neck, I'd be dead long before I could reach my steel no matter which blade I went for.

"Jacky went on and on about you. About *his Red*. What an *angel* you are—" His words, thick with a jealous hatred as he climbed onto the bed beside me. "Well little angel. You are about to get a taste of the devil."

The sword he promised met the skin of my neck as he climbed shifted his weight and climbed on top of me. His manhood's hardness pressed against my inner thigh like a weapon in itself. I shifted my hips to keep it as far away from me as I could.

Please, don't.

The contorted face of the one-handed man came to mind, followed by that of the smarmy Charles Swan.

No, the voice wasn't squirrelly enough for Swan and his thin moustache. Dark Water William, perhaps? The tall African hadn't spoken a lick to me or where I could hear since I'd been on board. Maybe, but this voice sounded like it belonged to a white man.

"My, you're a wiggly little whore, aren't you?" He pressed his knee against my thigh and sent a shooting pain down my leg. "That's all right, I like a little fight in my whores."

The skinny one-eyed man with the maniacal laugh? The bearded starer, Red Legs Roberts? Icy fingers of fear gripped my backbone as the sharpness of the blade bit deeper into my neck.

I struggled against his weight, but he dug his free knee into my other leg. "Ah, there we go now. Get ready to buck, little whore."

You're dead, Red. Dead Red. He won't let you live, even if you let him have his way with you.

I sucked in as deep a breath as I could manage as he maneuvered his body and struggled to enter me.

I held my breath.

It's now or never. You're dead either way.

"Help me," I shrieked. "Somebody—"

"Now you done it." My attacker grabbed my hair and positioned the blade under my chin. "You don't know how stupid you are. Nobody in *The Black Otter* fleet gonna believe your word over mine." He jammed the blade against my neck. "And adultery?" he seethed. "On the high seas, it's punishable by death."

The door to my room slammed open with such force that it banged into the wall with a sickening crack. Somebody roared an angry roar before the dagger fell away from my neck. A body thumped on the wooden floor of the captain's cabin I called home. When the clouds wisped away from the moon and a silvery light lit our room, I found myself staring into the dark, staring eyes of Red Legs Roberts.

He sheathed his sword and offered me a nod. "Ma'am."

We looked in tandem at the unconscious man on the floor. "It *was* the one-eyed man," I squeaked. Tears moistened my eyes, but I willed them not to fall.

Red Legs Roberts' voice was more scratchy than I figured. "Might want to put something on that neck."

Sure enough, blood dripped down my chest and arm in a steady, sticky stream. "Oh."

A lantern lit the doorway. "What in God's Blood?"

"Jack, thank heav—" The words squelched on my tongue when I saw Russian Jack's lantern-lit face. Those piercing green eyes were fiery black, while the gentle, boyish features I'd admired just this morning were contorted in angry, stormy planes. If not for his tell-tale fur hat, he would have been near unrecognizable, even to me.

"Solo," he growled, "bring these three up on deck."

Jack whirled and the light he carried faded as he disappeared up the steps. The one-eyed pirate's words buzzed in my ears.

Adultery is a killing offense. He won't take your word over mine.

"You're already dead, Red," I whispered.

Solo didn't look at me as he grabbed the one-eyed pirate by his collar. His britches were still around his ankles. "Up you," he commanded.

"He's called Piranha, Solo," Red Legs said. "Used to sail with Captain Kidd."

Solo ignored him. "Both of you who can walk. Best get up to the deck like Cap ordered."

No more sea shanties sounded from the deck as I trudged up the stairs behind Red Legs, the man who had saved my honor. And my life. Though that fact might not matter as much as I hoped it would as soon as we reached the deck.

When we reached the deck, there was no sound apart from the creak and groan of the ship as it sat lightly atop the waves. The gentle rocking was reminiscent of a cradle rocking in a nursery.

I was rocked as a baby when I came into this world. I suppose the ship will rock me as I leave it.

Russian Jack stood in the middle of the deck, a deep frown on his angry face. Moonlight bathed the haphazard and hangdog crews of *The Spanish Rose* and *The Black Otter* as they draped themselves around the railing.

This is what it must have felt like for the gladiators in Rome when they were pitted against wild animals, and certain death, in the coliseum.

My filmy nightgown, the one I hoped Jack would have relieved me of by now, was half soaked in blood. It did nothing to keep out the nighttime chill on deck. I hugged my arm across my chest. At least the bleeding seems to have stopped.

"Piranha!" Jack's voice was steely sharp.

Solo still gripped Piranha by his collar. With a fling, he tossed the one-eyed pirate at Jack's feet. The crumpled man groaned. Whatever Red Legs hit him with had split the back of his head open like a melon, though I hadn't noticed until now.

"Stand up when you are before your captain," Solo barked.

My back straightened at his tone. I thought about glancing to see how Red Legs was standing, but looking around at such a time seemed a criminal idea. I wasn't in line at boarding school, waiting for dismissal. No, this was a matter of live and death. Though who would be left alive and who would be dead was anyone's guess at this point.

Jack didn't look at any of us. The lantern glowed at his feet and gave him an otherworldly, almost divine, look.

This must be what Adonis looked like.

Something deep in my core longed for a kind glance from him. But it didn't come.

Piranha managed to get to his feet, but his pants stayed down around his ankles. His head hung at an odd angle and blood flowed from his split skull, soaking the back of his grimy shirt. A blind man could see that something necessary was irreparably broken inside the insidious pirate.

"Loyalty." Even the sea itself seemed to quiet when Jack spoke. "Loyalty is our creed, no matter the name of the ship we sail aboard *The Black Otter* fleet." Jack's jeweled cutlass hung hungrily at his side.

"Loyalty," he boomed again. "Loyalty to God Almighty. And, more importantly, loyalty to our *code.*" Jack turned his back on us and strode in front of his men, to the furthest reaches of the lanternlight. "Did each of you not swear this when each of ye first came aboard? Your hand upon God's own Word?"

"Aye," they grumbled.

"I said," Jack thundered, "did ye not *swear*?!"

"Aye!" The word resonated from the band of rum-drunken pirates and seemed to fill the whole of the sea itself.

With his hands clutched behind his back, Jack strode easily before his men. From where I stood, it seemed as though he made lingering eye contact with each one.

"And which man dares test that loyalty now? Step forward if you are he."

Not a soul moved. I wasn't certain if anyone even breathed.

"Very well," Jack said. "I take your silence as your agreement." He waited a moment. Only silence echoed above the ship.

"Because I will not tolerate a repeat of what is going to happen here tonight again." For an instant, I thought my husband was going to look at me. But he did not. "Or what already has."

Cold stones knotted in my throat and dropped down into my gut. *I am alone in the coliseum and the lions are roaring.*

I sucked in a breath. The world spun around me.

Don't pass out, Red.

Jack circled back around to us. "Nobody speaks until I ask, and when I ask you will speak."

Silence.

"Piranha." Jack situated his flinty black stare on the bleeding man. "First, I want to hear from you."

The broken pirate struggled to stand on his quaking legs.

"What happened tonight so that you found yourself in your commodore's quarters?"

Drool slimed from Piranha's mouth when he opened it to speak. "To satisfy your wife, at her request."

I closed my eyes. In a London courtroom, such a statement would elicit groans from the opposing party. On Russian Jack's deck, nobody made a sound.

"I see." Jack rubbed his chin thoughtfully. "And did she request that you cut her neck, too?"

Piranha tried to speak, but succeeded in only gurgling.

Jack turned away from the blood-spattered pirate with a *pshaw.* "Red Legs Roberts."

"Yes, Cap'n."

"Tell me," Jack started. "How did you find yourself in your commodore's quarters tonight?"

Red Legs spoke calm and easy, as though Jack had simply asked about the weather. "I was standing at the railing having a smoke when I saw Piranha come out of the wheelhouse. He crossed the deck, looked around, and took to the stairs. Your stairs."

Jack stopped pacing. "And then?"

Red Legs continued. "And then, I heard your woman scream.

She screamed *help me, somebody.* There was terror in her voice, but then the screaming stopped."

Jack stood with his hands clasped behind his back and his eyes the same shade of black as the nighttime sea. "So, what did you do?"

"Well Cap, I went to help her. I opened the door to your quarters. It was dark, and I had no lantern. I swung the butt of my blade and hoped I didn't hit your woman. When the moon came out, I saw she was bleeding from the neck. I didn't know it was Piranha till I seen him crumpled on the ground."

"Is that all you wish to say?"

Red Legs nodded. "Yes sir, except that's when you and Solo showed up."

"Liar!" The word was garbled as it exited Piranha's mouth. "Damned liar you are, Red Legs."

Jack didn't silence him. Instead, he tapped his foot. "Adultery is a killing offense when you sail the seas. So a killing we shall have."

Jack's black stare fell on me. "Redella. Step forward." His Russian accent flexed its fingers around the words—then strangled them.

He didn't call me Red.

Behind Jack, Poison Lightning studied the deck. For once, even Tommy was silent. Charles and Dark Water, however, stared straight at me. For the first time since coming aboard, I saw a smile curve Dark Water's lips into a sinister scowl.

I tried not to look them as I took the necessary steps toward Jack. I stopped when I was beside Piranha. In this moment, I wasn't his Red. I wasn't even his wife. Only one person aboard knew where I stood with him, and that was Jack. There was no question that I was at his complete and total mercy.

Careful to keep a blank face, I stared at his chest. "Yes, sir." My fingers laced together behind my back.

"Solo," he ordered. "Fetch her blade from my quarters."

I dared not move as we waited for Solo to return. A chill tickled my skin through my thin nightdress. I tried not to shiver. My neck ached, but at least it seemed the bleeding stopped.

"Here go, Cap." Solo held out the steel that I'd used just hours before to save Jack's life.

"*Niet.*" He shook his head. "Give it to my wife."

My eyes widened and I tried not to look surprised as I accepted the sword.

Jack continued his spiel once the blade was firm in my hand. "Redella, it is my belief that this man attempted to rape you tonight—in my bed." He paused. "In *our* bed."

A low murmur rolled through the men. My cheeks flushed with shame and I ducked my head.

"Was he successful in this, his abominable enterprise?"

"No." I licked my lips and prayed my voice didn't waver. "He was not successful."

The murmurs quieted.

"Very well." Jack kept his face and voice steady as the tide, but I saw his trembling fingers relax with my assurance. He blinked once and then he continued. "Then, a man who swore his loyalty to me and this fleet had the *audacity* to bear false witness about his actions to not only his captain, but also to all aboard."

The pirate crew grumbled their agreement.

"His punishment is death!"

The piratical grumble rose to a raucous cheer.

My head bobbed in a miniscule nod and my stomach turned over.

Jack paced the deck, his black eyes wild. "Do you agree, men of *The Black Otter* fleet?"

Their answer, in unison, came faster than I expected. "Aye!"

Jack looked at me as though he was explaining simple addition to me for the fourth time. "Aboard this ship, Redella, I am the judge. And you heard the jury." Jack's face was no longer scarlet. "But the crime was committed against you. Which makes you the executioner."

The Black Otter began to pitch and roll again, and with it, my stomach. "Jack, I don't—"

He erased the space between us, but did not touch me as he had before. I wished he would. "What's the matter?"

I stared into his eyes, which had returned to their normal green, but kept my voice low. "I don't know what to do, Jack."

"My darling girl." His chiseled, handsome face broke into a knowing grin. "You take his life."

Piranha broke the silence. "Lying whore," he managed. "She liked it, Cap."

I stared at my husband as his eyes clouded to the tell-tale stormy black. His hand began to tremble, and the notorious Russian whirled with a roar. The jeweled cutlass was in his grasp as all the pent-up rage he'd struggled to contain came to fruition.

Jack grasped the broken, would-be rapist by the hair. The shriek that came from the dying man as Jack yanked him up straight told of unimaginable pain. The cutlass moved so quickly, I thought Jack had done the deed for me.

"The lips of a liar!" Jack bellowed.

I stared in horror as a chunk of flesh from Piranha's face flew through the air like a comet trailing blood and fell to the deck with a sickening *smack*. Blood spread like a curtain of silk over Jack's cutlass blade. When he stepped aside, I swallowed back my horror.

Piranha, a man who Jack thought loyal, tottered there on the deck, his skull split, broken, and bloody. Beneath his nose, the flesh was gone. The bloody bones revealed there gave him the look of a grinning skeleton.

"He was going to do worse to you, Red," Jack bawled.

I held my blade in quaking hands.

"Even after his judgement was rendered, he tried to make you out the liar!" Jack's voice boomed like that of a cannon. "His dying wish was to break you down and kill you—or make *me* kill you—like any other pirate captain on the sea would have!"

I recoiled as though I'd been slapped. Jack's words stung with immeasurable truth. He was right, though, and his words were impossibly true. If any other man had come in judgement against me, I would have been found guilty before the trail even began. Strange enough, aboard this pirate ship, I'd received fairer treatment than I ever had as an honest landlubber.

"Do it!" Jack commanded.

I raised my sword. With the adrenaline from the earlier battle gone, I felt helpless and weak. Certainly not like a killer of any sort.

"His dying wish was that I believe him over you," Jack shouted. "That I take off your head and end your very *life*! As is my right!"

I looked at my shaking hands. Strangely enough, I thought of Sully. Sully certainly thought me weak and unable. Jack, however, found me to be nothing but capable from the moment we met. He rescued me from a life of shaking in fear when he took *The Scarlet Rose* and had never asked me to do anything I wasn't willing to do.

Until now.

He's trying to save you from yourself. To show you what you're capable of. This is your crew. You are capable, Red. Now, it's time to show them.

The tiny voice in the back of my mind was replaced by an image. Those sad, hopeless eyes of the dark woman in Sully's kitchen. There was nobody to speak for her as she endured her misery in suffocating silence. Nobody to force her unleash her inner warrior that seethed just below the surface.

This is my life now.

My ship.

My battle to fight.

As I raised my arms, the sword seemed to know what to do. The dying man before me was no formidable foe, at least not in this state, but he thought me a weak woman.

Prey.

A victim.

Some lowly *thing* to be used for his sick pleasure, then killed, or executed, in a heap of lies.

Already, I'd given him more grace than he'd shown me.

My blade slashed across his thin neck and his head lolled back. Piranha fell to the deck, never to move again.

The time for trembling was over.

When Solo and Red Legs had buried Piranha at sea, Jack stepped in the middle of the bloody puddle that nobody moved to clean. I couldn't help but notice the dead pirate's lips still lay on the deck.

"Our articles. So that nobody is unclear."

Jack held a ratty paper before him and read aloud.

I

*The giving of orders that did not come from your captain
is punishable by death.*

II

*Acts of disobedience against your captain is punishable by
death. No acts of theft or piracy against the villages that
supply or harbor pirates.*

III

*All booty is publicly inspected, then dispersed according to
universal law.*

IV

*Any man who loses a limb during the course of duty is to
be paid 600 pieces-of-eight and may retire if he so chooses.
Should he choose to stay aboard, he may do so for as long as
he sees fit.*

Jack looked up from the paper. "These are familiar to you, no?"

"Aye," grumbled the crew.

Jack waited until the crew again fell silent. "Now, as your captain, I am adding one more."

V

*The rape, or attempted rape, of any female aboard any ship
in The Black Otter fleet, is punishable by certain death.*

Stony looks fell upon me from Jack's—well, from *my*—crew.
Something twisted in my gut. If Jack couldn't get these men to
obey and not see me as the enemy, there was no hope. My life
would only be mine for so long. The crew would know when
death would come for me, as it was each of them who held the
my hourglass.

"Well said, Cap." Solo's voice chimed out like a bell, tolling
over the sea.

"Said well, it was," Tommy agreed.

Red Legs spat on the deck. "Aye. Well said. Shouldn't *have*
to be said, but as it is, it was said well."

Monica Joan crept up beside me as I scrubbed the deck with
a makeshift mop. Everything I thought was hard labor before
took leave as I tried in vain to scrub the blood from the grains
of wood on the deck.

"I brought fresh water, well fresh water from the sea anyway,
and rags," she whispered. "I can't believe you killed him. I
was watching."

I sat back, glad for a break, and offered her a smile. "I can't
believe it, either."

She pulled a rag from the bucket and wringed it. "Here, let
me tend your neck."

"He cut me good." I turned my head a bit. Not too far, but just
a bit. "I'm set to be a mess of scars by the time I'm thirty-five."

"What are they doing now?"

"They?"

Monica Joan stuck the rag back in the bucket. Having the
flaky blood washed away felt good. "Yes, them. The pirates."

I glanced over to where Jack stood. He held a thick brown
book before him. One by one, each of the crew came by and put
their hand on it. They exchanged words, then the next man came.

"Swearing in afresh, it seems." I wrung out my rag over the peskiest stain and started to scrub. "Swearing their loyalty and allegiance."

"On a book?"

"Yes. On the Holy Bible."

Monica Joan pondered this a moment. She shrugged. "At least they moved out of the blood to do it."

Chapter Seven

Swansea, Wales

Jack twined his fingers in mine. "I remember you two talking when she came to help you on the deck that evening."

The romantic mood that appeared with my husband's reappearance lifted. I stared out to sea and waited for the black veil of memories to come. "I can't help but remember it, Jack. When it comes to mind. Even if I try not—think of something else. To do something else. They wait until I'm quiet or alone, then come rushing out of their corners."

Jack's fingers trailed down my neck. I didn't respond. I couldn't. He pulled his hand away.

"She came out to help me that night, Jack. Do you know what she said?"

"What did she say?"

"That she found a dagger down below. She was going to try and kill anyone who laid a hand on me. After all, we were the only two females aboard. We had to look out for each other. If I went, she would gladly follow me into death."

I let my head sink onto the balcony railing. Jack's hand found the back of my neck and began to rub. I didn't stop him. I could stop nothing. The memories had stirred from their watery grave and demanded acknowledgement—no matter the hurt.

A hazy red sky stretched out before me as I stood at the railing of *The Black Otter*.

"Red sky at morning, sailor take warning. Red sky at night, sailor's delight." Jack's voice purred into my hair. "Why isn't the most beautiful woman to have ever sailed the sea still resting in her chambers?"

"It's hard to sleep without you next to me, Jacky." I closed my eyes and leaned into him. "Tell me, where does that verse come from? About the sky, I mean?"

Jack's arms circled about my waist. "Every seamen knows that. It means storms are more likely when the sky's lit red at sunrise. The opposite is true at night, when it means fair weather for nighttime sailing."

"Yes, I figured that much." I opened my eyes and scanned the world that was still so new to me. The world that had become my home. "What I meant was, where did it originate?"

Jack and I swayed together. "I figure the Bible. In the book of Matthew. Verse 16: 2-3. Where it all began."

I turned to look at Jack. This man amazed me more and more as days went by. "I have a confession. I never figured you to be a man of the Word. But when you swore the crew in on the Bible yesterday—"

Jack smiled down at me. "*He answered and said unto them, When it is evening, ye say, It will be fair weather: for the sky is red. And in the morning, It will be foul weather to day: for the sky is red and lowering.*"

My mouth fell opened and my eyes widened. I closed it as Jack continued. "Our Lord and Savior said this. One of the many reasons I believe He had salt in his blood. Like me."

He brushed my forehead with a kiss. I shivered. "Come to think of it, I believe Mr. Shakespeare mentioned it, too. In *Venus and Adonis*."

Jack's fingers twirled in my hair. "Is that so?"

I nodded. "Like a red morn that ever yet betokened, wreck to the seaman, tempest to the field. Sorrow to the shepherds, woe unto the birds, gusts and foul flaws to herdmen and to herds." I smiled at him. "I assume the meaning is the same?"

All the play was gone from Jack's face. "Recites Shakespeare from memory. My, my Red. I certainly do have a gem in you." He traced my cheek with his finger as light as though he were using a feather. "Pray tell, continue. I could listen to you all the day long."

Before I could call the next verse to mind, a black mass appeared on the horizon. "Jack! Another ship!"

"Aye, it is. But fear not. We know this ship. And they are friend, not foe." He gestured toward the mysterious ship. "Look at the flag, my dear, and you'll see that this ship is *The Molly Maiden*."

As we drew closer, I squinted into the sunrise. A heavy-bod-ied bare-breasted outline of a woman in white against a black background flittered proudly on the sewn material. I looked sideways at Jack. "*The Molly Maiden*?"

"Yes, she is harmless." Jack nodded.

I eyed the ship as it drew nearer. My stomach flipped as an odd emotion I couldn't place settled there. I licked my lips, which had gone dry. "You mentioned before, about your parents—"

I let my words trail off into the early morning fog.

Jack unfurled his fingers from my hair and stepped beside me at the railing. He propped one booted foot onto the lowest rail and gazed out to sea. "As you already know, my father was a pirate. The world knew him as the infamous Vladimir Nemirovsky."

Jack glanced at me. I shrugged and offered an infinitesimal shake of my head. "I've never heard of your father, Jack."

Jack nodded. "He was known among all those who called Mother Russian home. He led rebellions against the Rus-sia's Tsars."

"I see."

Jack drew in a deep breath, but kept his gaze fixed on the sea. "I've never spoken of this. Forgive me if my words are choppy."

"There's nothing to forgive," I whispered. "You've done nothing wrong."

Jack glanced at me again. His eyes shimmered with years of unrealized emotion. "It is so easy to love you, Red." He sniffled and cleared his throat. "My father was a pirate, like myself. His wanderings brought him to England, where he bought my mother's affections. And stole her heart. At least, that's the story she told me when I was old enough to ask."

"Your mother took care of you on her own then?"

"That she did, in her seaside whorehouse with the help of her fellow ladies-of-the-evening, as long as she was able."

I wonder if I ever passed his mother's whorehouse while running about for my own mother—or Sully?

Jack knitted his fingers together over the railing. "The coughing started when I was a young lad. She made sure I stayed in my little room in her closet, far away from her, around that time, lest I come down with the coughing, too."

It seemed Jack was treading on thin ice as he spoke of his mother with careful, deliberate words. I was equally careful not to speak, lest my words be the ones that made the ice break.

"The ladies kept me fed and clothed as her coughing got worse, then turned bloody. I learned early on to pick the pockets of the men who bought my mother while they slept."

"Wouldn't that have been dangerous, had you been caught?" The boards of *The Black Otter* creaked as the several waves crashed against the side without warning. Salty spray wet my lips.

"Yes. Deadly dangerous." Jack offered me a small smile. "It only took my being caught once to learn that."

"What happened?" My voice was a barely a whisper. I immediately regretted asking, for now I would have to hear the answer.

"I made the mistake of taking all the money from the john's wallet. Well, of course the next morning he noticed that all his money had vanished overnight. He immediately began beating on my mother, who was still asleep, accusing her of stealing from him."

I drew my hands to my mouth.

"I wasn't allowed to come out of my closet, no matter what

I heard or saw. But I couldn't let my mom take a beating for something I did. So I burst out of my closet and jumped on the man as he whipped my mother with his belt." Jack drew a shuttering breath. "He turned on me. Gave my mother time to get herself together and slip out the door. When she got back with help, the man was gone. Threw me through a glass mirror and left me for dead in a puddle of blood, so I was told."

I squinted into the rising sun. "My my, Jack—"

Jack ignored me and continued to tell the gruesome story of his past. "I learned then and there how to properly steal so nobody could tell they'd been swiped. My mother went downhill quickly after that beating and didn't last much longer. When she wasn't entertaining men, she took every spare moment to tell me of my father."

"She loved him," he continued. "He made her promises. They made plans of a life together. She was going to go with him on the high seas when he returned to Russia. In the end, he left her, with child, under the cover of night. She gave me the most Russian name she knew, Mikhail, and my father's last name. Nemirovsky. But of course, Russian Jack suits me just fine."

I felt like I was reading a storybook in my old nursery. "So tell me. How did you come to kill your father, Jack?"

Jack snapped out of whatever trance he'd retreated to. The mist cleared from his sea-green eyes as the giant wooden ship with the bare-breasted woman on the flag passed by. Half dressed women cat-called and whistled from over the railing of *The Molly Maiden*.

"Come now, my sweet Red, it's time we begin the day."

"The sky wasn't red tonight," I observed. The stars sparkled above us like diamonds on a black velvet pillow. This moonless night also lacked in breeze. All the day, I'd not been able to shake the image of a young Jack killing his burly pirate father from my mind. "Tell me Jack, how—"

My husband, who moments before had been standing innocently at my side, slapped his hand over my mouth with a smack. I chirped in surprise. Of all the things my husband might do that caused me shock, him hitting me never entered into my mind.

"Shush," he warned.

I tasted coppery blood, but nodded and dared not make a sound.

Jack lowered his hand. The shift in mood was almost tangible as we stood in shared silence. My husband lifted his face until his nose was pointed toward the sky like a bloodhound. I couldn't decide whether I felt safe—or afraid.

"Quickly, Red," he whispered. "Get to our cabin. Hide yourself well. Do not come out no matter what you hear."

"I will." I started across the dark deck. As I reached the doors that led down into our quarters, I heard Jack suck in a breath.

He let loose with a bellow so loud that I covered my ears. "Ships approaching, men!"

A high-pitched cackle split the tense air. "No, Captain. You are wrong. Ships already here."

Full grown fear drove me through the doors and down the stairs. When I reached our bedroom, I locked the door.

Where to hide? Jack said to stay hidden no matter what.

I glanced wildly about as *The Black Otter* pitched on the sea. A moment later, the anchor splashed down outside Jack's porthole window. My heart thundered in my chest.

What is going on? If it is bad enough to cause such a reaction from Jack then it must be—

My gaze fell upon our bed.

There!

Though I failed to notice before, mine and Jack's bed was laid out atop a flat, wooden chest. I pushed up the mattress and, sure enough, there was a handle. I gave it a pull. It creaked open just enough for me to get one leg in. Then the other. As I let the top ease down and seal me into what may prove to be my tomb, someone or something hit the locked bedroom door.

Chatter in another language, syllabic and short, echoed in the stairway.

Please God, let the mattress fall back over the top of this trunk. Let me stay hidden. Let—

Something sharp hit the locked door with such force, the wood splintered with a sickening crack. Hidden by darkness, an anonymous thing with many legs whisked across my hand.

Jack. Oh Jacky, where are you?

The incessant chatter grew louder.

Is that Chinese?

"You saw her come down here?"

"Ahhh—"

The tell-tale creak screeched as the mysterious invaders discovered my hiding place. Candlelight flooded into my tucked-away space. I glanced up. There, staring down at me, were the faces of men I'd never seen the likes of before. Slanted eyes, long mustaches, sharp swords. They certainly were Chinese. Chinese pirates.

"Take her to Jack," one ordered in twangy, broken syllables. "Let he watch us all take her before we kill her."

One of their swords poked into the flesh of my back as they forced me up the stairs.

"Behold," one of my captors hissed. "Your husband."

The doors flung open and I stumbled out onto the deck.

My throat tightened at the sight laid out before me. Russian Jack was there. On his knees, with a rope around his neck like a dog. Haggard and dirty Chinamen ringed him. All wore a look of murder in their eyes. Jack's icy eyes, however, were swollen almost shut. Scarlet smears streaked his cheeks. His chest rose and fell as though he'd just fought for his life, and was on the verge of giving up. When our eyes met, however, he bristled anew.

"Let her go, China Joe." Jack made no move, but the hatred for the rival pirate transformed his voice from one of a man to one of a bloodthirsty beast.

China Joe's crew laughed a twangy, inhuman laugh.

"Let who go?" China Joe's eyes glinted flinty black in the moonlight. "You mean her?"

The dirty Chinaman, presumably Joe, jabbed the steel point of a sword into my back. "You mean her? My new whore?"

He didn't let Russian Jack answer before continuing. "I wonder who will has her first—" His words mixed with the thick laughter of his men, until the sick sound blanketed all of us on deck. "I believe *I* will."

Jack sprang to his feet with a roar. He charged China Joe so quickly that the rope around his neck tightened like a noose, but the pirate holding the other end was taken off guard. He flew off his barrel and landed face first on the deck.

In that instant, Jack had the upper hand. Had the pirate with the sword in my back not jabbed it in further and grabbed my hair, I would have rushed to my husband's aid. Before I could figure a way out of my predicament, something crashed over Jack's head and he fell motionless to the deck.

I sat on the side of *The Black Otter*. Utter fear enveloped me as Russian Jack fastened the second and final cannonball to my legs. I was powerless to quell the tremble that knocked my knees together as I swallowed back the nausea that swelled in my throat. The stoic look on his face as he carried out the task forced upon him by the Chinese crew brought a tremble to my lip, as well as my legs.

He's really going to do it. My husband is really going to bury me at sea—alive.

"No Jacky, don't. Please." I tried to keep the fear out of my whisper. Still, the words hissed out of my throat with a terrifying finality. "Just tell me what to do and we can fight our way out of this mess. Together."

His face registered no emotion and he didn't answer.

"Go ahead Jack," one Chinese bucko chided. "Kiss your child bride goodbye."

Monica Joan's screams resonated in my ears as the Chinese took turns at her.

Will they kill her when they finish? Will they kill her as they finish?

She was terrified when we took her ship. I had personally assured her she was safe aboard *The Black Otter*—that nobody aboard would dare harm a woman with Russian Jack in charge. She was simply hitching a ride to the mainland under the guise of friendship and protection. And we'd let her down. We'd all let her down. But none had let her down more than me.

Jack leaned forward. "Let the cannonballs fall first. Don't jump with them." His lips, lips I was sucking and biting just hours before, brushed my cheek in a dry kiss. "Then swim. We passed a sloop yesterday, remember? *The Molly Maiden*? Swim to it. Swim in the direction of the setting sun."

"Jacky—"

His lips silenced my unasked question. My mouth worked against his, hoping against hope that, somehow, we would still come out on top. Tears wet my eyes and dangled from my lashes.

He pulled back. "I'll find you. I promise."

His callused hand brushed the side of my face and my eyes closed on their own. I bit my lip. The Chinese crew cat-called in their twangy syllabic way.

The grimy, grinning, gap-toothed face belonging to China Joe appeared over Russian Jack's shoulder. "Now push her," he instructed. "You do as China Joe say. I am your mah-stah now."

A whip cracked and Jack grimaced as the leather split the skin on his back. "Now!"

Jack hefted the cannonballs into his arms, one after the other, and placed them on the side of *The Black Otter*.

Will the weight break my legs? Will the fall alone kill me? Will I drown?

Another snap from China Joe's whip elicited a groan from Jack. Monica Joan's screams pinnacled, then silenced. Bedraggled pirates emerged, pulling up their pants and elbowing each other.

"Push her, fool, or I give her to my crew."

I stared at my husband and watched helplessly as his eyes clouded to stormy black. With a roar, he turned and dove again at China Joe. A tear rolled down my cheek as he wrested the cat-o-nine tails from his bony hand.

"Get his woman," China Joe commanded.

Time ground to a halt as the pirates, so freshly finished with Monica Joan, hunched and started toward me, their long-fingered hands outstretched. Hands that, should they touch me, meant death.

In the midst of the rushing pirates, there was Jack, my Jack, battling for my life and my honor, against a cruel nemesis that clearly had the upper hand. We were overpowered before Jack and I even knew we'd been overrun.

Faces flashed in my mind as my heart slapped against the inside of my chest.

Charles Swan. Dark Water William.

Thump. Thump. Thump.

The Poison Lightning. Handsome Solo.

Thump, thump, thump, thump.

Simple Tommy Tew. Ginger-haired Sully. My beautiful mother.

Thumpthumpthumpthumpthump

Russian Jack, the man I loved.

"Argh!" The pirates howled as they fought to reach me.

I didn't dare another glance at Jack. Instead, I shoved both cannonballs overboard. My fingernails, which had hours before passionately gripped the naked flesh of my husband, dug into the splintery wooden ship.

Three—

The chains went taut.

—*two*—

A pair of splashes met my ears.

—*one.*

A set of hands hit my back and sent me falling, flailing, into the briny blue below.

Chapter Eight

Adrift in the sea

My arms ached. The lifesaving chunk of driftwood that had no business being in the middle of the ocean in the first place bit into the flesh of my arms, leaving them bloody and raw. At least they *felt* bloody and raw. It hurt to open my eyes more than a squint to inspect them for myself. The sunlight reflecting off the endless sea that stretched out before me may well have been the sun's rays themselves. I squeezed my swollen eyes shut and didn't dare loosen my grip as I bobbed, helpless as a rotten coconut, in the blue expanse. Drops splashed my face as I went down, then up, then down again.

If it hurts, that means I'm alive. I drew in a shuddering breath and kicked my feet. *Thank you, God.*

Iron from the shackles my husband had clasped round my ankles bit into my flesh with even the slightest movement.

Bloody and raw.

Though they were still heavy, the cannonballs were gone. I drew one leg up and felt with my toes what weighed on me.

Chains.

My miniscule movements shifted my weight against the chunk of driftwood and I flipped round to my back. Heart thundering, I sputtered beneath the glassy surface only a moment before I righted myself again.

My breath came fast and rasped in my throat as I dug my fingers into the wood. Splinters pierced my flesh, but I didn't care.

If I lose my grip, there's no way I can stay afloat. I tried not to move my feet. *Even without the murderous cannonballs. The chains weigh enough that I'll be pulled down. I'll slowly lose the fight to stay above water, then I'll lose the fight to breathe.*

I bit my lip and pushed those troublesome thoughts to the far recesses of my mind. A flash of the creatures that lived in the depths forced my eyes open.

The night Red Legs Roberts and the other pirates had come aboard *The Black Otter*, stories of things they'd seen—unexplainable things—had been most enthusiastically told. Tales of monsters from the deep surpassed the tales of the treasure they'd taken. Rum was passed about and a hush fell as each men told their story.

"Sea devils, they was," Tommy had sworn over a fresh bottle of Spanish rum. "Swimming up from the depths and flying about the ship. Hundreds of 'em." Tommy spread his arms wide and splashed rum all over Red Legs Roberts, eliciting a groan from all the pirates. "A spear grew from each tail and they had wings, they did. Would fly for a bit, then ride beneath the water before taking flight again."

Normally, the pirates laughed at Tommy and his wild stories. But nobody aboard that night dared laugh at this one. After all, sea devils were no laughing matter.

Another pirate drew a long puff off a smoke. The end glowed orange and he exhaled before he spoke in a gravelly voice. "Seen sea devils. Had one leap on a boat when I was a young man. I was in the rigging." He flicked the ash and stared into the faces that watched his every move. "Me buddy approached it, and that spear Tommy spoke of? Speared me buddy. Straight through his chest and out the other side."

He sucked in another long drag and shook his head.

"Sharks," another offered. "Follow the doomed ships. See a shark? Death is not far behind. They smell it, before the soul is even gone from the body. And blood—they smell that, too."

Solo scoffed. "Smell in the water? Nothing can smell in the water."

The raggedy pirate looked at the blond prince. "When you've been a-bleedin' in the water as I was, you're likely to think a bit different, sonny." He held up his arm. On the end was fastened a hook where his hand once had been. "When you see one shark, there be ten more you can't see."

The smile melted from Solo's face.

Charles Swan shifted his thin moustache. "The Kraken," he squeaked.

Silence fell over the lot of them like a shroud.

"Ain't never seen The Kraken, meself. Heard the stories from the men that have." Charles glanced about the circle of men. "Tentacles, twice as long as a ship. And if the head comes up beneath you, you're capsized."

The familiar, uncomfortable silence returned. For to be capsized at sea is a death sentence. But to speak of being capsized—

"Seen a mermaid once," Jack chirped. His voice was much too chipper.

"Yes, we know," one pirate muttered. "And you married her."

Jack. Memories of my husband, some recent, and some not so recent, swirled in my muddled mind as I adjusted my grip on the wood. My shoulders ached and what skin was exposed burned like fire. *Did China Joe kill him?*

The none-too-distant memory of lying next to the strong, muscled man in the bed we shared as the early morning light spread across our blanket panged in my chest.

Was there something else I could have done? Did he give his life—to save my honor?

I twisted the horrid scene around in my mind.

I was hiding, they found me and brought me on deck. Then, there was Jack. There hadn't been a moment to grab my steel, or at least I'd have gone down fighting.

I squeezed my eyes shut again and leaned my face against the wood.

Then, I was on the side of The Black Otter with Jack before me, beaten and bruised.

China Joe's nasal, syllabic laugh made me cringe, even as a memory. But it was another sound that came soon after that froze in my mind and turned my blood to ice.

The helpless, hopeless screams from below deck.

Monica Joan.

She cried out for help that would never come. Tears welled up in my swollen eyes as I sobbed against chunk of driftwood as the memory of shriek after terrified shriek pained my ears afresh. I'd let down my only friend, and it had cost her life. And my husband, my precious husband. Promised to find me.

I love you, Jack. I'm not worth finding.

Before I had the chance to get too worked up, something bumped my foot.

Was that one of the chains?

The anonymous something bumped me from the other side and spun me around. I kicked but hit nothing.

The way Solo's smile had melted as the old hook-handed seaman swore by his theory that sharks smelled blood gripped my spine. Without warning, silver-bodied fish began to breach the water, jumping around me in a hopeless bid for freedom. *But from what?*

I dared a peek just as a gray dorsal fin broke the water before me.

"I'd say you was in need of some assistance." A woman's voice forced me to open my eyes. "You done found yourself in a bait of sharks."

I shielded my eyes. The outline of a person standing on the deck of a small boat blocked out the ceaseless sun. For a moment, I wondered if I was seeing a mirage.

However, mirages weren't supposed to talk. "Where am I?"

"Lost at sea, of course." The large, snaggletooth woman let go a laugh as she flung the rope ladder over the side of the boat. She grinned as she offered me a rotund hand and helped me onto the deck. "Now, you're safe aboard a vessel that is always in the right place at the right time. Some call us the Ship of Dreams."

I glanced back into the water. Sure enough, four fins circled the driftwood that had been my saving grace. I shuddered. "Many thanks."

"It's said those critters smell blood. Meself, I think I'd have a hard time smelling anything underwater." Her wide, tan face was decorated with a spiderweb of white scars. "Then again, I ain't no shark."

An impassioned groan from somewhere gave me pause. I rubbed my eyes and studied the ship where I'd found myself, or who'd found me. Rum-heavy air hung thick over the deck, like a drunken storm cloud. Men lolled about with half-naked, smiling women. Their money hungry giggles were reminiscent of those that came from the beds of the most downcast of the women in the London poorhouses. Women who decided they didn't want to be poor any longer and sold the only thing they had left to sell. Themselves.

She gestured up to the fluttering flag. The same black flag Jack pointed out to me the day before, with the white outline of a bare breasted woman. Up this close, I saw that she also sported a fish tail. "Welcome aboard *The Molly Maiden*."

I looked at the woman. Heavy-set like their symbol, her voluminous chest was barely concealed by fabric wrappings that were probably once quite nice. Stringy blonde hair was piled high, and salt-heavy tendrils dangled around her wrinkled face in an attempt to be seductive. She could have been somebody's governess in another life, or even somebody's grandmother. "Ships take a day off sailing to pay us a call. Merchant ships, pirate ships, soldier ships—they all stop for *The Molly Maiden*."

"I, um, see." I chewed my lip. "I suppose business is well, then."

"I'm Rhodesia." She studied me a moment through clear, brown eyes. The bags beneath them told of a lifetime of sleepless nights. "Speaking of passing ships—"

My eyebrows knitted together. Before I could respond, a naked blonde laid out on several barrels groaned as a man with greasy gray hair moved his oral attentions from her mouth to her breasts.

I glanced at Rhodesia, who wore a knowing smile.

Beside us, the blonde's eyes were shut as she took his hand and put it between her legs with a muffled moan. With his free hand, he struggled with his britches until his ripe manhood sprang free. At once, she turned on her side and took it hungrily in her mouth. The man began to thrust, but the odd position made such actions look ridiculous and painful. Still, I was powerless to look away.

"Tell me. A pirate ship from *The Black Otter* fleet stopped by, with news of one of our former best customers. Commodore Jack Rackham who refuses to be called such but will go by Captain Russian Jack until the day he dies." Rhodesia, the snaggletooth wench, ignored the blonde and her impassioned suitor. "You know, I think I have it figured. One of the pirates mentioned that Captain Jack married up with some young thing after he marked her face with his cutlass. To warn off other men, no doubt."

Jagged gasps and moans finally turned Rhodesia's head. We both watched as the man roughly pried his whore's legs apart and buried his face where his hand had been moments before. Somewhat awkwardly, he clambered atop her on the barrels. He bucked viciously, but with a hitch. It wasn't until then I noticed he was missing part of a leg.

Their passionate noises reached a climactic octave as Rhodesia turned back to face me. "Their ship will come back for them at sunset, once their business in Portugal is complete," she explained. "These prisoner transport ships always bring the business."

"Prisoner transport ships?"

"Taking convicts from London across the sea. To the New World."

I looked around the deck again. Sure enough, like the one-legged man, most of the men performing services to the woman—or having services performed upon them—were clad in the same dingy striped prison garb. One man caught my eye as he hitched up his blue hose and didn't offer so much as a glance to the brunette whore who wiped his seed from her face. With lust in his eye, he stepped to a black-haired beauty whose charms no blouse could conceal. He whispered something in her ear and she nodded before he dropped to his knees and disappeared beneath her skirts. She opened her legs wide and her head threw back as he obviously tasted the forbidden fruits of *The Molly Maiden.*

Strangely, I was the only one in chains.

"How do the prisoners earn the right to be turned loose in such a manner?"

Rhodesia shrugged. "It's a long haul across the Atlantic. Most men yearn for some bit of freedom before their sentences are carried out. Those who are favorites of the guards get to have just that."

"Aren't you afraid they'll try and take over the ship? Or jump ship and swim to freedom?"

Rhodesia laughed, sending a ripple across her ample bosom. "Jump and swim through shark infested waters? Let them have at it, if they're that idiotic." She sobered. "As for taking over *The Molly Maiden.* No one would dare go up against Irish Bon, no matter how hardened a criminal he—or she—be."

Irish Bon. Where have I heard that name before?

"Who pays?" I was powerless to stem the questions that flooded my mind as lust flooded the ship. "For your services, I mean."

"The prison system of Jolly Old England." She slapped my back. "So well they pay that they may just have *The Molly Maiden* on the payroll!"

Shock filled me as the prisoners filled the women who serviced them.

"Prison guards are hornier than the prisoners themselves." She cackled again. "Let's get you out of those wet clo—" Words fell dead from her tongue and she grabbed my chin. Rhodesia turned my face this way and that. "Say—how'd you get this mark across your cheek?"

I steeled my face and stared back into her questioning eyes as the innocent, shy girl I had been slowly melted away. Redella may well be dead in the water, with no hope of resurrection. "My name is Red. Left for dead by China Joe. Wife to Russian Jack. Co-Captain of *The Black Otter* and her fleet."

"You don't say." Her face flushed a robust pink, then broke into a sly smile. "Since you won't be needing a job to work off your room and board, you will have to make other arrangements. I'll see to it you get in to see Captain Bon straight away." She turned and hurried toward the cabin. Her fat legs smacked together as she ran. "Come along, Captain Red. Let's get you out of those wet clothes. It's almost time for dinner."

An emotion I couldn't quite place swelled in my chest as I strode along behind her, my broken chains clinking behind me. Nobody paid me any mind. Still, something told me I'd just been raised a notch on *The Ship of Dreams*.

"Get dressed and scurry on to the galley. Pantalets are in the dresser. Blouse is in there, too. Bon will know how to get you out of those irons."

After all that had transpired since coming to live aboard *The Black Otter*, from marrying a notorious pirate who wasn't my fiancé, to doing murder, to getting thrown overboard and picked up from amidst a shiver of sharks, nothing seemed as absurd as wearing pantalets on a boat full of whores.

I dropped my hands to my sides and fingered the wet fabric, heavy with salt water, that clung to my legs. Rhodesia let out a hard, toothless laugh.

"See there, you're pretty much wearing britches already." She clapped me on the back so hard I stumbled forward. "Least these in here are dry."

Chapter Nine

Aboard The Molly Maiden on the high seas

I pulled on the canvas pantalets and the only billowy blouse I found in the drawer. Thankfully, I maneuvered the clunky irons and chains through the too-big leg holes without too much difficulty. They clinked behind me like angry ghosts as I stepped out onto the deck.

Time to find the galley.

Still, convicts, guards and eager women conducted hasty business on the deck as the sun sank lower toward the watery, western horizon. A guard clambered off the black-haired woman I'd seen earlier. She stared at me hard as she pulled her skirts down.

"Heard you're Russian Jack's woman."

I set my jaw and nodded.

She glanced down at my leg irons before returning her piercing stare to meet mine. I didn't look away.

"I'm Red." I tossed my hair, which was just as dark as hers. "Where's the galley on this sloop?"

"Angel-Arse Hazel." She jerked her thumb over her shoulder, but still stared at me. Her golden eyes bore no promise of friendliness. "Galley's that way."

I nodded and started past her. My chains followed in metallic succession.

Scrape, thunk. Scrape, thunk. Scrape—

"You ain't no better'n me," Hazel barked to my retreating back.

"Still a whore, you are. Pirates don't take wives to sea. Just *his* whore, joining the ranks of many more before you."

I turned around slowly.

Hazel's smug smile wrinkled her pug nose and hid the smattering of her freckles that dotted her nose and cheeks. "You didn't believe him to be *virginal*, did you?"

This one's going to be trouble. But she has an advantage over me seeing as how she isn't weighted down with irons.

"You're right." I returned her smirk. "I suppose I'll have to track down all the whores that came before me."

"For what? Fight for his honor?"

"No. To thank them, of course."

The fake smile melted from Hazel's face.

"Because Russian Jack is the most considerate lover I've ever had the pleasure to bed."

No need to let on that I was the virginal one that came to the marital bed.

Something flashed in her eyes that warned me I hadn't had the last word in this unpleasant exchange. Still, I turned, heavily, and strode off into the direction of the galley.

Scrape, thunk. Scrape, thunk. Scrape, thunk.

The snaggletooth wench, Rhodesia, smiled broadly when I stepped into the galley. "Was wonderin' if you'd track us down. Never known a hungry gal to pass us by."

I nodded. "Rhodesia."

"Come on honey, sit by me." She waved her plump arm. "I'll introduce you around. After all—"

All activity in the galley stopped as I dragged my chains across the wooden floor. Careful not to duck my head or let my chin fall, I sank down onto the bench beside Rhodesia. I ignored the ache in my neck from the slash Piranha had given me and kept my face blank.

The old Redella would have balked at the women who scratched themselves freely and sat with their legs spread wide. Now, I was a pirate's wife and my name was known because of it. I left any fear I'd had back in that scarlet pool of blood on the deck of my ship.

"—any acquaintance of *The Black Otter's* is a friend of *The Molly Maiden*."

Rhodesia ignored the stony stares and unsmiling faces that seemed to say the opposite. "The prison transport ship will be coming back for the customers soon and the girls trickling in will be hungry."

"Rightly so."

"You know me, Rhodesia, and that lass who just ambled in? That's Angle-Arse Hazel. Irish Bon picked her up on a run to Nassau, along with Mary Carleton there."

"We've met," Hazel growled as she slid onto the bench nearest to Mary.

"I believe you have me confused," Mary chirped in a mock-ish voice. Her blonde hair was knotted in island knots across her scalp. Tiny shells dangled from the end of each row. Her dark eyes were deep set in contrast to her pale, European skin. "There is no Mary Carleton here. I am the orphaned Princess von Wolway of Cologne."

"Mary here is our woman of many names," Rhodesia explained. "If she's not careful, she'll find herself on one of the prison trans-port ships herself—and not as a service provider."

A thin woman with a tall, white judge's wig pulled off the hairpiece and scratched her bald head. "How many services did you have to provide to get your bigamy charge dismissed anyway, *Princess?*"

A gentle chuckle rolled through the galley as Mary stood up and swished around the tables. "A lady such as me never kisses and tells."

"Kissing doesn't get charges dismissed," the bald woman cat-called. "We all know that!"

Mary smiled. "Kissing doesn't earn judge's wigs, either, Nan."

The bald woman conceded with a shrug and pulled her tall wig back in place.

"That's Unconscionable Nan," Rhodesia whispered in her hoarse voice. "She goes for the high-placed men. Has served her well, so it seems, as she's stayed out of the clink."

I almost smiled as Nan gave her head a shake and wig powder rained down on Mary. But when I caught Hazel glaring directly at me, my smile hardened like stone.

A few more women sauntered in as the smell of gruel and rotted grog grew heavy in the enclosed cabin. The blonde I'd seen when I first came aboard was deep in conversation with a buxom brunette. When they entered, they both stopped as if on an unseen cue, and glanced around until their questioning expressions met mine.

"That be Buttocks-de-Clink Jenny with the yellow hair." Rhodesia raised her voice so all could hear. "Jenny, care to tell Russian Jack's wife how you earned your nickname?"

The blonde's lips tilted into an uneven smile. It wasn't until she began to speak that I saw she had relatively few teeth considering she looked younger than me. "When you don't want to go to the clink, give the guards what they want, something they ain't never had before. What nobody else will."

She shrugged, but didn't blush, as a laugh chorused up from the women who'd experienced a faction of men that I hoped to never know. "Aye, give 'em yer buttocks," they chortled.

Someone slopped two plates down in front of us. The laughing died down as the women dove into their gruel with ravenous appeal and a blatant disregard for any manners.

"The last one, the woman with Jenny, that be Salt-Beef Peg of Port Royal." Rhodesia stuffed a mouthful of slop into her mouth, obviously not caring that most of it slimed down her chin. "500 pieces of eight to see her naked at port. She's a bit of a legend, she is."

Hazel's voice met my ears through the talking and kidding. "It was the lightning scar that did it for me. Bloody 'ell, I'd give it to Captain Russian Jack Rackham for free."

The good-natured atmosphere died like a breeze in an

unwilling sail as I looked up. Sure enough, she was staring daggers through me. Something deep within crackled to life with fiery intensity.

"Come on now, Angel-Arse," Rhodesia began. Her attempt to lighten the heavy mood only made it worse. "Let her be now."

Hazel's black hair hung over her eyes like a sheer curtain. "Let. Her. Be," she spat. "Nobody asked her to come here. To strut about, acting like she's so much better." She dragged her hand across her nose and her words dripped venom. "Just because she married up with the only half-decent man on the sea."

I pushed back from the table. "Keep talking and I'll shut your mouth for you."

"Let what go?" Angel-Arse looked like a sea hag set on a fight to the death. "First she took my man, now she's on my ship."

"You should have done what the lady said and let it go," I snarled.

"Pshaw, a lady, she says."

"You will not like the ending of this story, but you can't stop writing it, can you?"

Like a woman freed from an asylum, Hazel sprang across the long table, knocking over bowls of gruel in the process. I was ready for her.

Hands snarled in my hair, but before I could be yanked to the ground by a woman who hated me with a pure hatred the likes of which I'd never known, something hit Hazel so hard and so fast, that she flew from in front of me like she'd been swept up in a hurricane. Handfuls of my hair went with her.

Dots of blood cooled my hot scalp. Someone was yelling. I shook my head and rubbed my eyes.

"Nobody's your enemy here, except maybe me!"

In the corner, Hazel sobbed on the floor and swiped at a bloody nose. Her jaw hung at an odd angle. I studied the long, lean body that stood over her. Unable to see the face of the person who'd intervened on my behalf, I only stood and stared. A canvas shirt hung loose over a pair of black britches.

Shoulder-length brown hair stuck out, this way and that, and the air of commanding confidence that came with the mystery sailor's appearance silenced the women.

"Oh, Red?" Rhodesia, who never moved from her seat, scraped the bottom of her bowl. She didn't bother to look up. "That's our captain, Irish Bon."

"You attack our guest aboard *The Molly Maiden*, I'm happy to put you back ashore in Nassau."

Hazel pulled her knees to her chest and hid her face. "I'm sorry Bon, don't put me ashore."

"Treat our guests with respect, Hazel. You could be replaced in a minute." Bon turned toward me. Eyes more purple than blue studied me with a warmness that took my breath. I blinked.

Irish Bon. Sully's voice was a shout in my ears. *Who sailed with Russian Jack before falling out over a game of cards and manning the whoring ship—The Molly Maiden.*

"Welcome, Red. I heard the wife of Russian Jack was among us. Stay. Enjoy your time with us, we're all family on the high sea."

Bon's rollicking Irish voice, harsh when chastising Hazel, softened like warm butter as it met my ears. A shiver danced down my spine as the captain of the sloop that saved my life stepped over to me. Lips tilted into a sly smile, Bon stuck out a hand. "Come on."

"Excuse me?"

Violet eyes sparkling, Bon spoke again. "I say, come on. I have something you need."

My stomach churned as I took Bon's hand. It was softer than I imagined it would be. Bon's fingers closed around mine in a gentle squeeze. Heat raced up my arm and I fought the urge to squeeze back.

Without a word, I let Bon lead me from the galley onto the deck. The prison ship approached from the distance and the men lolled about, watching and waiting for their ride with satisfied smiles on their faces. Still, our hands were interlocked.

"Lean up against the rail, there," Bon instructed.

I did as I was told.

Bon moved closer to me until our bodies brushed one another. I was powerless to tear my gaze away from the enchanting purple eyes that stayed locked on mine. My breath came faster as Bon finally released our grip. It wasn't until then that I realized how sweaty my palms had become on the short walk from the galley.

I felt Bon's hands on my legs as they tugged at my britches.

Why am I letting this happen—I should step away—

But I didn't.

"We have to hurry, we don't have much time." Bon's breath was warm on my neck. I gasped as Bon's mission was accomplished with a final yank.

Chapter Ten

Aboard The Molly Maiden on the high seas

"Johnny," Bon called. "Come 'ere." The prison ship pulled up along the port side of *The Molly Maiden* and lowered a plank bridge. "Hurry, Johnny!"

Bon's fists gripped my pantalets and had them hiked up above my knees. A strange sensation coursed through my veins and settled into my belly.

A large guard ambled over. "Ye Cap?"

"Remove my friend of her unwilling adornments, Johnny." Bon's fingers strummed my exposed legs gently as Johnny got to his knees with a grunt. "Seems whoever locked her up pulled a fast one on who made him lock her up."

Bon looked up at me.

"The chains were broken at the ends. The cannonballs fell off. Whoever ordered this, Lassie, thinks you're dead."

"You're exactly right."

Still, Bon's hand was on my thigh. I ignored the heat that throbbed within me and focused instead on Johnny. "How will you get them off? The key is no doubt aboard *The Black Otter*."

Johnny studied the irons a moment then produced a black key from his guard's uniform. "These be prison shackles, Miss," he began as he shoved the key into the lock. He had the first ankle clasp unlocked in a moment. "Don't tell the prisoners, but all the irons answer to one master key."

Johnny clicked open my second shackle and held up the key

for inspection. He kissed it before letting it drop back into his pocket. "If'n ye won't be requiring anything else, it's time to lock up my sheep for the long ride to the New World."

Bon let the legs of my britches drop and offered me a wink. I ignored it and straightened my clothing. "Thank you, Cap."

"Want to see something the likes of you'll never see again?"

Words escaped me.

"Look there." Bon gestured to the prisoners. "Never happens on dry land."

Johnny meandered sleepily across the plank that bridged the sea between the ships. No words were exchanged as the prisoners dutifully lined up and followed him. No resisting. No fighting. Not even any fanfare as they left the ship of dreams. Once each reached the transport vessel, the chubby guard leaned and clicked their leg irons into place.

My jaw went slack. Of all the sights I'd seen and experiences I'd had, this one was the most abnormal of them all.

Bon looked at me knowingly. "I told you that you were like never to see anything of these sorts again."

"And you're right again." I met Bon's violet gaze. "I haven't."

The plank creaked as Johnny pulled it back onto the transport ship, which moved away from *The Molly Maiden* without elaboration. Almost as though they hadn't even stopped at all.

I was about to say this very thing when Bon's hand on my cheek quieted my unspoken words. "It's no doubt been quite a day for you. Go to your cabin and rest. You have my personal assurance that no harm will come to you while you're aboard *The Molly Maiden*."

Assurances.

Monica Joan's trusting face flashed in my mind. I swallowed hard. "You're very kind, Captain, but I don't feel as though I deserve any special assurances."

Bon's full lips curled upward. "My dear girl. Any woman who is plucked from the sea after surviving what you did, after winning the heart and bed of a man such as Russian Jack—"

I didn't interrupt the words that hung, waiting, in the air like a fishing net.

Bon's fingers traced the curve of my cheek, but their caress felt nothing like my husband's. "You deserve everything special."

Jack. My heart panged. *Where are you?*

More knots wrapped around each other deep in my gut as Bon retreated across the deck and disappeared back into the galley. The voices in my head shouted at each other as I walked toward my cabin.

Someone on board is looking out for you, Red. Be grateful.

Do as you're asked, but don't delight in the flesh of another man.

I only want Jacky. But Bon is like no man I've ever experienced—

Be friendly, but not too friendly.

At least you weren't put to work, instead, you were put to bed. To rest.

Still—

Still—

The voices in my mind were winding down as I eased my aching body down upon my bunk. I flexed my ankles and leaned back. No sooner did my head hit the pillow than exhaustion turned my eyelids to stone. The ponderings over the curious nature of Irish Bon, Captain of *The Molly Maiden*, would just have to wait.

A vicious burning in my throat forced me awake. The moon shone through the round window of my cabin, bringing with it only the faintest of light into the blackness.

Am I awake? Am I dreaming?

I fought my fatigued muscles to sit up and rubbed my gritty eyes.

"I thought you might be thirsty."

My voice escaped in a croak. "Who's there?"

Someone shifted onto my bunk with a creak. Bon's face illuminated in the silver beams. "Don't worry," Bon whispered. "I brought you water."

Water ran musically from a pitcher into a cup.

"Here, Red. Drink."

Bon pressed the cup against my lips. My throat screamed for the promised coolness as the fresh water washed over my tongue. I gulped and gulped until the cup was dry.

Bon laughed. "I'll refill it then."

I grasped the cup with both hands as soon as it was full and tilted it upward. Bon laughed again.

"Glad I filled the whole pitcher."

"Thank you, Bon." My breath quickened as I drained the second cup. "Thank you." With the ravenous burning in my throat quenched, sleep threatened to overtake me again.

I eased myself back down onto the pillow, which may well have been made of seafoam, as soft as it felt. My eyes closed. "Thank you," I breathed.

Bon didn't answer, but a hand cupped the side of my face. Stroking, caressing.

Am I dreaming?

In that moment, I didn't care. Not even when I felt Bon's body as it lay down next to mine.

"You've slept for two days." Bon's voice was like a clear bell on a foggy morning from my doorway. "Rhodesia began to worry a bit about your health."

I adjusted my strangely-stiff body on the bed and stretched. "Mmmm," I groaned with a smile.

Bon returned my smile and swaggered across the floor before taking a seat on my bunk. "But you were fine, I told her so." Bon swept a lock of hair out of my eyelashes. "And I would know as I kept watch over you by day. And by night."

Before I could think of a response, Bon leaned down and effectively erased the space between us. Our lips met, and my eyes flew open. I pushed myself upward and, in the process, knocked Bon's hat to the floor. Brown hair stuck out this way and that.

Sensations I'd only felt in Jack's arms coursed through me as Bon's practiced fingers crept beneath the covers.

Jack. His handsome face and the memory his flesh against mine burst into my mind. Never before had I been more certain that no matter how kind Bon was to me, the only person I wanted kissing me was Jack.

Before I could stop Bon's kisses, they spread to my neck and whispered soft into my ear.

"I've fallen in love with you, Redella."

My eyes closed and I sucked in a breath. My fingers wrested in Bon's hair as her lips trailed down my neck. I lifted my free hand and pressed it against Bon's chest.

We both froze.

Bon sat back slowly, eyes locked on mine. Their violet color blazed bright with unspent emotion.

"Bon," I whispered. Ever slow, I began to work the buttons on the loose blouse my captain wore. I pulled it open with baited breath. "Bon is short for Bonnie, isn't it?"

The nipples that tipped her ample breasts hardened in the coolness of the morning air before she yanked her shirt closed.

"I'm so sorry," I said. "I can't do this."

Bon stood up and began slapping the buttons of her shirt through their holes. Her cheeks reddened with each button. "No, no. You don't apologize. It was me—"

I pushed myself off the bed and stood behind Bon.

She stopped buttoning and stood still. Finally, quiet words escaped her lips. "Is it because I'm a woman?"

Without thinking, I wrapped my arms around her and closed her hands in mine. "Anyone would be lucky to have you love them," I whispered into her ear.

She turned her face so that my lips brushed her skin.

"And no, it's not because you're a woman. It's because I love Jack. I must find a way back to him. If China Joe—"

"China Joe?" Bon's body stiffened and her words rang out loud and hard. "He's a madman."

I laid my head against her and rubbed my thumb along her trembling hand.

Bon shook free of my grasp and stomped across the floor. She paused for a moment as though she wanted to speak. Instead, she shook her head and stepped out onto the deck, slamming the door to my cabin behind her.

I melted onto my bunk. *The Molly Maiden* pitched and threatened to throw me onto the floor. My head drooped low, but no tears came. Instead, my mind tried to wrap itself around my predicament.

I lost my Jacky. Even though I was steadfast in my faithfulness to him, the ache of betrayal turned in my chest.

I lost my only friend aboard an unfriendly ship. The look of hurt upon Bon's face was like a slap to mine. She'd been nothing but kind to me, and I brought her only hurt.

Now, it seems I have lost my way.

The brief thought of Bon putting me ashore flittered in my mind like a wounded bird. I wondered what the noose would feel like around my neck when I was tried for piracy and convicted to hang by the neck until dead. I rubbed my throat.

If Bon doesn't put me ashore like she threatened to do Angel-Arse Hazel, I may just knot the rope myself.

Chapter Eleven

Aboard The Molly Maiden on the high seas

I sat alone in my room until night fell, alone with just my dark and brooding thoughts for company. Despite the growling in my stomach, I didn't dare set foot outside my door. Strangely, I didn't feel any sort of fear, even about Angel-Arse Hazel. But what I did feel was a looming regret of how things had happened with Bon.

What could I have done differently? I paced circles around my cabin as the infernal question swirled round in my mind. No matter what possible changes I made, every single one ended the same way—with Bon stomping out.

Angry.

Angry at something.

Angry at *me*.

The Molly Maiden stopped with a jerk so fierce, I tumbled off my bunk and onto the floor. Before I could push myself to my feet, something hit my door.

"Red? Red, it's Bon. Can I come in?"

I stumbled to the door and yanked it open. "Of course. You don't even have to ask." I tried to smile, but she refused to meet my eyes.

"We dropped anchor."

The smile melted from my lips and something sunk in my chest. "Dropped anchor?"

Marooned. I'm going to be marooned.

"Yes, alongside *The Black Otter*." Bon held out her hand and finally flickered her gaze to mine. If violet could be sadly blue, that was the shade of her eyes today. "We have to get you back to Russian Jack, don't we?"

A flood of emotion threatened to drown me as I placed my hand in hers. "Yes. Yes we do."

I let Bon pull me from my room. Just as she said promised, we were alongside *The Black Otter*.

My home I thought I'd never see again.

It was strangely silent, not even the sails fluttered. Nobody dangled in the ratlines, nobody sat in the eagle's nest, nobody puttered about the deck. The majestic ship that had been larger than life looked like nothing more than a shell of its former self; a forgotten ghost ship upon the sea. Hot emotion surged in my throat and I didn't know whether I was going to cry or cuss.

Irish Bon let go of my hand.

Jack's face flashed in my mind. That handsome face that kissed me gently and promised me forever before saving my life by botching my execution. My heart pounded against the inside of my chest.

The memory of Sully telling me the horrors of China Joe keeping captives alive for days, for torture lit my mind.

A fuzzy red ring tinged my vision as a foreign emotion came over me. In that moment, I knew I could kill again if it meant Jacky would be safe. *Or avenged.*

All the girls were there on deck, even Angel-Arse. She refused to look at me.

Bon kept her voice low. "*The Black Otter* is blacked out," she began. "China Joe's at the helm, so everyone's probably drunk. We're going over, girls. Just as we talked about."

Talked about?

Before I had the chance to ask what she meant, Bon reached over and grabbed the side of *The Black Otter* as it rocked gently on the waves.

Bon pulled a dagger out of her belt and slipped it into my

hand. I nodded in thanks. Something tingled in my fingers where our skin brushed against each other's.

There will be blood tonight.

Bon didn't speak, but motioned. Her intention was clear. It was time to board *The Black Otter.*

"You keep behind me Red, stay hidden," Bon instructed. "Rhodesia? Do your thing."

Rhodesia winked and sauntered across the deck, a distinct and unnatural swing in her hips. "Yoo-hoo," she sang. "Yoo-hooooooo!"

A wiry Chinese pirate rose from the deck like a ghost from a corpse. Slowly, he drew his dagger from his boot. "What you want?"

Rhodesia shook her ample bosom and strode right up to him. She plucked the dagger from his hand and sheathed it back into his boot. "Honey, we're from *The Ship of Dreams.* And what I want is—" She kissed her fingers and pressed them to his lips. "You."

The drunk pirate stood, stupefied, before realizing what he was being offered. A slow smile spread across this drawn face and lifted his moustache upward. "Ah, wench. Come wiff me."

He barked something in Chinese before guiding Rhodesia to a corner of the deck. His pants were already half down before the darkness enveloped the pair of them. Several more men straggled out from unseen places, rubbing their eyes, and some, still carrying their jugs of rum.

The girls of *The Molly Maiden* snapped into action. All giggles and swaggers, each fell onto the waiting arm of a horny, drunk Chinese pirate.

"Settle up with me after," Bon called. "For now, enjoy the wares!"

A few of the men grunted in acknowledgement.

"Come on," Bon whispered. "Let's go find China Joe."

I nodded. "And Jack."

Bon ignored my last statement. "You take the cargo hold." She flicked the dagger I'd tucked it into the waist of my britches. "I'll take Captain's quarters."

"Wait!" I grabbed her arm. "Do you know where the Captain's quarters are? I can—"

Bon covered my hand with hers. Her brows knitted together above her eyes and bespoke an air of sympathy. "*The Black Otter* used to be our best customer when we were in Caribbean waters."

A pang of jealousy clanged within me. I shifted my weight. The thought of Jack doing with Angel-Arse Hazel what he and I did in the confines of our cabin brought a swell nausea to my stomach, followed by a flash of anger at my absent husband.

Bon closed the space between us and pressed her mouth to mine. My lips parted and accepted her tongue. I returned her kiss ferociously, my anger at Jack for using whores still hot. With her lips against mine, something felt strangely right and supremely wrong at the same time.

Finally, Bon pulled back. Her hand lingered on my waist. I covered it with mine, not willing to let the moment end so quickly.

"You deserve to reclaim your true love, Red. Let's go find it."

I gripped the dagger as Bon and I crept across the deck. As we split ways, her bound for the bedroom I shared with Jack, and me bound for the cargo hold, a chorus of bloodcurdling shrieks made me freeze. "Bon?"

"It's all right, Red," she whispered. "Part of the plan. They're taking out China Joe's crew."

Ice chilled my veins as I started down the steps into the cargo hold. With no lantern, there was no way to see. I rubbed my eyes and eased the door shut behind me.

"Jack?" I called in a hoarse whisper. "Jacky? Are you here? It's me, Red."

Silence.

I inched down the stairs and stood at the bottom. The thought of striking out across the blinding darkness below decks gave me pause. A rash of tingles made the little hairs on the back of my neck stand on end.

My sixth sense.

A strangled breath rasped in the blackness.

Hands outstretched before me, I struck out across the gently rolling floor. "Jack?"

"Red." The familiar voice spurred me on with courage I didn't know I possessed. "Red!"

"Jacky!"

My foot struck something and I tumbled to the ground. Scrambling across the sparse floor, my hand finally came to rest on something warm and sticky. The metallic, heavy smell told me immediately what it was. Blood.

Fingers curled around mine. "Red?"

"Oh Jacky!"

A lantern sparked to life and illuminated the sick scene that lay before me. Jack, bound at the ankles and wrists and bloody all over, lay in a crumpled heap. Our hands tightened together.

His blonde hair was streaked red and his iconic fur cap was nowhere to be seen. Black clothing was slashed open from what looked like whip marks, revealing torn and bloody skin beneath. Jack's eyes were purple and swollen, only one opened just a slit.

Those soft lips that had tasted my kisses and explored my body were drawn and dry as though he hadn't had a drink since his capture three days prior.

I struggled to help him sit up and cupped the side of his face, as he'd done mine so many times. "By Jove, Jacky. Let's get you out of here."

I produced the dagger given to me by Irish Bon and cut his rope bindings.

"Red," he rasped. His chest rose and fell quickly and his hands began to twitch. "The lantern—"

Before I could process Jack's dire warning, realization hit me like an anvil.

Who lit the lantern?

The light grew brighter as I turned slowly to see who was behind me. Before I could register who shared the hellish space with Jack and me, a booted foot kicked my hand hard. My dagger flew across the cargo hold and landed with a clatter.

"I thought you dead when China Joe throw you overboard?" A wiry Chinese pirate I didn't recognize loomed over us. He unbuckled the latch of his britches and eyed me.

I rubbed my hand and glared at him.

"Strip," he commanded.

Jack growled and began to push himself to his feet. Another fierce kick from the Chinese captor put him down again. "You," he barked. "Watch."

He sat the lantern down and glared at me. "Now."

I looked at Jack and sucked in my lip. *He is no help. This fight is all mine.*

The brief thought of making a dash for my dagger swirled in my mind. *Or, I could try and strangle the wiry pirate when he comes close enough—he doesn't appear to have a blade—*

Jack returned my pleading glance before looking back at his captor.

"No," my husband whispered. He shook his head infinitesimally. "Don't."

The skinny pirate let his pants fall to the deck, exposing his want. From inside his stiff, grungy shirt, he drew Jack's jeweled cutlass. He crouched like an animal and held the blade to Jack's neck. The lantern light lit his slanted eyes. They were filled with hate.

His mouth twisted up into an evil smirk. "Do it. Or *Jah-ky* dies."

I looked at Jack, hoping he could feel my apology. My eyes trained on my husband, I did as the skinny pirate commanded and slipped one arm out of my shirt.

A feminine cough came from the shadowed recesses, just outside the ring of light offered by the lantern. The sadistic smile melted from the pirate's face as he turned his attention toward the sound.

This is it! Your chance!

I leapt at him and felt the jeweled end of the cutlass as it pressed into my back. I wriggled and arched as we fought for Jack's fantastic blade. Finally, the pirate bested me and sat astride my hips. His grin returned as he held the blade aloft. I glanced about wildly, but the weight of the pirate had me pinned.

I kicked as much as I could and flailed my arms. A sudden whoosh, like wind through the canvas sails on a still night, and the lantern light went out. We were cloaked in darkness once again.

I squeezed my eyes shut and waited for the sharpness of the silver to take my life.

Will it hurt when it slices through my skin?

Will he kill Jack next?

"Umph." Hot, foul breath slapped my face in a puff. The sound of a blade scraping bone as it was yanked from a body filled the dank silence of the cargo hold. The weight of the skinny pirate fell atop me.

The lantern illuminated again, revealing the stoic face of a woman.

"Hazel!" I pushed the pirate's lifeless body off me as she sheathed her blade with her free hand. I struggled to my feet. "You saved us."

"Us? You mean Jack ain't dead?" She shone the light in his direction.

Jack waved with a finger.

Hazel wrinkled her pug nose. "He sure looks it."

She sashayed over and squatted next to him. "Hear you're married up with now. Guess I'm not your favorite girl after all."

Jack groaned and tried to speak.

Hazel pressed a finger to his lips. "Hush up, Russian Jack." A pained smile contorted her freckled face, made almost innocent in the soft lantern light. "I never much liked servicing married men, anyway."

She stood and looked at me. The her lantern-lit face and revealed emotions I was sure she didn't want me to see. "Bon wants you up on deck. Him too, I reckon."

Bon's voice echoed from the stairs. "No need, I'll come to you guys." A smile, a touch too wide to be real, spread her lips.

"Can't find China Joe. Could be that he jumped ship when he realized he was without a crew."

A hand tightened around my throat. I let out a squeak and from across the hold, Bon's eyes widened.

"China Joe no run from boat of whores." I recognized the malicious voice as it slid over his teeth and out his mouth. From the corner of my eye, my fear was confirmed. China Joe, and he was wearing Jack's hat. "No more play."

Bon started toward us. "Let her go, Joe."

"Stop!" he shrieked. Something sharp pressed into my back.

I tried to pull the air into my lungs, but China Joe's hand was like iron. I yanked on his fingers, but they didn't budge. The world grew fuzzy, but I kept my focus on Bon's face. For the first time since I'd come to know her, she looked scared.

"Ahhhh!" China Joe cried.

That's it. The death cry.

I waited for the plunging steel to do its job, but it didn't.

Slowly, China Joe's grip on my neck loosened, and he sunk to the floor. I sucked in a shuddering breath and fell to my knees. The world began to come back into focus as I turned to see what happened.

Jack, my dagger in his bruised and bound hands, nodded at me.

"Jack!" I crawled to him and we melted into each other's arms. My tears came without warning. "You saved me."

"I love you," he whispered. "You and no other."

The strong sensation of being watched forced me to pull myself together. I wiped my face across the back of my hand and turned around, still wrapped in Jack's arms.

Bon and Hazel stood near the stairs. "You ladies—" I began. "I don't know how to repay you."

Bon shook off the awkwardness and strode over, a swagger in her step. "I say you owe me a ship, eh, ole Jacky?" She clapped him on the back. Hard.

He grunted but managed a smile.

"Get me that dagger, Red," Bon instructed. "Let's cut Jack free, shall we?"

Once he was cut free, Bon looped her arm through Jack's. "Come on. Red, get the other side if you would. And we'll get you to bed. *Commodore.*" She chortled as though everything that had transpired was nothing more than a jolly good joke.

"I detest that word," Jack managed.

Bon laughed. "I know."

I sniffled and did as I was told.

"Hazel," Bon instructed. "Draw some water and meet us in the captain's quarters. Stinks of Chinaman in there, but I'm sure the smell will fade with time. Grab that God-forsaken hat on your way up, too."

Jack got to his feet. He leaned heavily against me as Bon and I helped him shuffle to the stairs. "Think every bone I got in there is broke, battered, or bruised," he whispered.

I smiled into his puffy face and pretended not to see the tears on Hazel's cheeks as we passed her by.

"Looks like you have your ship back." Bon's voice came from somewhere behind me. "Why aren't you down there taking care of lovey?"

I leaned against the railing of *The Black Otter* and ignored what I knew wasn't really a question. "Getting a bit of fresh air before I go back down to the cargo hold." I glanced at Bon as she slid up next to me. "Before Jack fell asleep, he asked me to find his cutlass. Told me to get some food and bid you thanks and farewell."

Bon laughed as her hand brushed mine. "The only thing that's worse than that ugly hat. That damned sword." I joined her laugh and our voices melded musically to the tune of the crashing waves. When the moment passed, a strange smile tilted my lips upward. "Is the crew accounted for? Both yours and mine?"

Bon nodded and spit into the sea. "All accounted for. Glad to be untied and out of their quarters where China Joe had 'em locked up. Glad to get some fresh water. And fresh women."

"You mean your girls are working right now?"

"No rest for the weary, I'm afraid." Bon winked at me. "And like I said, we've always been partial to this ship."

I pushed back from the railing and ignored the odd emotion that surfaced. "I've got to go find that sword."

"We'll be leaving once business is done."

I stopped. Something inside me pained at the thought of Bon leaving. She offered me a smile. "You're welcome to come with me, Red."

"I don't think I'd make a good whore."

Bon reached out and took my hand in hers. "I didn't mean to work for me, Red."

I froze, our fingers intertwined. She wasn't asking me to come be one of her whores. She was asking me to come *with* her. "I can't do that, Bon, tempting as it may be."

"I know." Bon rubbed her fingers along mine. "Here, I'll go with you to find that sword. Never know when you'll need some saving grace."

Still, our hands were locked together. "Red, grab that lantern there by the door."

I licked my lips and let her lead me down the stairs and into the darkness.

"Poison Lightning and Solo hauled those two bodies out of here," she reported as I sat the lantern on the bottom step. "Shackled 'em to a cannonball each, if I saw correctly. Then dropped them overboard."

"They deserve it," I muttered. I ignored my pounding heart as the glint of something against the far wall, between the stacked wooden boxes, caught my eye. "Look there. That was easy."

I broke from Bon's grip and made my way across the floor, careful to step over the pool of China Joe's blood. "Found it."

I turned to call out to my friend, but she was already there. Right behind me. Closer than she should have been.

We were outside the ring of light, so her sea-roughened features were muted and shadowed. Something flickered across her violet eyes. "I don't want to leave you, Red."

"Bonnie." I sat Jack's blade down on the nearest box.

She nodded and bit her bottom lip. "I don't have the words." She squeezed shut her eyes. "If I said I love you—"

I pressed my finger to her lips until she opened her eyes. I took care to keep my voice low. "Then I would say I love you, too. A love I could never feel toward Jack or anyone—though I love him in a special way, too. You're my best friend."

She exhaled and kissed my fingertip. "I didn't know how to say it, but yes. I understand." Still, she didn't move away. And I didn't force her to. When her calloused hand touched my cheek, I didn't turn away. Instead, I turned into her touch and kissed her palm. "Bon—"

Her body was pressed against mine in an instant, and her free arm circled around my waist. "I love it when you say my name, Red." Her breath was warm on my throat. I closed my eyes. "Say it again."

Her fingers traced their way from my cheek to the back of my neck before twirling into my hair. She gave a slow pull that pulled my head back and exposed my throat. "Say it."

The word whisped from my lips in a throaty whisper. "Bonnie."

Bon growled as her lips met the skin of my neck. I expected her to be rough—but she wasn't. Her lips were soft and her kisses ravenous.

"Bonnie," I moaned as she pulled my hair harder. "Oh Bonnie."

"Let me make love to you, Redella." The arm that circled behind me was, at once, hiking up my heavy dress. I tried to ignore the want that stirred in my most secret places as her fingers gripped the inside of my thigh. "Let me show you how much I love you."

Jack's face, so freshly rescued, burst to the forefront of my mind. *Red, what are you doing?!*

With both hands, I pushed her away, my breath coming in awkward gasps. The warmth on my neck from Bon's lips cooled with her sudden absence. I fought my tied tongue for words and tried to ignore the look of want—and hurt—in her violet eyes. Bon's shirt was half unbuttoned, revealing her voluminous, dark-tipped breasts, which no matter how masculine she chose to dress, would forever reveal she was all woman.

I reached out across the sudden expanse between us and grabbed the sides of her shirt. I smiled into her face and pulled her close. My skin brushed her exposed breast and she shivered. I placed my hand over her thundering heart.

"I love you, Red." Bon's voice was heavy. "I fell in love with you the minute I saw you." Something hitched in her chest, I felt it and heard it. "But you love Jack."

"I do love Jack." I erased the space between us and pressed my lips to hers. Her mouth worked against mine hungrily, but I pulled away. "But that doesn't mean I don't have feelings for you. Strong feelings."

"I don't want to leave without you."

"I can't leave Jack, Bon. He's my husband." I forced a smile. "And you risked everything to bring me back to him."

I let my hand slowly fall from over hear heart, down her chest. "I'm indebted to you, beautiful Bonnie."

Bon sucked in a deep breath, her breasts swelling into my hand. "If I wasn't married to Jack, I would leave with you in an instant."

Her violet gaze met mine.

"But I have to remain faithful to my husband."

"I'm a madame on a whoring ship. Faithful isn't really in my line of work." She looked away. "I suppose I can understand your wanting to stay faithful to Jack. If you were mine, I'd want you all to myself, too."

"However—" I caught her fingers in mine and brought them to my lips. "I can be intimate with you in another way."

Bon scoffed. "Is there another way?"

I held her hand in mine and stared into her eyes. "Bonnie?"

She smiled and arched her brows. "Red?"

"I'm going to share something with you that nobody knows. Not Jack, not anybody. I'm not even sure of it myself, really."

She flexed her fingers in mine. "Go on?"

I took her hand and placed it on my stomach. We stared at each other for what seemed to be the longest while.

"I don't have any proof, really. But I think—"

"Lord above!" Bon tore her hand from mine and let out a whoop. "We're havin' a baby!" She danced a little jig. "Ain't never been in that predicament myself."

A wide smile pushed up the corner of my lips. "Neither have I."

"If I was still a good practicing Catholic, by God, I'd say make me the godmother!"

I wrinkled my brow and tried to picture Bon in one of those ornate Catholic churches of my childhood. I shook my head and pitied he priest that would hear her confession.

"Reckon I can still be godmother anyway? I mean, I could teach the little tot to climb ratlines—"

I started to laugh.

Bon continued, working the buttons on her shirt. "To set the sails."

I slapped my hand over my eyes.

"And of course, how to choose fresh girls—"

"Bon, really!" I let go a belly laugh. "I suppose we'll have to see what Jack thinks—" The smile melted from my face and my laughter died on my lips. I froze as I tried to make out the crumpled shape across the hold.

"What's the matter, Red?"

I squinted before the bile rose up hard and fast as the shape came into focus. I choked back the vomit. "Oh no—oh God, please no."

Bonnie looked behind her.

I hurried across the cargo hold. "It's her, oh Bon it's her," I managed. "I mean, it's her remains." I sank to my knees and drew my fists to my mouth. "She was my friend," I explained as I stared into the lifeless, still-open eyes of Monica Joan. "The Chinese killed her before they threw me overboard. I heard them have their turns at her—" I sucked in a breath. "Then I heard her die."

A tear eked from my eye, followed by another. I fell into Bon's open arms.

"Come on," she whispered. "Let me take you to Jack. I'll take care of Monica Joan."

I stifled a sniffle and looked at Bon as we made our way back to the stairs. "How did you know her name?"

"You called her name when you were asleep. Promised you were coming to help her." Bon picked up the lantern and helped me up the stairs. "Tell Jack I'll bring his precious sword up later."

Jack stood at my side as we stitched the last of the thirteen stitches into the old hammock that had become Monica Joan's tomb. Thankfully, Bon had been the one to find the hammock and place Monica Joan's body inside, along with the cannonballs that would ensure she sank to her rest and didn't float for eternity– so I didn't have to be the one to do so.

Bon joined Jack and me. "She had some personal effects on her." Bon produced a folded sheet of paper. "This letter. Sealed and hidden in a pocket in her torn shirt. Don't know how the pirates missed it, but I'm glad they did."

Fresh tears spilled down my cheeks as Jack accepted it. He turned it over in his hands. "It's addressed to someone. It's only right that it reaches its intended."

We stood at the side of The Black Otter. Jack cleared his throat. "I am going to try and do this from memory as I've presided over my fair share of burials at sea." Jack cleared his throat again. "For as much as it hath pleased Almighty God of his great mercy to take unto himself the soul of our dear sister, Monica Joan, here departed, we therefore commit her body to the deep, to be turned into corruption, looking for the resurrection of the body, when the sea shall give up her dead, and the life of the world to come through Our Lord Jesus Christ who at His coming shall change our vile body, that it may be like His glorious body, according to the mighty working, whereby He is able to subdue all things to Himself."

He nodded to Bon, who returned his nod and pushed Monica Joan's body into the sea.

A splash resounded as the remains of my friend, whom I failed when she needed me the most, fell to their watery grave. A sense of finality hung about the deck. After what seemed an eternity, Bon coughed.

She pointed to her girls as they boarded *The Molly Maiden*. "We're going to port for supplies. I'll make sure Monica Joan's letter is posted."

A smile flickered across Jack's bruised face. "I'm much obliged." He handed it back to her. "I've no doubt you will."

Bon looked at me and grinned. I could tell she was forcing it. "Hard enough being a woman in a man's world. Us gals have to stick together, don't we?"

I tried to smile, but my lips failed to comply. In fact, they began to tremble.

"Ah, come now Red." Bon grabbed my hand and spun me around in a circle on the deck. "Chin up, girl, life is only life. Live it and let it be."

She laughed as she danced me over the deck of my ship until I had no choice but to laugh, too.

Bon whirled me round and round then dipped me backward. Jack was there, upside down. He was smiling, too.

Bon pulled me up and pressed her lips to mine. My heart pounded in my chest and a heat surged through me.

Jack.

Jack's voice met my ears. "Kissing my wife, eh Bonnie?"

Bon released me, my cheeks aflame.

"You know I hate that name, Jack." Unlike me, Bon never blushed. Now was no exception. "Ole Jacky. You wouldn't have your ship, your life, or your woman if not for me."

Jack extended his hand. It was then I noticed that he was smiling, too. Bon took it and gave it a shake.

In jest, Jack looked up Bon's sleeve. "Still got a card or three hidden in that sleeve, Bon?"

She jerked her hand back and laughed. "Still can't accept that I beat you at cards, eh?"

"I wound up paying you all of my debt and then some!"

The pair shared a laugh.

"Debt?" I smiled through the confusion.

Bon and Jack shared another look. Bon scratched her nose and looked away. "Like I told you, Red, *The Black Otter* was once our best ship."

My stomach went queasy as Angel-Arse Hazel's freckled face dominated my mind. *I wish I hadn't asked.*

"Anyway," Bon continued. "I tried to get this wife of yours to sail off with me, and she wouldn't do it. Guess she loves you, or something."

Uneasiness gone as quickly as it had come, Jack shook his head. "Trying to recruit my woman as one of your working girls, Bon? I'm relieved she said no!"

Bon slapped her knee. "You think I'd let a gem such as her go to work? Bah, I invited her to come with me and share my ship. And my bed!"

Both captains shared a roaring laugh while I stood, confused, with my face flaming.

"Goodbye, old friend," Jack said. "I think I'll retire. Red, take your time in saying goodbye." He offered me a bruised wink. "Just make sure she doesn't challenge you to a game of cards."

He gave my hand a squeeze before disappearing down the stairs with a limp, into the quarters we shared.

"I suppose this is—" I started. Before I could get any semblance of a proper goodbye off my tongue, Bon quieted me by pressing her lips to mine. She kissed me with such force, that I found myself pressed up against the side of *The Black Otter* with Bon's body pressed against mine.

One of her hands cupped the side of my face while the other rested high on my waist. Her mouth, gentle yet firm, worked against mine. Her tongue slid between my lips. I opened my mouth wider to accept it.

A flash of want tightened my muscles in forbidden places. I wondered, in a brief moment, what making love with Bonnie would be like. Would she be gentle and sensuous, caressing my body with her fingertips, both on the outside and on the inside? Would she be rough, taking charge and doing whatever she pleased with me as her willing partner? Had she been with many lovers or was making love something special instead of something to just pass the time?

As her mouth worked against mine as she kissed me deeply, and I let her, something told me it making love with Bon would prove to be exciting, rough, and gentle all together.

Shocked by her sudden display of affection, I tightened my arms around her.

She broke from our kiss, and trailed them from my mouth down my neck. "Your invitation doesn't end here. Come away with me any time, Redella." Her voice was a sensuous, throaty whisper. "I can't bear the thought of leaving you."

I took her face in my hands and looked her in the eyes. "You have the most beautiful eyes I've ever seen, Bonnie," I whispered. "And such a beautiful heart."

I pressed my lips to hers again, then pulled back. "Thank you, for everything."

Bon sniffled, stepped back, and hitched up her pants. "Take care of yourself, Back from the Dead Red. Guess this is goodbye."

I stared at *The Molly Maiden* from the railing as they prepared to set sail for the mainland. Bon caught me watching. Instead of waving, she kissed two of her fingers and held them out to me, before drawing them back to her heart.

My breath came faster as I kissed my two fingers and held them out to Bon before covering my heart, too. A brand of sadness I'd never felt before twisted in my gut as I watched them leave, my two fingers still pressed to my chest. With heavy legs, I trudged down to the captain's quarters where my injured husband lay waiting. Irish Bon was gone.

Chapter Twelve

Swansea, Wales

I don't pretend to understand women. Didn't then, don't now." Jack stroked my cheek as we stood together on the Welsh balcony where he interrupted my wedding to another man. "But that was good advice Bon gave you."

I blinked and tried to clear the fog that enveloped my brain when I dared think of Bon. "Advice?"

"About life. How life is just life. Live it and let it be."

I nodded and studied the stark white railing. Jack's stare was almost tangible as I traced the fancy molding with my finger.

"I know that you know, Jack."

I glanced up at him. Shame veiled my eyes.

"About you and Bon?"

I sighed. "Yes."

"Let me guess. It's your feelings toward her that have you worried." Jack chuckled. "Good God above knows the whole of the deep blue sea knows about hers toward you."

My voice escaped in a whisper. "And you're still here? Wanting to be with me?"

Jack shrugged. "I suppose if I have to share your affections, I can't think of one better to share with than Irish Bon. Trustworthy, she is. With a good heart."

"Yes, she is all those things." I glanced at the ocean and tried not to choke on the words that had strangled in my throat for so long. "Jack—I need to tell you something."

His fingers wound together in my hair. "I'm listening."

"I've never wanted another man to touch me. Never did until I met you, actually." I licked my lips. They dried again. "I never wanted anyone except you. Then there was Bon."

"Darling—"

I dared a glance at my husband.

Something in his eyes softened as he looked down at me.

"Like I said. I don't pretend to understand women. Even squirrelly ones like Irish Bon."

"She's special to me, Jack. More special than anyone else. Except you." The invisible weight of guilt I'd carried with me like a cross lifted as the words took their leave. Something more sinister took its place. Burning guilt. "I'm sorry for not telling you before."

Jack sighed. "I know how physically affectionate you two were, Red."

Words strangled in my throat.

"I know you could have had her, made love with her, as easily as you and I did in our bunk. But you that didn't. I know you stayed faithful to me."

"How did you—"

He held up a hand. "A captain, or commodore as she calls me, damn her, knows everything that happens with his crew—and his wife. Let's leave it, shall we?"

I nodded. Still, my head hung low.

"Red. I love you. And I know you love me. Whatever kind of friendship you have with Bon—it doesn't change what you and I have." He paused. "No more than anything, or anyone in my past changes my feelings for you."

Angel-Arse Hazel's face flashed in my mind. I wondered for a brief moment how many times Jack had taken her over the years before he came to find me. And if he felt for her what I felt for Bon.

I exhaled and smiled. This time, I didn't have to force it. "I love you, Jack."

"I know you do." He swept my black bangs back and tucked them behind my ear. "And I, my darling girl, love you."

The days passed quickly and, under my care, Jack healed quickly. One morning, I eased myself down on our bunk with Jack's breakfast in tow.

"Good morning," he purred. "I smell salmagundi."

I sat his plate on the small table that was built in beside the bunk. He was right, the scrambled meat bits, fish, vegetables and fruit did have quite the pungent smell. "Red Legs was the cook today. I expect we'll have salmagundi whenever he decides to cook again."

We shared a laugh.

"Are you feeling up to getting out of bed today?"

Jack propped up on his elbows. All the bruises were long healed and he seemed to suffer no ill effects from the beating China Joe had given him, despite being so close to death when I finally found him that he was more dead than alive. "I can't get out of bed 'till I have my daily dose of medicine."

Lust lit Jack's green eyes to a fiery twinkle.

I slid my blouse off my shoulders as I strode across the room. I turned to face Jack as I pushed shut the door. He flipped back the blankets and patted the bed next to him. With his busted ribs, we'd been careful in our lovemaking. Until now.

When we'd finished, Jack held me tighter than usual. "There's something I have wanted to tell you, my love."

My breathing was still coming fast from our morning romp and sweat dripped down my naked back. Jack's fingers slid down my backbone and made me shudder a delicious shudder. My breasts swelled against his chiseled chest as his softening manhood slid from between my legs. "Tell me?"

"You asked before. About my father."

I looked up into his face. He smiled down at me as I snuggled into his arms. "Yes I did."

"Is this still a story, dreadful as it is, that you want to hear?"

At once, I was a child again. Nestled safe and warm in my nursery while my governess told a bedtime story. "I do, Jack. If you're of a mind to share it with me."

"Me mother died of consumption. So I took what money I'd stolen from the men who bought her and what little bit she'd left me." His fingers strummed my slick back as he spoke. "The girls, as my mother had called them, did their best to look after me, but they weren't my mother. I was not their affair and, quite frankly, my presence wasn't good for business."

I tightened my arms around him. His back was healing up nicely from the beatings China Joe had given him, and all that was left now that the scabs had fallen off, were white slashes here and there across his skin. I traced them nonchalantly with my fingertips as he spoke. "I understand, I suppose."

Quite frankly, I hoped I would never have to understand the life Jack lived before coming to captain *The Black Otter*. I wasn't a mother, at least not yet, but the thought of having to sell my body to men to make a living while my child hid in the closet—it made my stomach turn. My heart went out to Jack's mother, and all the other mothers who had to live a life in such a manner. My thoughts began to swirl.

What would I be like as a mother—

Emotion burned in my throat as Jack continued.

"Once I came to see that I answered to nobody, belonged to nobody, and nobody was waiting for me to come home to them. That nobody cared if I ate, bathed, combed my hair, or had fresh clothes—or any clothes at all. . ." Jack shrugged. "The decision almost made itself for me. I had to go find my father—the only other kin that I knew of in this world."

"So I claimed a dock as my own, down in the roughest part of town. Was no matter, I was a whore's son and expected to be rough and wild." Jack sat up and pulled a smoke out of his shirt pocket. I'd never seen him smoke before, not even when other pirates would. I didn't say a word, and chose instead, to prop up on one elbow and listen to a story that I was sure had never been told before.

Jack struck the flint he produced from his shirt pocket and lit his smoke. He took a long drag with his eyes closed before he continued. "I already knew how to take a beating, and I was learning how to dish them out, too. Not bad for a lad who was not yet a man."

"I learned all I could from anyone I could watch or from whoever would teach me. Fencing I picked up straight away. I would challenge drunk men to a duel and make it known people should place their bets. I earned quite a hefty sum since nobody ever bet on me." He exhaled and turned and offered me a wink. "Hell. I wouldn't have bet on me, either."

I would have.

"One day a ship came through, a cargo ship of some sort. From the Orient. The men who disembarked spoke of a Russian pirate who boarded their vessel, took their rum, silk, and spices, and left them a mess of gold coins in trade. Of course, the men were to keep the gold for themselves—not pass it on to their masters, who would be sorely disappointed when they discovered they were robbed of their Oriental goods." Jack flicked the ash of the smoke onto the floor. "That was the first time I saw Spanish gold, when the men went ashore with their pirate loot, much too rich to bother sailing the seas for someone else any longer."

I cleared my throat. "The Russian pirate, it was your father, wasn't it."

"Aye, it was." He took another long drag before continuing. "I figured it was Providence that a ship looted by my own dear father pulled into my port. Since I was rootless and burning for adventure, with a healthy dose of anger at my father, I sought out the man they hired as the new Captain and informed him that I was his newest hired hand."

Jack laughed and stood. The sweat on his naked body had dried and I drank in the sight of him. So many scars, so many stories. And so beautiful, all the while. He made his way to the porthole nearest our bed, unlocked the tiny round window, and flicked the butt of his smoke out into the salty sea. "Of course, he thought me nothing but a young fool and called me such. So I swiped his dagger from his hip."

My eyes widened and I pulled our thin blanket up to my chin. Stories of young Jack were so much more lively than those of young Redella.

"I told him that I could kill him with that dagger if I had a mind to, but killing wasn't why I needed a job just then. Instead, I'd throw it wherever he pleased. Into an empty barrel, through a ratline square, wherever he pleased. If his dagger made it, then I came aboard. If not, I would leave."

"Did he take you up on your challenge?"

"This sailor, a man by the name of Vane, was no ordinary Captain."

Vane. Vane—where have I heard that name before? My eyebrows knitted together as I puzzled over the familiar name.

"He told me where I could stick that dagger, which was most ungentlemanly, and informed me that he would relieve me of my head before I had a place on his ship."

I sat up and snapped my fingers. "Charles Vane!"

Jack sat back down next to me, his lips turned up in a knowing smile. "Ah, I see you've heard of him."

"His wanted posters, I've seen them. They offered a handsome reward—called him an English-born pirate."

"So you see where this story goes." His hand came to rest on my knee as he continued. "I informed Mr. Vane that he would not have my head and that I was going to sail with him—with or without his blessing. Do you know what he did?"

"What?"

"He had the audacity to laugh at me. Asked me what kind of business did I have to conduct by way of his new ship. He called it the *Lark*."

I let my hand fall over his.

"Since a challenge didn't work, and threats didn't work, I decided to try something even more insane."

I was powerless to stem my curiosity. "What's that?"

"The truth." Jack chuckled at the memory. "I told him I was the bastard son of Vladimir Nemirovsky, the Russian pirate who probably looted this rig. My whore mother was dead and it was high time I found Vladimir and called him out. Either make him respect me as a father respects his son—"

"Or?"

"Or kill him. For breaking my mother's heart."

I studied the blanket, suddenly shy and at a loss for words. *Is it possible to love this man even more?*

"Vane took me at my word. He promised to teach me what I needed to know, so that when we met Vladimir on the high seas, not only would my presence be humiliating to him, but I would have the skill to back up my mouth. And he did."

"Vane was my mentor, and soon became my friend. He helped me perfect my fencing technique, my fighting, and everything else. And any time we passed a ship, I learned on my feet how to relieve a ship of their goods. Much like you are."

"The day finally came, we spotted Vladimir's ship once we reached Caribbean waters. We sailed alongside, and they allowed this, thinking we were an English trading vessel, ripe for the plundering. Once we pulled down the English flag and ran up a black flag, they realized this wasn't the case."

Suddenly, I wasn't sure I wanted to hear more. Jack's voice was coming quicker and with fire behind his words. No, not fire. Venom. Deadly venom. "Does it bother you to speak of this, Jack?" I shifted on the bed and briefly considered slipping my shirt on. "Because if it's painful to recall—"

Jack didn't hear me, or if he did, he didn't let on. "I boarded first, sword outstretched. The same sword I gifted to you when we married."

My blood turned icy and I shivered a bit, though there was no reason at all why I should be cold.

"I told them, I am Mikhail Nemirovsky, and I was in search of Vladimir. He appeared, of course. It was like looking in my own eyes, a few men aboard gasped. There was no denying I was his son. I told him, just as Vane and I rehearsed, that I was there to sail the seas and plunder their riches as his son."

I wanted to reach out to Jack, to hold him as he told this horrible tale. He'd begun to shake a bit, and something in my gut told me to stay put and keep my hands to myself for the time being.

"The lot of them laughed so hard, tears streamed down leathery faces. One pirate, closest to me and wearing a tall, fur cap—"

I glanced about until I set eyes on his iconic headpiece that consumed an entire corner of our cabin.

"Not one to enjoy being laughed at, especially at such a pivotal moment in my young life, I swung my blade and sliced off his ear."

I was incredulous. "Your father's?"

"No. The pirate with the tall, fur cap," Jack smiled. "So not only did they stop laughing at me, but I earned my cap which I still wear to this day."

"What did your father do?'

Jack's head drooped a bit. "He said the day he took a whore's son aboard his ship as anything but a slave would be the day he met his Maker. I told him that could be arranged."

"We drew our swords, him smiling all the while. I know he was toying with me to gauge my abilities and to see if I was a worthy opponent. He even instructed his crew to stand down, no matter the outcome. Vane and the men who sailed with us stood down, too."

Someone banged on our door and made me jump. Tommy's voice rang out from the other side as my heart thumped in my chest. "Are ye alive in there, Cap? Ye and th' missus?"

"Yes, Tommy. We'll be up in a moment." Jack stood and plucked a fresh shirt from the chest of drawers in the corner. He slapped his arms into the sleeves and began buttoning furiously. "Our duel ranged all over. From helm to helm, bow to stern and back again. On top of boxes, through the rigging. I was ready. I was young and full of fire. His smug smile melted from his face the longer we dueled, and he began to tire. The longer we dueled, the angrier I became. Every smack of every john who bought my mother spurred me on, every time I heard her cry when she thought I wasn't listening, or cry *his* name in her sleep."

Jack's fingers shook as he spoke. "I thought I had him. I flipped his blade from his hand and fed it to the waves below and held my own steel to his neck. I looked into his face, up close, and forgave him for almost two decades of hurt and abandonment. So I lowered my blade, having won the fight, and turned to walk off his ship and leave him be, safe in the knowledge that his bastard son could have relieved him of his head. As I walked toward Vane, I saw something flicker in my mentor's eye, and realized that in that instant I forgot the first rule of being a sea gypsy."

"Never trust a rival pirate," we said in tandem.

No wonder that's the first rule of the sea you made me memorize.

Jack nodded. "One of his men tossed him a blade. If I hadn't moved when I did, he would have driven it deep into my back. But I side-stepped his death blow, which made him even madder. He was no longer smiling and his eyes were black—"

"Your eyes get black when you're killing mad." My voice was a whisper. Immediately, I regretted saying anything. Jack, thankfully, ignored me. It seemed the more he talked, the more he wanted—no *needed*—to finish this story.

"I knew this was the end. One of us would leave, the other would be buried at sea, the loser of this familial duel. I stabbed my blade into his dueling arm and asked him the question I had been dying to know the answer to. Why, Father? Why?"

"Why?" I leaned forward. "Why what?"

"Why all of it. Why did he leave me mother, why did he leave me. Why did he make promises and not follow through, why weren't we good enough for even a letter." Jack picked up his black britches and held them there. "Why did my mother die loving a good for nothing son-of-a-bitch like him."

He gave his britches a shake. "He knew what I was asking.

And he answered me, too. Why, he said, would I want to recognize a whelp like you, a son of a good for nothing whore."

The pain in Jack's words was almost tangible and his voice had
started to shake. Still, he continued, his words coming faster and
louder. "I made those promises to a dumb whore, he said, and
he smiled as it said it. If they think you love them, they don't
mind fucking you for free."

I exhaled the breath I didn't know I'd been holding.

Jack exhaled, too. "When he said that, I knew he was no man.
Certainly not my father. Not worth killing, not even worth a
second look. But, I knew he wouldn't let me live. So, I said, for
my mother's honor, and plunged my steel through his heart. Or,
where his heart would have been, had he had one." Jack slid his
legs into his britches and pulled them up, but didn't button them.
"He work a look of surprise, as he bled out his lifeblood all over
my boots. It took him a moment to die, so I asked him one last
question. One he could carry with him into eternity. 'Who is
the dumb whore now?'"

I stood, still stark naked, and went to my husband. I wrapped
my arms around his middle and pressed my head to his chest.
"Jacky, I—"

He stroked my hair a moment. "Now you know the story of
my sordid past, Back from the Dead Red."

"What happened after you killed him?"

He twirled his fingers in my hair. "Vane and I extended an
offer to the men on Vladimir's ship—join us or go down with
your ship."

"That's a kind offer, I would think."

"Would you believe every one of those Russians joined our
ranks? And just in time before we sunk my late father's ship,
with his sorry body aboard." Jack pulled back from our embrace.
"Tell me something, Red."

He cupped my face in his hands.

"Anything."

He pressed his lips to mine. Our mouths worked against

each other, eliciting fiery passion that sparked to life once again. Our breath, coming faster, intermingled in the muggy cabin air when Jack pulled away.

"Do we have to go up on deck now, or do you have a few moments to spend in the arms of your husband?"

"A few moments?" Without hesitation, I began to work the button's on Jack's shirt. "You have all my moments for the rest of my life, my love."

"See that ship there?" Jack's easy tone matched that of the calm evening. Days at sea were my favorite of all the days. With frothy grog, sea breezes, and Jack instructing me on this or on that, I preferred these days to the adrenaline-filled ones that came with taking ships.

Besides a few pelicans and a pod of dolphins, we'd been completely alone on the Caribbean Sea. Until Jack spotted the wayward ship.

"Notice the flag." His hands tightened around my waist. Memories of our rough love that played out in the confines of our cabin this morning flamed within me. Aches from forgotten muscles only Jack could stretch made me shiver.

"It's a Spanish flag." My voice was sultrier than I intended. Still, I was powerless to look away from Jack's chiseled jaw. Had he not spotted this ship, I would have been inclined to pull him below decks to continue what we'd started earlier.

Jack, though, was oblivious to my want. "Yes, it's Spanish. But it's no ordinary ship." He looked down at me, his eyes sparkling anew. "It's a rum ship."

Those aboard the Spanish rum ship stood on the deck, all smiles, and waved as we sailed alongside them. As Charles Swan pulled down our English flag and ran up Jack's flag Jolly Roger, however, the waving slowly stopped.

Jack's flag was quite foreboding, even to me. A solid black flag boasting a white outline, much like *The Molly Maiden*, except Jack's white outline was a grinning skull over a pair of crossed swords. Rightly so, fear shrouded the Spanish faces that had moments before been welcoming and friendly.

"I am Russian Jack of *The Black Otter* fleet. There's nowhere to hide, nowhere to go," my husband shouted. "Throw down your anchor and let us board."

A bearded man with a young redheaded woman clinging to him nodded. He waved to his men who tossed the anchor overboard.

"Good," Jack said. "We're coming over."

Jack nodded to Poison Lightning, who drew his dagger and nodded in return. The tall African waved his arm. Dark Water, Tommy, and Charles followed him as he stepped from the side of *The Black Otter* onto the captured ship. Red Legs dashed up from below decks and tossed a sword to Solo and kept one for himself.

My heart thumped in my chest as Poison Lightning stepped up to the big, bearded man in charge. He held out his black hand and accepted the man's sword without uttering a word. The others aboard the rum ship followed suit and surrendered their arms.

Solo stepped up beside us. "Always nice when it goes down easy, ain't it Cap." He glanced at me and winked. "There's a time for bloodshed, and then, there's a time for just stealing some rum."

"Agreed, Prince," Jack said. His chest puffed with pride. "Looks like the boys will have it handled before we go over and finish the deal."

The redheaded girl, who couldn't have been that far out of her teenage years still clung to the old man. She glanced from face to pirate face and showed no fear Still, something about her body movements wasn't natural. I furrowed my brow and studied her until her nervous gaze met mine.

"Jack." I tugged at his waistcoat. "Something's not right."

Jack turned his beaming face down to me. Slowly, his smile faded. "What is it?"

"I don't rightly know—" I studied the girl. Her long red hair flowed with reckless abandon over her shoulders and her young face was shadowed with fear.

Her arms were wrapped about the big man as though she meant to meld right to him. But her hands—

Wait! Her arms!

"Jack, she is tied to that old man!"

"What? Surely—" Jack let his words trail off as he struggled to see what I was seeing.

"Look at her hands! She's trying to get away."

Solo, who'd been listening as Jack and I spoke, nodded. "She's right, Cap. I see it."

Jack and Solo shared a look so bold that even I heard the unspoken word.

Headhunters.

Jack drew his cutlass and marched all the way to the edge of *The Black Otter's* deck before he turned around.

"Come on, Red. Time to see if your hunch is right."

Solo pressed his steel into my hand. "I'll grab another, you may need this."

Jack and the men of *The Black Otter* had the rum ship boarded in seemingly no time. "Poison Lightning," Jack called. "Tie them up, the entire lot of them. Ankles and wrists."

Poison Lightning's expression didn't change as he carried out his orders.

"And Poison Lightning," Jack added.

The tall African turned to face his Captain. "Beware of stowaways."

Poison Lightning nodded as Red Legs joined him with a handful of new ropes. They lashed each man at the wrists and ankles, as Jack commanded, while Solo managed the transference of the rum from their vessel onto *The Black Otter.* Jack paced the deck before them, like a hungry dog before a feast of fresh meat.

After each man was tied, Poison Lightning pushed him down onto the deck in a kneeling position. I stood off to the side, Solo's steel in my hand, in case I was needed. The young girl had in fact been tied to the old man. As soon as Jack set foot on their rum ship, he'd strode over and cut her loose. Now, she stood behind the men, her red hair blowing in the thick sea breeze, her hands and feet untied. And she hadn't taken her eyes off me.

Our eyes met. The emotion that flashed in hers was no longer one of fear. It was one of pleading.

When Poison Lightning and Red Legs tied the last man, they marched across the deck and took their place behind Jack, who immediately stepped forward. "A simple rum ship you claim to be, eh?" My husband's eyes flashed black. "Then I say you are a boat of liars!"

The tied men hung their heads.

"How about someone tell us who you *really* are."

The hairy man spoke in a wavering voice. "We are but a simple Spanish rum ship, Captain Jack."

Jack let go a roar. "The truth, man!" His cutlass was pressed to the man's neck in an instant. "Tell me you're a slave ship."

Surprise lit the man's face. Ignoring the cutlass, he looked up at Jack. "A slave ship? No sir. That we are not."

Jack stood in silence but didn't move his blade. "Then why was the woman bound to you?"

Finally, the redhead tore her gaze from mine. "S-sir? Captain? May I speak?"

Jack didn't look away from the hairy man. "Yes madam. I pray you do."

"Funny you say that, Captain. I pray, too."

A quizzical expression flashed across Jack's face. "Pardon?"

"It's just that, once we reach England, I am suppose to marry the man that you are about to relieve of his head."

"Marry him?" Jack sheathed his cutlass, The man kneeling before him exhaled hard.

Jack ignored him and stepped in front of the girl, who had

respectfully sat down when Jack began speaking. He extended his hand and helped her to his feet. "Tell me, do you love this man?"

She didn't even flinch or look at her intended. Instead, she looked directly at Jack. "No sir, I do not. His name is Sir William Appleby and he took me in place of my father's gambling debts." She blinked big, green blinks. "You can call me Rusty."

Jack looked at me, bemused. "Red, come talk to this young lady. This Rusty."

I sheathed Solo's sword in my belt and stepped to my husband's side. "Rusty. I'm Red."

"Back from the Dead Red," Jack corrected.

Rusty's eyes brightened. "I've heard of you, Back from the Dead Red. You were thought dead when your pirate husband, Calico Jack Rackham, murdered you to save you from a ship of Chinese pirates. But you came back to him!"

I was speechless. And apparently, famous.

"However, the legend says you're a murdering savage. You don't look like a murdering savage to me."

I exchanged a look with Jack. His lips were tilted in a half-smile. I ignored it, lest I break into a grin to match my husband's. "Rusty. Are these men carrying any slaves aboard, from the Caribbean back to Spain?"

She shook her head. "The only slave aboard is me."

My eyebrows shot skyward. "Rusty. Why were you tied to Sir William?"

She didn't balk or even stop to think. The words flowed off her tongue as quickly as they came into her brain, it seemed. "When he saw your ship approaching, he was afraid you were pirates. We were told to act friendly, perhaps you'd pass us by. Nobody else had to be tied up. Only me, so you couldn't steal me, he said."

"So he tied you up to protect you?"

Rusty's stared hard at me. "He thinks I'm stupid, Miss Back from the Dead Red. Probably because I'm a girl. He tried to make me believe that being tied to him was to keep me safe.

But he tied me up to get me on this boat in the first place. He would creep down into my quarters to spend the night with me." She closed her eyes and made a disgusted face.

Sully's smug face flashed into my mind without provocation. My blood heated to a low boil. I walked over to Sir William.

He didn't look up at me.

"Tell me, sir. Would you keep her tied when you were away from the house, too? Once you're married, I mean? Perhaps you might shackle her up so she couldn't slip away when you weren't looking?"

I drew my sword in a swish.

"Red," Jack warned.

I ignored him and plunged the sharp steel through his shirt, knocking him backward on the deck, and pinning him there. "Now you're the one who's tied up."

"Captain Back from the Dead Red, please." Rusty's voice gave me pause. "I prayed, you know. Prayed for a way out of this—this life of slavery. Then you appeared."

I turned and looked at her.

Her face was contorted in planes that made something twist in my chest. "Please don't make me go to Spain and marry a man my grandfather's age."

I shifted my gaze to Jack. He was smiling. "Reminds me of a younger version of someone we both know," he said.

A chuckle escaped my lips before I could stop it. I extended my hand to Rusty.

"Come on, Rusty. Sail with us aboard *The Black Otter*. I personally guarantee your safety—" Before I could finish, Rusty flung herself into my arms and wrapped her arms around my neck.

"I promise, I'll help out and do whatever's asked of me. I know it will be a more fair life than I was going to live."

"Fairer," I corrected. "A *fairer* life."

Rusty giggled. "Fairer."

Jack snatched my borrowed sword from Sir William's shirt. "Normally, I would lock you in your cabins and sink your ship."

The men trembled and shifted their weight.

"However, since you were honest with me, I'll simply take your rum and let you keep your lives."

"T-thank you, C-captain." Sir William's voice shook.

"Ah, Sir William. To you, I give you some advice. Look for a woman your own age, not a girl as this. And do not buy her. Love her, and she will love you."

Sir William nodded.

"And furthermore, I must ask. How much of a gambling debt did Rusty's father owe to you?"

"Fifteen pieces of silver, Captain Jack."

Jack let out a low whistle. "Quite a sum." He looked at Solo. "Cut them free."

Solo did as he was told as Jack rummaged in his pocket. "Just so we're even, I'll pay her father's debt to you."

Jack flicked a handful of pieces-of-eight at Sir William, counting as he flicked. He didn't stop until he reached twenty. "Extra for your trouble," he said. "And a fresh shirt once you reach shore."

Sir William sat in his pile of silver, a look of bewilderment on his bearded face.

"Are we square?"

The old ship captain nodded.

"Good. Consider it a dowry then." He jerked his thumb toward where I stood, Rusty still clinging to me. "Apparently my wife and I have just inherited a daughter."

"Where are we going?" Rusty's voice was edged in curiosity as she stood between Jack and me. "To do more pirate things?"

I glanced at her. With her fair complexion and smattering of freckles across her nose and cheeks, I guessed her to be about fourteen years of age. "How old are you, Rusty?"

"Rusty O'Malley's my name. And I'm sixteen years of age. Seventeen in June."

Jack's lips tried to conceal a smile. "We're in the month of June, Rusty. Perhaps since you've been adopted by Redella, which means you've also been adopted by me, you'll consider taking our name. Rackham."

"Rusty Rackham." She gazed into the distance and tried the name on her tongue as though it was a new and exotic dish to be sampled. "Rusty. Rusty Ra-a-ackh-a-mmmm." She linked her arm through mine and smiled up at her adopted father. "I like that."

Jack glanced down at her. "Tortuga."

"Rusty Tortuga?" She crunched up her face and closed her eyes. "No, that doesn't go as well. Does it?"

I let go a laugh. My cheeks ached from the near constant smile that had appeared with Rusty. "No. What Jack means is Tortuga is where we're going. Rusty Rackham fits perfectly."

She smiled. "What's Tortuga?"

"Pirate paradise," I whispered. "Come on. Let's go get you settled into a room."

Jack chuckled as we strode across *The Black Otter* together, arm in arm. He muttered something that sounded like, *like mother, like daughter*, but I couldn't be certain.

Red Legs Roberts yanked off his hat as we approached. "Red, she can have my bunk."

My eyes widened. "That's awfully considerate of you, Red Legs, but—"

Red Legs interrupted me. "I didn't figure you'd want to put her in the cargo hold after what happened to your friend down there."

My lips thinned to a hard line.

Red Legs, who had never spoken more than a sentence to me or anyone, continued. "So I'll move my quarters down there and Miss Rusty can have my bunk. It's off by itself and don't smell too much."

Rusty nodded at him and extended her hand. "Many thanks. I'm Rusty Rackham, daughter to pirates Back from the Dead Red and Russian Jack. Who might you be? Red Legs, is it?"

I rolled my eyes as Red Legs' face went fiery with Rusty's direct attention. "Rusty, help Red Legs move his things. Just remember," I caught Red Legs' sleeve and dropped my voice to a hoarse whisper. "Rusty is my daughter. She will be respected as such."

Red Legs' droopy eyes widened, as though accusing him of possibly being improper was truly a shock. "Of course, Red. I would never disrespect Jack. Or you."

Something crossed that pirate's face that made me believe him.

I stood and watched the pair of them walk away, lost in chatter. "Come, wife." Jack's voice interrupted my staring. I turned to face my husband. I'd returned Solo's sword that he'd been so kind to lend me. Jack held my steel out before him.

I accepted the thin blade. Now that I knew the full story that came with it, I accepted it gently and returned my husband's knowing smile.

"Thank you, Jack."

He gave me a sizzling wink. "Let us sail on to Tortuga."

Flags of pirate vessels I'd not yet seen lined the bays and cays around the pirate-friendly Caribbean city of Tortuga. Jack docked us in the midst of several other *Black Otter* ships by moonlight.

"Care for a taste of rum, Red?" Jack's eyes sparkled. "Seems the boys are already imbibing. Now that we're here, we can join them. My husband handed me a jug.

Tilting it upward, I took a long swill. "Mmm. Spanish rum." I handed it back to Jack and licked my lips. "Let the celebration begin."

Rusty and Red Legs were on deck, passing a jug between them. "This rum tastes sweeter since I'm not having to drink it at my wedding party."

Solo, jovial and grinning, sat down beside them. "Pass that jug," he sang.

Red Legs laughed. "You mean you didn't bring your own?"

"I had one," the pirate prince said. "Can't seem to recall where I left it!"

The three dissolved into a fit of drink-heavy giggles. Jack wrapped his arm around my shoulders. "Shall we join them?"

I nodded. "We shall."

As the night wore on, several *Black Otter* fleet hands from ships that marauded in the waters of the Orient, the English Channel, and along the coast of The New World came onto their flagship to greet Jack and divvy up their amassed booty—and rum.

Several wasted no time in joining the ranks of Tommy and Poison Lightning and passed out on the deck amid the boxes and crates, while others sat up with Charles and Dark Water. Sharing several jugs, they sat together until talk turned to mermaids, The Kraken, and other ominous creatures of the deep.

Red Legs, Solo, and Rusty, about three jugs into the evening, broke into song. Sea shanties echoed over the dark sea as bonfires lit the shoreline.

I laughed from the railing. Though I hadn't imbibed as much as the others, my body felt warm and fuzzy.

Didn't I have just the one drink with Jack when we pulled into port?

With my eyes closed, I leaned out over the sea and sucked in the cool breeze that swirled off the waves as my mind pitched and whirled.

Jack's voice was somewhere. "I'm stepping over to *The Revenge* to divide up a hefty haul they made in Oriental waters. I'll be back." His dry kiss brushed my forehead and I smiled, my eyes still closed.

"I'll be here," I slurred. I tapped the steel that hung on my belt. "To protect our schip."

Jack laughed a monotone, otherworldly laugh. "You best go below decks and sleep it off. We're safer here than anywhere."

Jack's footsteps retreated across the deck. I slunk down against the railing and willed the world to stop spinning. One leg dangling over the side seemed to help. The happy sounds of *The Black Otter* danced around me and, despite having my eyes closed, I knew all was well. A smile found my lips as I drifted off to sleep.

An odd sound sparked me awake. A quiet grunting, out of place. The singing of sea shanties was no more and the sounds of happy laughter had been replaced by silence. Only the sounds of the sea, lapping at the side of *The Black Otter*, perhaps beckoning her back out to the deep, remained.

Did I dream that?

I rubbed my eyes. Still, my vision blurred. I closed them again. Another odd grunt jarred me awake.

There it is again!

I pushed myself to my feet. A mess of drunken bodies were strewn across *The Black Otter's* deck. I bent slightly and examined each face.

Poison Lightning.

Charles Swan.

Dark Water William.

Solo.

Tommy was curled in a corner, whimpering in his sleep.

Was that the sound I heard? I listened for a moment to Tommy's whimpers.

I shook my head. *No, that's not it.*

Red Legs Roberts clutched a jug between his legs and snored deeply.

A couple of men I didn't recognize split into four. I rubbed my eyes and they went back to normal. My heart thudded to a gallop. "Rusty."

The sound came again. This time, more urgent.

I straightened my back and touched my steel. A flash of movement from behind the wheelhouse caught my attention. I held the railing with my free hand and staggered over. The anxious grunting was louder.

"What's going on here," I slurred.

A pirate I'd never set eyes on before, pale and bald, rose to an enormous height. He didn't speak, but from under him, Rusty scooted across the deck toward me. With her hands finally free, she pulled a knotted rag out of her mouth. Tears streaked her face.

My vision tinted red. "Did he—"

She grabbed my legs and sobbed. "No. But he tried. I was sitting, looking at the stars. Everyone else was asleep." Her voice twinged from scared to hysterical. "He came up behind me and stuffed this rag in mouth."

I unsheathed my sword. "Who are you?"

"How dare you talk to me. Worthless woman." His voice was a growl and his shirtless body was ripe with muscles. Scars criss-crossed his face and his large hands gripped into fists. "Now get out of here. Let me finish my business. Or you're next."

He grabbed for Rusty, but my steel moved on its own and bit into his wrist. His hand froze.

"Go on Rusty. Get out of here." I felt her let go of my legs and I heard her skirts rustling as she obeyed without question.

The world pitched around me, but the giant of a man stood strangely still. I glared at him. "Get off my schip."

He jerked his hand away. Blood sprayed across the deck. As though he wasn't even injured, he retrieved his blade from his side and stood at ready. Scarlet oozed down his arm. "You want me gone? Make me gone."

I assumed the position. The voice that slid over my teeth didn't sound like my own. "To the death."

He nodded and struck out with his sword. Mine intercepted. Still, I didn't move my eyes from his. My lips twitched into a smile.

His mustached face went scarlet and he attacked again. My steel clanged against his as I thwarted his sword. With a flick of my wrist, I plunged my tip into his shoulder. He let go a roar as his face contorted into a grimace.

Booted feet pounded the deck behind me, but I didn't take my eyes off the monstrous giant of a pirate that stood before me.

Tommy's voice rang out first, then Solo's. "Let her be, Nikolai. That's Captain Jack's wife!"

I yanked my sword free and held it at ready.

"She's dead now," Nikolai growled. "Don't give a damn who she is."

Metal clanged again through the still night air as his sword crashed into mine. I broke free and ducked as his blade slashed across where my head had been.

The brief thought of protecting my belly swirled into my mind. The possibility of being pregnant had occurred to me before. Once I told Bon, the thought sort of drifted away with her. But now, it was back. When one swill of Spanish rum made my stomach turn, I just knew. Now here I was, drunk and pregnant and dueling the biggest man I'd ever seen.

I pushed the thought away.

Of all the times to be distracted, now was not one of them.

"Red, look out!" Rusty's voice was dripping emotion. "Please stop!"

I dropped instinctively to one knee, my sword before me. As Nikolai hulked over me, him an ancient mountain and me a helpless little pebble, I saw my chance. Holding my sword with both hands, I jammed it up hard through Nikolai's chin. The big man dropped his steel to the deck with a clatter. Surprise widened his black eyes. He sunk to his knees.

"By God's Blood," Solo whispered.

I yanked out my blade, and Nikolai crumbled to the deck.

"He's dead!" Solo finished. He sounded shocked. But I wasn't.

I listed against the railing and hung my head.

"And you're dead drunk!" Solo stared at me, his eyes wide. "Not one of us could beat Nikolai sober—God knows most of us have tried."

"He tried to rape Rusty," I slurred. "Then said he'd kill me, the old brute." My blood, which had been cooling, began to boil anew. When the red ring tinged my vision, it was as though I stepped out of myself and into the skin of a killer—who would stop at nothing to win.

I shook my head, then immediately regretted it. Instead, I held up a finger to my crew and wagged it like a schoolmarm might. "And *that* will never be allowed."

A couple of men chuckled, but I couldn't tell who they were.

"Red?" Solo stood there, staring at me. "I'm a little drunk. But—am I dreaming?" Finally, Red Legs waddled over. "I'll get Rusty safe to her bunk, Red." He looked at me, then looked at me again. "You need assistance gettin' to yours?"

I patted my belly as my vision cooled and the red ring faded. As the adrenaline ebbed, I became myself again.

We did good, baby.

"I'll take care of Red." Solo's voice comforted me on some level. My knees started to shake as the adrenaline ebbed.

I sank over the railing as my stomach threatened to revolt. "Jack?"

Solo helped me to sit down, feet dangling over the side. The gentle lapping of the water against the side of *The Black Otter* made my eyelids flutter. "He's not back yet, Red. He'll be proud to hear of your fight."

"Need to tell Jack—"

Solo rested his arm across my shoulders as a wave of nausea swelled in my stomach. I retched into the sea until tears streamed down my face.

"I'm sure everyone will be telling Jack about this fight," Solo assured me.

I batted his well-meaning hand away and wiped my mouth. "Not that." Despite emptying my stomach, I felt even drunker than before. "About the baby."

"Um—" Solo's boots scraped the deck beside me. A moment later someone's hands were under my arms. "Let me help you get to your bunk, Red. Tommy!"

"Tommy's here, I am. What does Solo need me help with?"

Solo's voice had sobered as he babysat his inebriated co-captain. "Help me get Red to her's and Jack's bunk."

Tommy, a head and a half shorter than Solo, ducked under one arm while Solo held the other. On Tommy's side, my arm rested on his balding head. "That was the cleanest fight I ever seen, it was." Tommy's voice was full to bursting with awe. "The way you jibbed, and you jabbed. You killed him right fair, you did."

I tried not to giggle as my feet seemed to tie themselves in knots on the short walk across the deck. "I appreciate all the help—"

"After we get you tucked in, Solo and me, we's gonna chunk this Nikolai feller over, we is. Time that big lug was put to rest, it is."

Slowly, two of my crewmates helped me navigate the steps into the captain's quarters. "Tommy," I slurred as we reached the bottom. "Fank you, for all your help.

"It be no problem Miss Red, it—"

"Your pa," I interrupted, "would be mighty proud of you."

Solo and Tommy deposited me at my door and retreated up the stairs. I waved to them, then toddled to my bunk. I didn't even bother with disrobing, not that I could have if it'd have tried. Instead, I fell asleep with my clothes on, sprawled across the bunk I shared with my absent husband.

After what seemed like an eternity, the door to our quarters creaked and slid across the floor. I opened one eye. The sun's rays peeked through the porthole. My head throbbed. I closed my eye again.

"I heard you had an eventful night." Jack eased himself down onto our bunk and rubbed my back. "I'm so sorry I wasn't here."

"Told you I'd manage," I said. "Me and the baby, we did just fine."

Jack stopped rubbing. "Do you mean you and Rusty?"

I smiled and rolled over. I took Jack's hand in mine and placed it over the slight curve of my belly. "No Jacky. I mean *our* baby."

"You mean—" Jack's voice trailed off into the early morning dawn. "I'm going to be a *father*? Someone's *father*?"

I giggled, but Jack wasn't there to hear it. The door at the top of our stairs banged open. "I'm going to be a father!" His words were a bellow in the early morning haze, and no doubt, those still feeling the effects of the rum didn't appreciate his fervor.

A moment later, Jack thundered back into our quarters. "Come on!"

I raised an eyebrow.

"If you're having my baby, I must keep you fed. To the galley."

I stared at him. His glowing face dimmed. "Or should I bring it to you? In bed?"

I pushed myself onto my elbows. "To the galley we go," I managed. I let him help me to my feet. "My, you're going to be a protective father, aren't you?"

The smells in the galley made me belch. Or perhaps it was the remnants of last night's rum. Either way, my knees were weak and my stomach felt like the sea before a storm. I sank onto a chair and lay my head on the table.

Rusty's voice chimed from somewhere. "Don't you believe that God can answer our prayers?"

Red Legs' voice answered from somewhere. "I never gave it much thought."

"I do. I know He can actually. He did for me."

Red Legs must have been on galley duty, because the odor of meat and fish assaulted my nose. Normally, I would have relished the scent. But not today.

"I prayed for a way off that boat, Red Legs. Every morning, every night. All day. Then a ship appeared." Her voice dropped. "Your ship."

"It did?"

"It did." Rusty sounded as certain in her declarations of God's existence as I was in my absolute nausea this morning. "And I recognized you right off."

"Me?"

The sizzling of meat hurried my stomach's revolt. I hiccupped and groaned.

"Yes. I recognized you from a dream I had. I was praying and fell asleep. Of course, I was locked in my bunk. In my dream, I saw you." I could hear a smile in her voice. "You didn't look so *angry*, though."

If Red Legs replied, I didn't hear it. Unable to hold my stomach at bay any longer, I dashed up the stairs and to the railing where its final revolt came to fruition.

Jack was beside me in an instant. "Darling, what is it?"

I coughed and wiped my hand across my mouth. "No more rum. Ever."

"Cap? Cap!" Solo's voice was frantic, very atypical for the most level-headed pirate on board. "Oh Cap. We've got trouble."

"You're telling me," Jack grumbled. "What is it, Solo?"

Solo huffed, as though he'd been running all about deck to find Jack. "It's Tommy. He's gone."

"Gone where? On shore?"

"No. He was very drunk. He took *The Revenge*."

"He *what*?!"

Solo's voice went higher pitched the longer he talked. "He was talking about his father, and wanting him to be proud of him. So he got it in his fool head to sail to Madagascar." Solo paused. "To kill his half-brother, Prince Ratsimilaho."

Chapter Thirteen

Swansea, Wales

The balcony door flung open and smacked against the wall of the church. Charles hovered in the doorway. He looked as though he didn't know whether to run or vomit. Or both. Instead, he spoke. "Might I inquire as to the state of our matrimony, Drucilla?"

Jack looked down at me with a bemused expression. "Drucilla? Did I manage to crash the wrong wedding?"

I ignored Jack. "Charles—" My hands wringed on their own. "I must apologize. I wasn't quite honest when I told you my name was Drucilla."

"Dru*cilla*," Jack scoffed.

"*Drucilla,*" I began as I glared at the tall, blonde pirate, "was my late mother's name. She could have been a Saint. She died of a cancer instead."

Jack's face softened and the jovial smile melted into a look of concern. "I'm sorry, Red."

"Who's Red?" Charles' confused old face made my heart pang. The Welsh copper baron had been nothing but kind to me, while I had told him nothing but lies. Flutters of guilt filled my gut.

I sucked in a breath. "Charles, my name is Redella. My late mother was Drucilla. After a pirate by the name of China Joe overran our ship and pushed me overboard, everyone, including my husband Russian Jack—" I nodded to Jacky, who touched the edge of his fur hat in smug greeting. "Well, they thought me dead. When I made my way back to Jack, and to our ship, instead of calling me Red, they began calling me *Back from the Dead* Red."

Charles' face paled. "I've heard of Back from the Dead Red. Heard that she was—*is*—a murderess." He stuck his finger in his collar and tried to swallow, but choked. "With quite a handsome reward on her head," he managed.

"Rumors travel quickly, Charles," I began. "That is why I couldn't tell you my real name."

Charles coughed. It seemed he couldn't draw in a proper breath. He dug his gnarled old finger into the collar of his shirt.

"Excuse me," Russian Jack began. "Charles, is it? We weren't quite through here. Perhaps you can let yourself back inside for now."

Still choking, Charles did as he was instructed.

Jack looked very satisfied with himself. "Now my dear, where were we in our reminiscing? Somewhere on the high seas, I believe?"

"Solo and Dark Water—go on shore and procure what supplies you can as quickly as you can. "Get as much ginger root as you can find. Maybe off one of our ships that caroused in the Oriental waters."

I watched Jack bark orders from my spot on the deck. Crammed between two barrels of ale, I was hidden and supported at the same time, with an easy shot over the railing for my still-churning stomach.

"Hurry men! Off with the old and on with the new. We have to catch Tommy." He reached out and grabbed the spineless Charles Swan by the stained canvas shirt. "Did you see him last night?"

Charles' head whipped back and his thin moustache looked somehow sweaty. It was as though he couldn't pull a thought out of his head without Dark Water William to exchange glances with first. "Yes Cap."

Jack tightened his fists and pulled the shrimpy pirate closer. "And?"

Charles glanced around. I knew he was looking for Dark Water. His eyes fell upon me and he pulled his thin lip up in a scowl before turning his attention back to Jack. "I think he took Poison Lightning with him when he left, Cap. That *woman* dueling with Nikolai got him all upset. Especially when she started talking about his *father*."

I opened my mouth to dispute him, to tell Jack I'd only been attempting to compliment simple Tommy, but instead I leaned over the rail and relieved my stomach again.

A wry smirk twisted Charles mousey lips into a grotesque excuse for a smile. "Yeah," he continued, "after Red starting chiding him about his father, Tommy went on shore. I thought he was going to kill someone, or kill himself. As you know, Cap, the crew of *The Revenge* went into town—with *you*—and Tommy saw his chance."

Jack went into town without me? I pulled rogue stories from deep recesses of my mind together. *Pirate captains go into to drink—and whore.*

By now, Charles was fully animated. "Yeah, and then he jumped on board and said, '*I'm going to Madagascar and I'm going to kill that sorry brother of mine, Prince of the Rats*'."

Jack gave Charles a sharp shake. "Nobody was with him? He was all alone, without provisions?"

Charles shrugged, unfazed. "Like I said, The Poison Lightning was with him."

A deep cough squelched the one-sided conversation. The Poison Lightning stood beside Jack, a look of thunder on his face. "Poison Lightning never go *nowheres* that Captain not know. Charles Swan is a liar. Black liar."

Everyone's eyes widened. To my knowledge Jack, along with everyone else aboard *The Black Otter*, assumed that Poison Lightning simply couldn't speak. But talk he did, and with a low, grumbling voice.

"Tommy go because *Charles* tell Tommy to go. Dark Water help Charles. Tommy set up to die." Something flashed in Poison Lightning's eyes, an emotion I thought foreign to him. Hate. "Bad men, Charles Swan and Dark Water."

Jack's eyes blackened. He'd told me before that The Poison Lightning was a seer who could tell the future and something that he was seeing now was enough to get him mad enough to talk.

"Charles, go below decks. Make sure we've enough fresh water for the trip to Madagascar."

Charles slunk off like a whipped pup, all the while throwing pouty, doe-eyed glances over his shoulder. I studied the pirate who preferred to stay in the shadows if his cohort, Dark Water William, wasn't around.

Never accused of being friendly, Charles was distinctly cold. Not just to me, but to anyone except Dark Water and Jack. Though, everyone knew where his loyalties lay.

From the moment I came aboard The Black Otter, Charles struck me as a feminine man. His face was feminine, his look was feminine, even how he carried himself, not to mention his doe-eyed glances that seemed to beg something, compassion perhaps, from whomever they were aimed toward. Because of that and his attachment to Dark Water, who was muscular and burly with a hard stare, I wasn't at all shocked the night when I witnessed for myself Charles and Dark Water, who were much more to one another than simple crewmates.

Solo had been teaching me to climb the ratlines. The moon was long risen and the sun long set as Jack sailed by starlight. Solo had finished instructing me for the day and assigned me the task of climbing the ratlines, from the deck to the crow's nest on the tallest mast, ten times before I could retire for the night. *Climbing will toughen up your hands,* he promised. It was on my seventh trip up the ratlines that I spotted them, Charles and Dark Water, locked in a lover's embrace, hidden away behind a stack of crates and barrels. A place where they thought they could express their feelings for each other without being seen. Only they were seen. By me.

The Poison Lightning stood, unmoving, before Jack. "Bad men, Charles. Dark Water. Loyal to each other. Not Jack. Not Red. Bad."

Jack nodded. "You know I trust your sense in these matters. But we have to sail to Madagascar to intercept Tommy, who has quite a lead on us. And if he means to kill their prince, we will need all the manpower we can get—Charles and Dark Water included."

Poison Lightning nodded.

"But if they're as bad as you say, keeping them around will lead to a problem. If not now, later."

Poison Lightning spoke as though he was using all the English language he could muster, perhaps from some grammar school lessons he'd overheard as a boy, or simply from his listening to people speak throughout his life. He seemed to be using all the rules of the language, but at all the wrong times. "Need Charles. Need Dark Water. Bad can be good never, Captain."

Jack rubbed his chin. His black cape fluttered in a sudden breeze. He looked to the sky, then back to Poison Lightning. They shared a smile.

"A storm's coming," Jack observed.

"Sail. Now."

Jack clapped his hands. "I have a sneaky feeling that we'll intercept Tommy before he has time to get himself killed."

I heard the anchor being hoisted as I made my way down to our cabin, and in no time, we were on our way.

The storm raged on outside, furthering the righteous nausea that had gripped my gut. It seemed like days passed before Jack came down to our bunk.

"Here, ginger root. To help settle your stomach."

I peeked out from under my pillow with a groan. Jack held out a wrinkled white root that looked strangely like a gnarled hand. "Just chew a bit at a time."

I took it and nibbled at the end of what looked like the thumb. Once I got through the papery outer layer, the inside was juicy and had a strange spicy flavor. In no time, my mouth was on fire. I chewed quickly and swallowed.

"Whatever ails me will likely be burnt out by this likes of this devil root."

Jack sat down on the foot of the bed and rubbed my leg. "How long do you reckon 'till we have our child?"

"I've been trying to figure that myself. Close as I can come, my guess would be about five more months?"

Jack's face transformed to that of one a man might wear in a shop, confused between two prams, not knowing which is best for his unborn, but delighted all the while that his child would be sleeping in one soon. "Five months you say. So shortly after we reach Madagascar, if we don't catch Tommy before."

I pushed myself up and ran my hand through Jack's hair. "I suppose it's time to start thinking of names. Father."

"How have we still not caught Tommy? Did he have that much of a lead on us?"

Jack steered the giant wooden wheel and stared out over the choppy sea. "He had a bit of a lead on us, but it's this weather that's against us. He seems to be catching the good winds and leaving the sour winds for us."

"Surely that can't happen, Jack. Truly."

Jack cut his glance down to me. "Tommy's no expert sailor. He had a good lead on us and has kept it. Something is working in his favor."

I pulled my shawl about my shoulders and handed Jack the steaming cup I brought for him. He accepted it with a sly wink.

"I think Rusty is falling in love with Red Legs."

Jack sipped the steaming coffee. "Surely you're not just figuring that out."

I gave Jack a playful nudge with my elbow. "I wasn't done. I was *going* to say I thought at first, he might feel the same for her. But now, I'm not so sure."

"You may be right. I noticed him being a bit more stand-offish, too."

I rubbed my swollen belly. "Any idea why?"

Jack nodded. "Rusty, sweet girl that she is. She's always talking about God and praying and dreams."

"That she is. Devout." I stretched my back. "Funny, she sees a boat full of pirates as her saving grace."

Jack chuckled and took a longer swill of his coffee. "As did you, if I recall."

I arched an eyebrow and shrugged. "Perhaps you're not pirates after all. But a band of marauding angels, rescuing damsels in distress."

"And you and Rusty can convince the Powers-That-Be of that very thing if we ever get caught."

My smile faded. "Jacky, please. Don't say such things."

He drained his cup and held it out to me. "Of course. I'm sorry, Red."

I took it and stuck it in my britches pocket. "Why do you figure religion to be off-putting to Red Legs?" I stepped to the bow of the ship and gripped the railing. "He swore in on a Bible, didn't he?"

"He did. Everyone did. But Red Legs had a hard past. Probably has a beef with God. With Rusty telling everyone how good and merciful He is all the time—"

"Yes?"

"Well, Red Legs probably wonders where God was when he was getting the daylights whipped out of him for no good reason."

"Oh." I took a step back and froze.

"I know it's hard to hear, Red, but—"

"Oh!"

Jack turned his attention to me. "What is it? Are you all right?"

I held my belly in my hands as a smile spread over my face. "Oh!"

"Red?"

"Feel here." I grabbed Jack's hand and placed it where I felt our baby kick.

Nothing.

"What am I feeling for?"

"Talk to her."

"Who?"

"Your daughter." I tapped his hand. "She's shy now. Talk to her. Tell her to kick her father's hand."

Jack dropped to his knees and caressed my belly. "Mama thinks you're a girl. Most fathers would want a boy—but not me. I want a daughter, just as pretty as her mama."

Thunk.

"See that? Jacky, did you feel it?" My voice rose on its own. "Oh Jacky, she knows your voice!"

When my husband looked up at me, tears shimmered in his eyes, brightening their already green hue to the color of England in the springtime. "Redella, I believe we have a daughter."

"Jack, what was your grandmother's name?"

"I've never told you? In all the talking about my past we've done?"

I shook my head.

"Her name was Loreena. Loreena O'Malley."

I chewed my lower lip. "Mother's middle name was my grandmother's middle name. Jacqueline."

Jack looked up at me, emotion ripe in his eyes. "I believe we have our name."

"Loreena. Loreena Jacqueline Rackham." I stared into my husband's face and waited for his approval. "If, of course, that's a fitting name for you."

He stayed squatted down for what seemed like an eternity. "I never figured to find myself in such a way, Red. A husband, a father." Jack rose and wrapped me in his arms. "You've given me a gift I'm not worthy of, Red."

I covered Jack's hands with mine. Loreena kicked again, bringing a smile to Jack's face. "Loreena Jacqueline," he whispered into my hair. "I think that's the most beautiful name on any land, on any sea."

"We'll be in Madagascar by nightfall."

"Time passed quicker than I thought, what with my ginger root to gnaw on." My belly had grown so large over the course of our journey that it felt as though I had a giant Caribbean melon stuck under my canvas skirt constructed from a torn sail. Thankfully, Rusty was a skilled seamstress and was able to make my clothing dilemma as painless and comfortable as possible. I sucked in a breath and a deep cramp across my back furrowed my brow. "Have you seen any sign of Tommy's—well, *your*—ship?"

"I caught a glimpse of *The Revenge* this morning, then she was gone again. I figure we'll catch her when we dock."

"I'm quite tired, Jacky. Would you please wake me when we get there? I'd like to see Tommy—and apologize, if it was me who set him off on this silly quest." I pressed my hands into my lower back and leaned into them. "Even if it wasn't me, I'd still like to apologize to him."

It seemed I had only just laid my head down upon the pillow when Jack's voice echoed through the cabin. "Redella. Redella, we're here. And it looks like we're too late."

I dragged myself out of the bed. The cramp in my back wasn't helped by my rest. *Perhaps once I get up and move around it will feel better.*

I was wrong. It hurt just as much.

No matter. Tommy was out there and needed our help. I followed Jack, slowly, up the steps and across the deck. Before we were even on shore, I could hear him.

"Prince of the Rats! Where ye be, I say?"

I let Jack help me down the rope ladder as I tried to watch over my shoulder. The deckhands of *The Black Otter* lined the beach, while Tommy stumbled about with his sword drawn at the mouth of the Malagasy jungle. Funny looking little animals, gray with long black and white tails, stared at him with bemused, catlike expressions.

"Jack, do you think Tommy's been drunk this entire trip?"

My husband helped me to the shore and shrugged. "I don't know. He found his way here and faster than us. But he's certainly drunk now."

Tommy's voice grew to a hysterical shriek. "Prince of the Rats! I, your half-brother Tommy Tew, challenge you to a duel! To the death, it be!"

The cat-like creatures scattered as a man stepped out of the jungle understory. I gasped.

Decked in shimmering gold and threads I'd never seen colors of before, he wore an air of regality over everything else. A throng of shirtless women followed behind him, their eyes downcast. "You come to my kingdom and threaten me with death? This is not how brothers behave."

"Prince of the Rats," Tommy seethed, then stopped. "We have the same nose, for God's sake, we do!"

"Why have you come, Brother?"

Tommy's face turned from white to red to purple. "Brother! You cannot call yourself my brother!"

The women knelt so quickly that Tommy jumped. When they rose, each held a spear. Still, their eyes were downcast, but their message was clear.

"Why," Tommy began. "Why did Father love you and not me? Why did he give you all this, and me? I just got his name and nothing more, I did."

Prince Ratsimilaho started to speak, but someone stepped up behind him. The women dropped their spears.

"What's all this talk of blood and death and noses?"

Tommy's face transformed from furious to shocked. "Father!"

My eyes widened. I leaned closer to Jack. "I thought his father was killed?"

"So did I."

Tommy dropped his sword and hitched up his britches. He

started toward his father, but one of the women picked up a spear. He stopped short, a confused look on his rotund face. "Father?"

A white man by all accounts and dressed in pirate garb from yesteryear, the elder Thomas Tew spoke with a regal tone. "Tommy, it's time you knew the truth."

A black woman, slender and tall and shirtless, stepped from the jungle with a cat-like creature riding on her shoulder. The long, striped tail curled down around her breast. "This is my wife, the Queen of Madagascar. With her, I had the prince."

I half expected the prince to smirk. Instead, his downcast face mirrored Tommy's.

Thomas continued. "Your mother was a whore, Tommy. She insisted that I was your father and went so far as to give you my name. I never claimed you as my own, and if I could, I'd take my name from you now, lest you disgrace is more than you already have."

Thomas, the apparent King of Madagascar, bowed. "As for the rest of you. Restock your water, enjoy our food, and please, be gone by morning."

With that, he turned on his heel and disappeared back into the jungle, his woman only a step behind him.

Tommy turned his toe in the dirt. His hunger for the truth had outweighed his humiliation. Within the span of a few minutes, he'd gone from killing mad to—

Prince Rats waved a hand and dismissed his throng of women. "Brother, I—"

Tommy shook his head. His pants had slid back to their normal position, revealing his paunchy belly. "I thought he was dead, having died a hero's death on the high seas, he did," Tommy whispered.

The prince started toward him, but Tommy backed up.

"He recognized you as his blood, he did. I guess I should have come to kill Father—or love him."

Prince took another step forward, his hand outstretched. I saw a tear drip down Tommy's cheek, followed by another.

"Brother, please stop. Let us talk. You've come a long way. Come into my hut and rest. Please."

"Would you kill me, Prince of the Rats," Tommy managed. He swiped at his damp cheek and sniffled. "Death would be better than being the unwanted son of a whore and a pirate, it would."

I saw his shoulders start to shake.

"Jack, I can't let this go on." With my hands on my back, I waddled forward and nodded in greeting to the Prince before putting my arm around Tommy's shoulders.

To my surprise and probably everyone else's, Tommy melted into my embrace, crying like he'd no doubt cried for his father all his life.

"Come on Tommy," I cooed. "Let's go back to our ships. To your *real* family."

Tommy nodded but didn't look up.

"I'm so sorry for telling you that your father would be proud of you. I didn't know what a fool he was, or I never would have said such a thing."

Tommy stopped sobbing. "What?"

"On deck that night in Tortuga. When I told you your—"

"No." Tommy waved an arm. "You called him, my father, the legendary pirate Thomas Tew, a fool?"

"Yes." I looked Tommy squarely in his puffy face. "Yes I did. Because anyone who would talk to a loving son in such a manner *is* a fool. Don't you agree, Prince?"

Tommy glanced over his shoulder. Prince Rats had followed at a respectable distance, careful not to get too close—or too far—from his brother.

"Yes," Prince Rats said. "Yes I do." He erased the space between us and placed his brown hand on Tommy's shoulder. "You were right. We do have the same nose."

Tommy broke from my embrace and extended a hand to his brother, who took it and pulled him into a warm hug.

"Won't you stay? Tell me of your travels, and of your fleet?"

The cat-like creatures with their long, thin bodies reappeared, peeking out from between the branches of the understory that lined the beach. Their large, yellow eyes peered intently at the curious goings on between the pirates and the locals.

Tommy hesitated. Slowly, he turned his tear-stained face toward Jack and me. A look of want and heartbreak contorted the features on his pudgy face. "Can we, Cap?"

"We may as well stay," Jack started. "After all, we did sail round the horn of Africa to get here, did we not?"

"We may as well." I pressed my fists into my back. "If that is what you wish to do, Tommy."

Tommy turned back to his brother. "Father didn't seem to want me here, he didn't. He said so himself, he did."

Prince Rats squared his bare shoulders. "Father—" He cleared his throat. "Father will not be King of Madagascar forever. He rarely comes out of the hut he shares with my mother, the Queen. I see him about as often as you have, I'd say." He glanced at Jack and me, and smiled. "And I want you here."

The morning came too quickly. Prince Rats and Tommy, all smiles, sat on the beach together, just as they had all night. The little creatures, or ring-tailed lemurs as Prince Rats called them, skittered about between them. They laughed and passed a jug between them as Jack and I approached.

"The crew has restocked supplies on both ships, thanks to the kindness of the Crown of Madagascar." Jack stretched his arms wide. Another twinge in my back made me grimace. "The time has come, Tommy. For us to be on our way."

Prince Rats handed Tommy the jug. "Or you can stay. With us."

"Brothers we be," Tommy agreed.

Prince Rats stood and helped Tommy to his feet. "I'm proud to meet you, I am."

With tears in his dark, almond shaped eyes, the prince pulled his brother, our simple Tommy Tew, into a righteous hug. "Stay with us, Brother. In time, Father will come round."

Tommy pulled back and shook his head. "No, we'd best be going. Sorry I challenged you, Brother, to the death and all."

I cocked my head and smiled. Tommy nodded goodbye to the prince and let his watery gaze flitter back to mine. His lip quivered.

"It's your father's loss, Tommy. He'll regret it, someday."

Tommy nodded and walked beside me across the shores of Madagascar to the rope ladder that waited to carry him home. I was very proud of him. He didn't cry again until he was safely locked in his bunk aboard *The Black Otter*.

"Red Legs? You, Rusty, Charles, and Poison Lightning. Take *The Revenge*. The rest of us will stay aboard *The Black Otter*.

Charles started to protest, probably he wanted to sail with Dark Water, but he thought better of it and closed his mouth.

"Let us go now, my darling," Jack whispered into my hair. "Our work here is done."

I stood on the deck and watched as Madagascar, its topless, dark women, the lush green jungle, and the funny little lemurs grew further from me. Prince Ratsimilaho stood on the bank and waved as we left. Everyone ignored him and Tommy was below decks in his bunk, so I waved back. He stood there, unsmiling and waving, until we were each but a black speck in each other's vision.

My heart ached for Tommy. I knew my father about as well as he knew his. The one time I asked about my father, Mother sat me down in our London home and told me things that broke my heart. I was about seven years of age when I asked, but when she finished, I felt I'd aged a decade or more. He was a merchant sailor who, when he learned of Mother's falling pregnant with me, spoke honestly to her for perhaps the first time.

He had another family. A loving wife and three children in Scotland. His family, the one to which he would be returning, had money. Even though he never came to call on Mother again, or much less ask after me, he bought us a home in London before he left back to his real family. The home where Mother and I made happy memories, where I grew up, and where Mother passed from this earth.

In a way he took care of her, and of me. Perhaps in some way that was love. Perhaps that was all the love he was capable of. However the way he loved and the way my mother loved were starkly different. Mother, the daughter of a late Protestant preacher, loved me with every fiber of her being, every bit of her soul. And I knew it, for she showed it every day with every decision she made. I was certain that Tommy's mother loved him, too, even if her way of providing for herself made her less of a person in society's eyes. If she didn't love him, she wouldn't have given him the name she did. Something to aspire to, live up to. Sure, she didn't set him on the path to becoming a businessman or merchant sailor, but she had done the best she could with what she had.

Go tell him so, Redella. Tommy needs a mother's love now, and you're set to be a mother any day now.

I turned around to go do just that when a cramp seized my back. "Oh. Oh my," I chirped. An odd pressure crushed down on my insides. Before I could make sense of what was happening, a splash of water down my legs and over my feet made me freeze. "Oh no."

"Jack," I called. My voice shook, and that scared me. "Jacky!"

"Coming," Jack called from the wheelhouse. He dashed around the corner, his black cape flying behind him. "Yes?"

I must have been standing funny because my husband was at my side in an instant, his hand on my back and the other holding my hand. "Red? What is it?"

"We're about to have a baby," I managed. Another cramp tightened in my back. I grimaced.

"A baby?" My husband's face went ashen. "But, you said we had—" He ticked his fingers against his thumb.

The water that had broken and burst down my leg oozed still. "Yes, I know. It's too early. Much too early."

"—several more months," Jack finally said. He held up his fingers helplessly.

I ignored the fear that surged and burned in the back of my throat. "Jack, get Rusty."

"Darling, she's on the other—"

"Jack." I stared daggers at my husband. "Do you want Tommy, Solo, and Dark Water William to deliver your child?"

Jack shook his head. His green eyes were wide and clear. "Get Rusty."

"As you wish." Jack looped his arm about my waist and called out loudly. "Solo! Help!"

Solo helped me down to my bed. "Jack told me he was going to get Rusty. I don't know how he is going to do that, but when Captain sets his mind to something, he doesn't give up." Solo helped me adjust on the bed I shared with Jack and pulled the blanket up to my chin. "Probably he'll take the rowboat. *The Revenge* is but a little ways behind us."

I nodded a strained nod.

"I helped my mother deliver my two of my sisters." He sat down at Jack's writing desk and propped one leg up on the other. "If something happens before Jack gets back, I'll help you bring the baby."

Solo's warm smile made me feel safe.

"Thank you." I tried to return his smile, but another cramp seized my middle. "Ah!"

Solo jumped up and grabbed my hand. "Just squeeze. Squeeze my hand when it hurts."

I breathed in big, panting huffs. "You know," I managed. "It's too early." I glanced up at him. "I'm scared."

"Let's just take it one step at time." He smiled again and seemed confident that everything would be fine. "Jack will be back soon."

I felt myself relax.

"Now, if there's one thing I do remember from helping my mother, is that you're supposed to rest between the pains. Close your eyes now. See if you can even sleep a bit." He stroked my forehead like a husband would. My eyelids fluttered.

"I meant to tell you," Solo whispered. "It was fine of you and Jack to take on Rusty the way you did. You're already a wonderful mother, Red."

"Mmmhm."

"And the way you took care of Nikolai, then took care of Tommy," Solo stroked my forehead. "You're going to be a wonderful mother to this little chap, too."

Footsteps grew louder and the door to our quarters banged open. Jack's breathless voice met my ears. "We're back, I got her. I got Rusty."

Another pain gripped my middle. I arched my back and reached out. Solo grabbed my hand. "Squeeze, you won't hurt me. Squeeze, Redella."

"You're a natural, Solo." Jack's voice was revenant.

Still, I hadn't opened my eyes. "Jacky," I breathed. "It's too early."

Jack sunk down beside me. "I know. We'll get through this."

"One step at a time," Solo said again.

I felt Rusty's hands on my knees. "Good news, Back from the Dead Red. I'm about to have a little brother or sister."

Another pain tightened my belly. "Ah!"

"Breathe now." Rusty peered between my legs. "Hey, I see something!"

"Rusty?" Jack's voice was hesitant. "Have you ever delivered a baby before?"

"Nope. I've never brought a baby before." She sounded strangely chipper. "But what better time to learn than now?"

I closed my eyes. *I do not want to be a teaching case. Or this will turn into a tragedy.*

"Solo has, Jack." The waves slapped against the side of *The Black Otter*. It was easy to hear that a storm was brewing. "Mmm," I groaned.

"Solo!" Jack's voice was tinged in urgency. "Would you let Rusty help you deliver my child?"

"Yes, Cap. Is that all right with you, Redella?" Solo's voice was calm and ever gentlemanly. So much so that I didn't balk at him calling me Redella. He could have called me the Queen of England and I wouldn't have cared.

"Yes, please" I gasped. "Something's wrong, Solo. I can feel it. Bad wrong."

Solo joined Rusty at the foot of the bed. "Let's not focus on anything but breathing right now, Red. You'll hold your baby today. But for now, breathe. Think of the place that made you the most happy."

I felt for Jack's hand and finally opened my eyes. He brushed my hair from my sweaty forehead.

My words came in huffs. "I've been happiest here."

Solo pushed my knees apart. "Good. Imagine we're sailing calm waters through the Caribbean. The sun is shining, dolphins jumping, and soon, we'll take a rum ship."

"My ship," Rusty chimed. "You'll take my ship again and rescue me!"

"Ah yes." Solo's voice, so calm, gave me no choice but to relax. "Is that what you saw there, Rusty?"

"Yes. But it doesn't look like a head?"

Solo stood up. "That's because it's not." He wiped his hands on his britches and rolled up his sleeves. "Redella, listen to me very carefully. Your baby is trying to be born feet first."

"Solo." I huffed through another pain. "I have to push."

"Not yet."

Jack interjected. "Solo, have you ever seen such a thing before?"

"Yes. Once."

Jack's voice was as anxious as I had been before Solo took over. "Tell me Solo. Did the baby live?"

For the first time since I'd come to know him, Solo didn't answer his captain. "Redella, I need you to change position. Get on all fours. Rusty, you help her."

Jack's voice sounded nothing like the mighty ship captain but had taken on the fearful tone of a new father. "Solo, I asked you, did the baby—"

"Captain," Solo interrupted. "Help your wife. Hold her steady."

Jack did as he was told. "It's going to be over soon," he whispered. "And I'll be here the whole time, by your side."

Inside, worries and thoughts mixed together until I was afraid I'd be sick. So many things to worry about, to plan, to fix, to prepare—

"Jacky," I managed. "Where are we?"

"Sailing south along the coast of Africa. Why do you ask?"

I curled my fingers into our bedsheets. I managed a smile as I leaned against him. "So we can tell our Loreena Jacqueline Rackham where she was born."

Solo's voice came from behind me. "Push with the next pain, Redella."

Something deep inside me that shouldn't have been bothered burned like fire with a sudden, sharp burn. I let go a yell before I could help myself.

"No. No yelling." Solo's voice was sharp. "Take all that breath and use it to push your baby out."

Rusty's excited voice tolled like a church bell. "I see feet!"

I leaned against Jack on wobbling elbows. Big drops of sweat dripped down my nose, wetting our sheets. "I'm going to split in two!"

"One more big push and we'll be almost finished." Solo's voice was calm again as he reported from between my legs.

Someone banged on the door. "Cap? Cap!" Dark Water's deep, throaty voice sounded worried. "We have a problem."

"Rusty, can you come up here with your mother?" Jack stood up, but didn't move from beside me until Rusty was there. He dropped his voice low. "Dark Water wouldn't have come down unless it was life or death."

"Is—is—all right?"

Rusty sounded like she was smiling. "Everything's fine. Probably just the storm, is all."

I gripped the blankets into sweaty knots as the next pain took hold of my body. I gritted my teeth and tried not to yell. Instead, I pushed with every ounce of energy I had left. My insides were on fire and I may well have been pushing a bag of rocks out of me.

With my bottom half in the air, I lay my head on my pillow. "She's born."

The lack of emotion in Solo's voice didn't go unnoticed. "Why isn't she crying?" I tried to move, but Rusty stopped me.

"Don't move, Mama. The afterbirth has to come." Her usually chipper voice was notably muted. "I know that much."

"What's wrong?"

Rusty mopped my forehead and smiled at me. "I love you, Mama."

Tears welled in my eyes, but it wasn't because of the final pain that delivered the afterbirth. It was from something else.

"Solo," I begged.

"Rusty. Go get Cap. Now." He patted my lower leg. "Red, you can lay down."

I let my quivering frame fall into the sweaty sheets and sniffled. "What's wrong? Please tell me."

Solo sucked in a breath as Jack flung open the door. The hopefulness in my husband's eyes drained as he looked at both Solo and me. I saw Solo shake his head before turning his attention back to me. "How long ago did she stop kicking and moving about, Redella?"

I licked my lips and tried to remember the last time I felt my daughter move. "Well before we landed in Madagascar. I thought it was normal for her to calm down. Felt a bit like she dropped. Thought it was normal. Wait—" I struggled to sit up on my elbows. "You said *she*."

Solo's hand fluttered down to my arm as Jack reappeared. "Redella, she didn't make it."

"No." I pushed his hand off my arm. "Let me see her." I glanced to Jack for help. He stood at the foot of our bed, arms crossed across his chest. "Jacky, let me see her."

Jack's eyes shimmered. "She's been gone awhile, Red. She doesn't look like a baby." Jack pointed down to her. "Solo, what's that?"

"A knot. In the cord."

"My God," I whispered. "Loreena Jacqueline."

"Loreena Jacqueline Rackham," Jack echoed. "Let her mother hold her, Solo."

Another bang on the door made me jump. "Cap. Cap!"

Jack let out a huff.

"What's going on out there," I asked. Though my insides were so numb, I didn't care to listen. However, I wanted Jack with me, not out there with them.

"We're in Blackbeard's waters."

"I've heard of Blackbeard—"

Jack shared a look with Solo. Even in my state, in our stuffy stateroom, I sensed doom. "He is also known as Edward Teach. At least that was what he went by when we were acquainted before."

I looked up at my husband, silently begging him to continue.

"He is under the impression that my—that *our*—ship, *The Revenge* is, well—" Jack took a deep breath and let it out slow. "His."

I chewed my lip. "Is that why Dark Water came down? To tell you?"

Jack nodded. "Blackbeard sent over a dinghy and kindly gave us an hour to get out of his territory. Or give back his ship. Though it was never really his. It was a misunderstanding."

Solo's brow furrowed. "An hour? By God that's impossible and he must know—"

Jack looked at Solo and flipped back his cape. His steel caught a glint of light from the porthole and shone in his scabbard. "He knows. And our hour is up."

Something shrouded Solo's face before he remembered the task at hand. He forced a smile and placed my daughter in my arms. From the corner of my eye, I watched as Jack turned on his booted heel and whisked from our room.

"T-thank you, for everything Solo," I managed. But the emotion came quicker than I imagined and drown my words. Deep sobs roiled up from the painful depths of my tender gut. Rusty circled her arm around my shoulder.

"Loreena Jacqueline is a beautiful name for a beautiful baby sister," she cooed.

I sniffled.

Get a hold of yourself, Red.

Slowly, I look down at the bundle in my arms studied my dead daughter. Her tiny blue eyes were open wide. When I adjusted, her little jaw went slack. I pushed her mouth shut gently and held it there. Her lips were full, as though they were ready to plant a kiss on the cheek of her mother or father.

Or sister.

"She doesn't weigh nearly as much as my sword," I breathed.

Rusty's voice was muted. "She's just a bit longer than my hand. And her tiny fingers are so long and thin. And those little nails—"

Rusty fingered her little sister's lifeless hands, each one perfect, with an almost invisible nail tipping each one.

Loreena's skin that didn't look like skin appeared somewhat bubbly and dark. I chewed my lip. "Pray for her, Rusty."

Rusty was deep in a Latin recitation when Jack whisked back into the room. He slammed the door behind him. "Can you walk, Red?"

I made no move to swipe the tears from my cheeks. "Here Jack, would you like to hold her?"

Jack didn't answer. "Darling, Blackbeard was toying with us. He had ships waiting, though I don't know how he did it."

Solo, who'd been keeping vigil in the corner, leapt to his feet.

"Red, if you can walk, we need to get you down to the cargo hold. I'll lock you down there, and you too, Rusty, so no harm will come to you."

Rusty scooped Loreena from my arms as I swung my legs over the side of the bed. "Jack," I managed. "Please bring my sword."

I saw his lips tilt into a sad smile. "As you wish."

"Rusty." I jerked as something crashed above me. The thunderous cacophony that rumbled on deck was too much to bear. "I can't stay down here while everyone else fights."

And dies.

"Mama, you can't go up there." Rusty had wrapped Loreena in a sheet and placed her in a crate. Before it held my daughter's remains, judging by the stamp on the side, it had held potatoes.

I struggled to my feet. "The cargo hold only locks from the inside." I sheathed my sword and tiptoed across the floor. The world pitched and spun, but it felt good to walk and stretch my legs. I rested my fingers on the lock.

"No Mama, please." I didn't look over my shoulder at Rusty. I'd put on pantalets and stuffed the crotch with old clothes since the blood wouldn't quit coming, so I stood at an odd angle, with my legs wider than they should be.

I sucked in a breath and flipped the lock. "You stay here. I'll be back with news of victory."

"Mama!"

"What is it, Rusty?" I looked back over my shoulder at my adopted daughter and immediately regretted my harsh tone. I smiled at her. "Thank you for everything today. I don't know what I would have done if not for you. You're our blessing, child."

Rusty's voice was small. "I—I love you."

I opened the door. "I love you, too. Lock this door behind me."

The scene on deck was all it had sounded like from the cargo hold. Pools of blood left red rings in the thirsty wood. From atop the wheelhouse, someone roared. I drew my sword and spun on my heel. The world kept spinning and a roil of nausea surged. I hiccupped.

Red, you're in no condition to fight. You're going to get yourself killed.

Dark Water William glared at me. "Witch," he seethed. "Only a witch could give birth to a monster. The devil's seed. Then come up to fight."

I backed up a step as Dark Water squatted down atop the wheelhouse as though he meant to spring down atop me. Something flashed in his eyes that gave him a beastly look. As I backed up another step, something hit my shoulder. Charles Swan's foul breath, with a slightly fishy odor, met my nose. He made no move to shift out of my way.

"Witch," he agreed. He twitched his nose. His greasy moustache moved across his lip like a limp worm.

I swallowed back the nausea and put my hand on my sword. Slowly, I drew it from its scabbard. My vision grew fuzzy and I suddenly wished I had something to lean against.

Outnumbered.

One of Blackbeard's men crept up behind Charles, but all his attention was fixed on me. Without a second thought, I tossed my sword to Charles. "Behind you!"

Charles turned and stabbed my steel through the approaching pirate. Something changed on his face when he turned back to face me. His features were somehow softer, almost human. I think if I'd have been a man, in that moment, he would have pledged his allegiance to me over Dark Water.

He glanced up at his cohort, still crouched atop the wheelhouse, and jerked his chin. The tall African with the hate-filled eyes melted backward off the wheelhouse and disappeared into the throng of the fight. My insides chilled. Somehow, some way, this fight was just beginning.

Charles handed my bloodied steel back to me before disappearing behind Dark Water. I sank against the wheelhouse, not really sitting and not really standing.

It's not over with Dark Water. Or Charles Swan.

"Redella!" Jack's voice met my ears. "Watch out!"

Metal clanged together and my hair blew back in a whoosh as a hidden pirate's sword met mine. His dark eyes flashed and his beard, so black it was almost blue, hung stringy from his face. Tiny shells and beads dotted the gnarled mess that hung from his chin.

"So it's true," he growled.

He slashed again, and with a flick of my wrist, I blocked it. "What?"

"Back from the Dead Red." He reached for me, but I slipped out of the way. The world pitched again as I stumbled, but somehow, I found my footing.

"You'll make a wonderful wench aboard my ship."

I jabbed for his throat—but missed.

"I'll have to share you with the crew, of course. But a girl like you won't mind. Will you?"

My guts ached and I regretted coming up here at all. Still, my words escaped my tight lips in a growl. "You'll have to kill me first."

"That can be arranged."

The cacophony that had reigned upon the deck as Blackbeard's crew tried to take *The Black Otter* dulled to silence as I stared at the scarred pirate. I felt the blood escape my body and disappear into the cloth between my legs. The brief thought of being caught by the smarmy pirate and made to lay with the men upon his ship brought with it an icy trickle of fear down my backbone.

I'm not at my strongest, he may win this battle.

He took a step closer and tossed his sword from one hand to the other. I reached out with my steel and attempted to catch his and flick it away, but I missed completely. Everything went double in my vision. I blinked my eyes and flexed my fingers around my sword's handle.

Blackbeard laughed, a mean spirited, cackling laugh. "Stupid girl. How long will you continue to try and fight me off?"

I'll kill myself before he takes me alive.

I thought about trying to answer, but Blackbeard was moving his sword around slowly. It took all of my concentration to watch his blade. A chilled veil of sweat cropped up across my forehead and I sunk to my knees.

"Get up, wench," he growled.

I struggled to focus on him, but everything went sideways.

Don't faint, Redella. Don't faint.

I jabbed blindly with my sword, as though I was fighting an invisible enemy. As his image drew closer, my sword met resistance.

Blackbeard growled and let go a string of curses. "How did you—" His voice was tinged in incredulity. "Me leg! You slashed me leg!"

"Just need to lay down—" The words sounded garbled even to

my ears as I tried to watch death as it came for me in the form of Blackbeard's steel.

Death or worse.

Jack's face fuzzed over Blackbeard's shoulder as the old pirate grew nearer to me and slashed wildly with his steel.

"Jacky," I whispered. "I'm so sorry."

Blackbeard's steel slashed wildly before me. I lost sight of it until I felt a trickle of blood drip down my arm.

"Ow," I whimpered.

"Surrender to me."

Everything went dark. A strange sense of peace shrouded me. "I'll be with Loreena," I said. Or perhaps I thought the words. "You won't take me alive."

Jack's voice interrupted my internal reverie. "Gaaaaah!"

A death cry. Was it mine?

I struggled to open my eyes, which felt as though the lids had turned to stone. I watched as Jack sunk his dagger into Blackbeard's neck. The older pirate fell to his knees, his eyes still alive with hate as I lay helpless before him.

Blackbeard stared through me and gurgled something, but the words were lost to the blood that filled his throat. When Jack pulled out his dagger, Blackbeard fell over. Dead.

Jack crouched at my side. "You need to be in bed, Redella."

"I couldn't," I began. I closed my eyes again and may have slept for a moment. "Couldn't leave you alone." The world pitched and rolled, like a ship on an angry sea.

Jack pulled me to my feet. I kept my eyes closed, though I kept my fingers tight around my blade's handle. "While the boys clean up from the fight, you and I have some business to attend to."

Beads of sweat stood out from my forehead like pearls on a necklace. As I allowed Jack to pull me through the macabre scene that was our deck, I felt them slide down my neck in a ticklish descent. My body felt hot and, with the adrenaline ebbing and my heartbeat slowing to a somewhat normal rate, I felt shaky and weak. "Jack, I don't feel well," I started. "Can you tell me where—"

I saw it before we'd even reached the far side of the deck. A small crate with the word potatoes stamped on the outside. I ground to a halt. "No Jack."

Emotion burned in my throat, but no tears came. Everything hurt. My woman parts, my guts, my arms and legs. Even my insides felt to be on fire. But nothing hurt more in that very instant than my very heart and soul.

"Come wife," Jack said. His voice was gentle, not at all commanding as it had been in the past. "It's time we bury our daughter."

"I don't know how—"

"We became parents together." Jack's hand covered mine. "We will this learn together, as well."

I stepped closer to the box. A dark swatch of skin was visible just inside. Strange bubbles were visible just under her skin that gave her an otherworldly look. I knelt down and stroked my daughter's head. Someone has mercifully closed her blue eyes. Probably Rusty, as the fight raged with Blackbeard's men.

"She had blonde hair, Jack. Like you."

Jack's hand massaged my neck.

I wanted to memorize everything about her. The tiny details that made her who she was. The curve of her nose, the length of her fingers. "We will never gotten to hear her squeak," I whispered. "Or hear her first cry."

I stared at her little offset mouth. "She never got to smile." Her first smile, if it even happened inside me, would never happen again on this earth. "I'll never get to feel her wrap her little hand around my finger."

I covered my eyes with one hand. While I wanted to drink in every detail of my firstborn child, I also wanted to forget. Forget the excitement. Forget the pains. Forget the moment when she was born. Forget everything, because remembering—*knowing*— hurt with an excruciating force in an unseen place deep inside me.

Jack cleared his throat. "Solo found your old blouse. The one you came aboard wearing." He squatted down beside me. "He thought you might like to let Loreena rest in it. In case it was a family heirloom."

"Solo," I began, before emotion broke my words. "Was the first to hold her. He has been correct about so many things since I've come aboard, Jack. And he is correct here again."

I chewed my lip and bowed my head. Jack leaned over and gently picked up our daughter's body, which was wrapped in the blouse that had accompanied me from my former life. "I wore it to my mother's funeral," I whispered.

I dared a peek at Jack. He smiled down into Loreena's face. A smattering of silent tears glistened upon his cheeks. "That settles it, then. Our daughter will rest in her grandmother's arms in Heaven, and in a blouse her mother wore to honor her own mother."

Rusty appeared silently at his side, a sewing needle in her hand. "Shall I, Father?"

"Say goodbye, Red." Jack looked down at me. "Say goodbye to our daughter, until we meet again someday."

Emotion hitched in my throat as I allowed Jack to pull me to my feet. Ever obedient to my husband's command, I leaned over and kissed my dead child on her precious forehead. "I love you, little one. I am sorry you never got a chance to see the ocean."

I melted into Jack's side as Rusty sewed my blouse over her little, stillborn sister. "Thirteen stitches, Father," she whispered. "Correct?"

Jack nodded. "Yes, that's correct."

Tears flowed from my eyes and soaked my face, and Jack's blouse. An unwelcome, unbearable pain seared hot in my chest. "Oh God, please," I managed. "Please. Please, please."

Suddenly, a horrible realization hit me. "Rusty, stop sewing!"

"Mama?"

"What is it, Red?" Jack's loving voice was tinged with concern.

I peered up at him, fully aware of my quivering lips and trembling voice. "Jack, baptize her. Please."

"She was gone before she was born, Red," Jack started.

I shook my head violently. "No. No!"

"Red!" My husband's hand cupped the side of my face. "Red, calm down. Your wish is my command."

"Rusty, bring Loreena to the side of the ship, please." Jack knelt and scooped a handful of sea water into his palm as Rusty squatted down, the little bundle securely in her arms. "Redella, say the words."

Jack tipped his palm so that the sea water streamed down onto Loreena's head. "Your father and I baptize you, Loreena Jacqueline Rackham, in the name of the Father—"

Jack scooped more sea water and continued to let it stream onto our baby.

"And in the name of the Son—"

One last scoop.

"And of the Holy Ghost. Amen."

My face crumpled. "Oh Jack, it was supposed to be holy water. Oh Jack, what have I done? Have I damned her soul with my—"

"Redella." Jack's voice had morphed from gentle to commanding once again. "Ask any seaman who has ever sailed the sea." He took my face in his hands and forced me to look at him. "There is no holier water than that which the Almighty created Himself. He created the oceans, did He not?"

His words made sense. I nodded and patted his hand. "Pray for her, Jack. Please."

"Rusty, continue sewing please."

A slew of consecutive splashes made me jump. I glanced over my shoulder as Poison Lightning readied himself to push the last of Blackbeard's men overboard. He must have felt me watching because he turned and held my gaze—mine, hopelessly watery while his, all business. He offered me a nod before turning back to complete his task of burying a rival pirate at sea. I turned back to my own funeral proceedings as my heart continued to break in fresh, unimaginable ways with each passing moment.

"The sewing is complete, Father." Rusty's voice was impossibly formal. "Loreena is ready for the journey.

"She mustn't float for all eternity," Jack whispered. "Place her in her crate, Rusty."

Red Legs sidled up beside me. "Shall I nail the coffin shut, Cap?"

Jack sniffled. I didn't look up, but it sounded as though he was crying. "Yes, Red Legs."

Without fanfare, Red Legs stepped over to Rusty and patted her shoulder. "Go to your parents, Darling."

Rusty nodded as her own emotions roiled up and over, reducing her to a blubbering female, not unlike her mother. I opened my arm to her, where she melted into my side as I had Jack's.

Red Legs, perhaps in another life, would have been a fabulous undertaker. "Tell me, Jack," he began in his trademark easy style. His words lightened the mood over our end of *The Black Otter* considerably. "Do you reckon Loreena would have grown to inherit *The Black Otter* fleet?" He pounded nail after nail into the boards. "What a silly question, of course she would have. And what a leader she would have been, coming from the two of you." Red Legs stood and tucked his hammer into a pocket of his britches. "My she rest in peace, Captain Red. Captain Jack."

"T-thank you, Red Legs," I whispered.

"May I do the honors, Captains?" Solo's tranquil voice appeared from nowhere. "I brought her into this world. I feel it's my duty to see that she gets properly planted."

Jack cleared his throat. "Yes, thank you, Solo." He unwound his arm from around my shoulders and produced a book from the inside pocket of his duster.

"The Book of Common Prayer, 1662 edition." I glanced at him. "From The Church of England."

Jack cleared is throat and began to read. "Jesus said to her, "I am the resurrection and the life. The one who believes in me will live, even though they die; and whoever lives by believing in me will never die. Do you believe this?" John 11:25-26."

"Yes," I whispered in answer. "Yes I do."

"Me too, Mama," Rusty whispered back. She squeezed my shoulders.

Jack continued. "I know that my redeemer lives, and that in the end he will stand on the earth. And after my skin has been destroyed, yet in my flesh I will see God; myself will see him with my own eyes—I and not another. How my heart years within me. Job 19:25-27."

Jack cleared his throat, then cleared his throat again. Red Legs stepped over to his captain. "I can read, Cap. May I?"

Jack nodded and wrapped both of his arms around me. His shoulders shook, as did mine.

Red Legs' voice was more commanding than Jack's when reading from the prayer book. "For we brought nothing into the world, and we can take nothing out of it. First Timothy 6:7."

"Aye," Tommy said. "That be true, it be."

"Naked, I came from my mother's womb—" Red Legs' gaze flickered to me before focusing back on the book. "And naked I will depart. The Lord gave and the Lord has taken away; may the name of the Lord be praised. Job 1:21."

My thoughts swirled in my mind, like a tempest. *God, please keep Loreena in Your loving hand—*

Red Legs continued to read from the book, Psalms 39 and 90, then First Corinthians chapter 15, but I didn't hear the words. *My baby. My baby is dead.*

Red Legs' voice roused me from my daydream. "When they come to the grave, while the corpse is made ready to be laid into the earth." He shifted his weight. "Mortals, born of woman, are of few days and full of trouble. They spring up like flowers and wither away; like fleeting shadows, they do not endure. Do you fix your eye on them? Will you bring them before you for judgement? Job 14:1-2."

It's time to bury my child.

Jack's voice was loud and commanding again. "Solo, please bury our daughter in the ocean, that was briefly her home and is now her home for all eternity."

"Yes, Cap." Solo picks up the little makeshift coffin to begin to lower it into the water when Tommy, his dirty hat pressed to his chest and a coil of rope over his shoulder, and Poison Lightning appeared, toting a cannonball. Wordlessly, Poison Lightning attaches the cannonball with a short length of chain to the bottom of the crate.

"So she'll rest and not float, she will," Tommy whispered. "She will," he repeated.

The trio of pirates laced the rope through the crate, with Poison Lightning and Solo each taking an end. Tommy lifted the crate gently and placed it outside the ship. Solemnly, Solo and Poison Lightning began to lower Loreena's little casket into the waves.

"Sleep well, little baby," Tommy whispered. "Sleep well."

A boom from our cannon, which we were never forced to use, made me jump. I grabbed Jack's coat. One, then two, then three booms. I glanced at Jack. "French volley of fire. One for me, one for Loreena, and one for you."

Jack cleared his throat as the smoke from the cannon fire hung low around us and continued, emotion crackling in his words as he read the same piece he'd read when we'd buried Monica Joan at sea. "For as much as it hath pleased Almighty God of his great mercy to take unto himself the soul of our dear daughter Loreena Jacqueline Rackham, here departed, we therefore commit her body to the deep, to be turned into corruption, looking for the resurrection of the body, when the sea shall give up her dead, and the life of the world to come through Our Lord Jesus Christ who at His coming shall change our vile body, that it may be like His glorious body, according to the mighty working, whereby He is able to subdue all things to Himself."

When Poison Lightning and Solo nodded to Jack and held their rope, now emptied of its contents, my world began to spin. I heard Rusty call my name, but it sounded as though she was yelling in a dream. The feeling that I was falling, falling, falling was strong. But I never hit the ground.

I woke up tucked into my bed in the quarters I shared with Jack.

"Don't try to move," Rusty warned. "You passed out. You're not well, Mama."

"Where's Jack?" I licked my dry lips. Everything in my mind was fuzzy. "The battle with Blackbeard—"

"They're gone. Most of them dead. We won." Rusty mopped my forehead with a wet rag. "You and Jack did Blackbeard in."

"Loreena." Her name brought an ache to my chest.

"We buried her, Mama."

"I thought it was a nightmare." My voice was a whisper. "Where's Jack?"

"Jack'll be back soon."

"Back?" I tried to sit up but became so woozy that I collapsed back onto the bed. "Jacky?"

Solo's face hovered above me, like faces do in dreams. "He's gone ashore for you a doc."

"Ashore? Where are we?"

"The Cape of Good Hope. South Africa."

A smattering of tears fell from my lashes. "No, Solo. Not ashore—" I whimpered. "Pirate hunters—" I sucked in a deep breath, but more words wouldn't come.

"He took Poison Lightning with him. They'll be fine." Solo patted my hand. "He gave us strict orders to look after you. You do what Jack wanted and just rest."

My eyelids fluttered closed, but my mind refused to rest.

When I finally woke up, it seemed that I hadn't rested at all. I sat up. "Where's Jack?"

The room I shared with my husband was empty. I looked out the porthole.

Nothing for miles, only the open sea.

My stomach turned up in knots.

Weren't we in port in South Africa? Did I dream that?

My aching muscles allowed me to move only so fast, but I finally made it up on deck. "Where's Jack?"

Pitiful looks stared back at me. Rusty stood up and strode across the deck, a pout on her full lips and her thin arms outstretched.

"I'm sorry, Mama."

I stepped back. "What happened?"

Solo drummed his fingertips on the side of the ship. "You were right about the pirate hunters, Red. Jack was spotted in town before he could get the doctor."

I pulled my hands to my mouth. "No."

Solo held up his palms. "Now hold on. They tried to get Poison Lightning, but Jack pretended he was a beggar. Kicked him and cussed him. Saved his life. Poison Lightning got away and came back to report to us. Jack's on a pirate hunter ship bound for England. We're trailing them."

"Thank God." I exhaled and shook my head slightly. "I knew we wouldn't have just left him—"

Solo offered a smile. "We'll get him back, Redella."

"No." Dark Water William rose up behind Solo like a demon. "We won't."

Before Solo could turn around, before anyone aboard could fathom what was happening or make a move to stop it, Dark Water raised a chunk of wood and brought it down hard on Solo's head.

My princely friend, who had proven most loyal no matter the stakes, sunk to his knees, then fell over.

Dark Water's thin lips pulled up into a wicked smile. "This is *my* ship now."

Chapter Fourteen

Aboard The Black Otter, on the high seas

Thank God I came up on deck when I did. My eyes widened. *If Dark Water had overtaken the ship with me still passed out in our quarters—* Something icy slid down my spine, but I didn't bother with trying to discern what it was.

It's now or never.

I leapt forward and grabbed Solo's sword from his belt and landed in a crouch. I met Dark Water's eyes, silently thanking God for however long I'd slept. *At least I had some energy back, despite the deep ache in my muscles.* "This is my ship. You can't have it."

Dark Water raised his upper lip in a snarl from the end of my blade. "Only a witch would take over a ship."

Something hit me from behind and sent Solo's sword clattering across the deck.

Charles Swan.

I stumbled but didn't fall. Still, the world pitched around me. Fingers grabbed at me, fumbling, curling in my hair, yanking, but not making a clean grab.

I rolled onto my back. Dark Water's eyes were black with hate as he stared at me, his dagger held high and ready to finish me.

"Dark Water! Help!" Charles plea twanged upward and with a whine.

"I got him Mama!" Rusty shrieked.

Dark Water glanced toward the scuffle. That was all the time I needed.

I clasped my hands together like a club and swung with everything I had.

For Jacky.

For Solo.

For Monica Joan.

For Irish Bon.

For Rusty.

For Tommy and Poison Lightning.

For Loreena.

Society may group us together as sniveling pirates, whose lives weren't worth a red cent. But I knew better. I knew good could be found in strange places and evil was everywhere, even in rich doctors' London homes. But there was no place for evil aboard *The Black Otter.*

We might all hang in the end, but I wouldn't let myself dangle from the yardarm without knowing full well I'd fought my hardest.

Better to fight like a man than hang like a dog.

My forearms connected with Dark Water's fist. His dagger flew from his hand and clattered away.

I dared a glance at Rusty. Sure enough, she'd jumped on Charles' back and had him pinned to the deck. Dark Water, seeing his nearest and dearest in such a predicament, charged her.

"No!" I roared. I reached for his booted foot as he momentarily forgot about me. But I wasn't quick enough. "Rusty, watch out!"

Her pretty eyes widened as the tall mutineer sprinted toward her. Something flickered across her freckled face, but it wasn't fear. Not by a long shot.

Red Legs burst from nowhere and banged Dark Water in the chest with his shoulder before he could close in on Rusty. Dark Water Williams' feet caught air before he hit the deck with a resounding *oomph.*

Tommy, sensing his time had come to be a hero, thundered across the deck with a yell and plopped down atop Dark Water, a proud smile on his pudgy face.

Chest heaving, I pushed myself to my feet. As I stood, I picked up Solo's sword from where it lay. I set my jaw and held the blade to Charles' neck.

"Red Legs," I growled. "Tie them up and lock them in the jail below decks."

I stood on deck, staring, as Red Legs lashed the arms and legs of the would-be mutineers before me. Both stared hotly at the woman who'd bested them. As Red Legs dragged them away, I could see in their eyes they would make good on any chance of escape—and this time they wouldn't fail.

The time for mercy was over.

"Rusty."

My adopted daughter straightened her back and stared at me. "Mama?"

"You saved us all." I flickered a smile at her. "Again."

"Of course I did." She flung her hands up in exasperation. "You're my family."

"In the cargo hold are bolts of cloth. Find all the red you can and sew us new sails. Blood red sails."

"Yes ma'am." She disappeared like a streak of lightning. There one minute, so bright and tangible, then gone.

I held Solo's sword in front of me and scowled. "Tommy. Poison Lightning. Also in the cargo hold is paint. Find all the black you can. It's high time that my husband's flagship lived up to its name."

"Consider it done, because we'll do it, we will." Tommy led Poison Lighting to the cargo hold with a jovial bounce in his step.

I planted my feet and stared at the remnants of my crew. "Now that the more innocent among us are gone, only us killers are left.

Solo groaned and rubbed his head, and Red Legs' face was scarlet and unsmiling.

"I want to add two articles to *The Black Otter*." I shifted my gaze from my men into the distance. "I-if you're married, you're faithful. To the end. To death. No matter what."

"Aye," Solo gurgled. He cleared his throat and squinted at me. Red Legs nodded a stiff nod.

"I-if you're not faithful, you die."

"Aye aye, Cap." Solo smiled, like a big brother would smile when his little sister threw her first punch at a boy who unwelcomingly tried to kiss her.

Red Legs scowled, but nodded, the fire still not gone from his face.

"Till Rusty gets the new sails sewn, we'll set these here to catch every wind. We *will* catch Jack—and bring him back home to his ship."

"Aye aye, Cap," Solo said again. I knew he meant it.

Chapter Fifteen

Swansea, Wales

Jack let his fingers dance down my backbone. Even through the fabric, his touch left me craving more of him and longing for the familiar caress of his skin against mine, without the cumbersome dress to get in the way. I inhaled his exotic scent as I lay against his chest and listened to the steady thud of his heart.

Rum.

Spices.

Sweat.

Sea.

My eyes closed on their own.

"If I'd have figured any way to save your life, Jacky," I began. "I would have right then."

Emotion clogged my throat and threatened to choke me like it had choked my elderly fiancé. "But I couldn't figure a way, not even with Rusty's help, to get through the trap."

Jack tangled his fingers in my hair at the back of my neck. "I know you would have, Back from the Dead Red. Defying odds is what you do best, it seems."

I was careful to keep my voice soft. "I did try, you know. Later. But it didn't work."

His fingertips on the nape of my neck were intoxicating. "So I heard."

I tightened my arms around Jack's middle.

"How did you get away?"

"I'm afraid you won't believe me," Jack said. "To be completely honest, I'm still not sure how she pulled it off."

My eyes sprang open. I pushed back from his grasp. "*She?*"

His arms fell away from my body like dry leaves in a winter wind. Jack's face was soft and his eyes steady, despite my sudden fervor.

The hurt on Angel-Arse's face when she learned I was married to Jack had haunted me, off and on, without reason. Sometimes during the day, other times in my dreams.

The fuzzy memory of Jack going into Tortuga without me the night I killed Nikolai often accompanied that memory.

Had he gone into town to meet her and have a free farewell hurrah?

"You mean to tell me, Russian Jack Rackham, that you were rescued by a *woman?*"

"We're too late." I couldn't look at Rusty as I adjusted the white cloak I'd swept over my head and shoulders before coming ashore. If I started crying, everyone would see that Russian Jack's wife was there—present at his makeshift, coastal English trail.

We hadn't been able to catch the pirate hunting ship, though all of us had tried every trick we knew to catch fair winds. Since we failed to catch Jack's ship, followed the pirate hunters right up to the English coast.

I'd left Solo in charge of *The Black Otter* while Rusty and I came to try to free Jack without getting ourselves caught. And hanged.

"Guilty of piracy," one of the judges yelled. My throat tightened and my eyes fluttered shut. A chorus of townsfolk joined in, pumping their fists and all affirming my husband's doom. I pulled the cloak tighter about my head and shoulders.

"Dear God, no," Rusty whispered beside me.

"Come on, this way," I said. We pushed our way to the front of the throng. "I have to see Jacky."

Several of those who had served as both judge and jury spoke amongst themselves. One slapped a black blindfold over Jack's eyes while another shackled his already bound hands. He wore a look of defeat that mirrored the one he'd worn when China Joe made him attach cannonballs to my legs before throwing me overboard.

Even then, Jack had a surprise or two in store—but what could the surprise be now?

His hat was nowhere to be seen and his blonde hair was streaked with blood.

What did they do to you on the ship's ride here Jacky—

I sidled up to the scaffold as thoughts swirled viciously in my mind.

There must be a way to get Jack out of this—

"That wife of his, Back from the Dead Red. She'll try to rescue him." The man's voice hissed from between his clenched teeth. "And we'll be ready for her."

I froze.

Another of the men, who wore a tall powdered wig reminiscent of the one Unconscionable Nan had worn aboard *The Molly Maiden*, nodded in answer. "She won't come if he's dead, so we can't kill him. Put him in the gibbet. And we'll wait for her at the bottom. She has that scar on her face. She'll die trying to break him out."

"We'll see to that."

Those who played judge and jury also got to play executioner. "The sentence for the condemned," one shouted to the ravenous crowd.

The tittering crowd silenced in eager anticipation.

"Left to rot in the gibbet!"

The man who'd promised to catch me gave Jack a kick. "May God have mercy on your pitiable soul."

Rusty and I trailed the mob to the docks as they led Jack— bound, shackled, and blindfolded—like a dog to his death. By the water's edge sat a nest of iron. Rusty grabbed my hand.

The gibbet.

Shaped like a man, the strips of rusted iron bound with

grommets were made heavier still by the memory of those who were there before. Once they locked you in, you never came out. One of the men unlocked the shackles and cut the ropes that bound Jack's wrists.

"In with you," the kicker shouted.

Blinded by the knotted fabric, Jack crawled blindly across the ground as the jeers from the onlookers grew louder. Some threw stones, others threw kicks. Rusty and I watched, but my attempt to show no emotion was futile. Tears eked from my eyes and the urge to dash into the crowd and help my husband was almost tangible. I prayed nobody would notice.

Finally, Jack managed to crawl into his metal tomb. The man in the white powdered wig slammed it shut. Jack jump when the metal slapped together. I did, too.

"Reel him up," someone shouted.

Slowly, the metal prison began to rise to the yardarm, where he would dangle until the blistering heat, the freezing cold, the incessant wind, and relentless birds slowly took his life. If the lack of food or water didn't kill him first.

The man in the wig turned to the others. "Now, we wait for that wife of his, Back from the Dead Red. Remember, she's said to be scarred across the cheek."

I pulled my cloak tighter and chewed my bottom lip. Rusty and I shared a glance that rang with a shared truth.

Hopelessness.

I smacked the balcony and stared at my fluttering veil. "There was no way to get you out, Jacky. If there was—"

"If there was, I sure didn't see it." His green eyes were gentle. "Once I got that blasted blindfold off, that is. Here, let me tell you what happened."

"Well Red my dear, once they had me hoisted up, and once I got that blasted blindfold off, I had a decent view. I overlooked the docks and could see the sea stretching way out before me. The pull to be on the sea, where I belonged, hurt the worst. God Almighty, I wanted to be on it."

Jack drummed his fingers on the balcony. "I knew any attempt at rescue was over. Even if you came, you would be overpowered by the trap that lay in wait. So as strange as it sounds, I prayed you wouldn't come." Jack glanced about. "I would be forced to watch you die. I couldn't bear that."

I nodded. "I understand."

"That first day was the worst. I knew it would be bad and I knew it would be hot—" Jack's eyes met mine. Slowly, he began to roll up his sleeves.

I gasped.

The flesh was red and the ghosts of blisters dotted his forearms.

Jack continued, unfazed. "But I didn't figure to burn clean through my clothes."

"Jacky, that must be agony."

Jack rolled his sleeve down again. "It was moment by moment. I couldn't bear to look forward to being rescued."

"No?" I felt very ignorant to hear Jack say the words. And a bit hurt.

"Like I said, I couldn't see any way of my getting out alive, or you getting in alive. So to look forward to being rescued, or finding a way out, was too much."

My head hung on its own. You're a failure Red. Jack needed you, you let him down.

Jack, though, paid me no mind. "So instead of wishing in vain for any hope of getting out alive, I focused my attentions on other things."

"Like what?"

Jack leaned back against the railing of the balcony. "I tried to keep each moment as comfortable as possible. When I came to an uncomfortable moment, or moments, I looked forward to when it would be comfortable again."

"What was it like, Jack?"

The picture Jack painted in my mind was a vivid one, full of sights, smells, sounds, and feelings. With each word, I wished he would say no more, while still praying that he would go on.

"What I didn't account for was the spinning."

I must have looked confused.

"When they hoisted me up on the yardarm, my comfort was the last thing on their mind. Actually, the least comfortable I was, the better, in their eyes." A slow smile spread his lips into a wide smile. "From the moment they hoisted me up, I was spinning. There was nothing I could do to stop it. Reach out, stick out a leg, nothing. I vomited twice and immediately regretted it. But when I looked down—" Jack visibly shuddered. "Once the gibbet finally stopped spinning, I realized how hot it was. The sun reflecting off the waves below me. Oh, the metal. It didn't take long for it to get too hot to touch. And you know as well as I—"

I wanted to hold him. I wanted to take away these horrible memories that I failed to save him from. I wanted to fix it all. But instead, I stood quietly and let him continue.

Jack twiddled his thumbs. "When you get hot, you get thirsty. I tried to ignore that at first and concentrate on when the next breeze would blow through and give me a little respite. They didn't come as often as I would have liked."

"There I was, crammed in that little hot, iron coffin. Couldn't stand up, couldn't sit down. So I crouched the only way I would fit. When the sun set and that first cold, damp chill set in, I thought I was hallucinating when I saw it."

"Saw what?"

"*The Molly Maiden* when she sailed into port, her flag fluttering."

My breath caught in my throat.

"I couldn't pay much attention to what Captain Bon was doing, even though I had a pretty good view from where I hung. By then, the birds had taken a liking to me, thanks to the vomit. And let me tell you, when your throat aches from thirst and your bones shake from cold, fighting piercing beaks through metal slats is even more miserable. And damned near impossible."

Jack caught my chin in his hand. "Don't look so downcast, my love. This story has a happy ending."

I nodded and tried to smile.

"I was fighting off the birds, incessant bastards that they are, when I heard it. Down below. Bon hadn't come to procure more girls like I'd figured was a happy coincidence. Instead, Irish Bon and the girls of *The Molly Maiden* were involved in an absolute massacre—and they had the upper hand."

I thought back to when we took *The Black Otter* back from China Joe. The way Rhodesia sauntered onto my captured ship and took control of some of the most ruthless men on the sea, with nothing but what God gave her between her legs and a simple dagger, and my lips flickered upward. "They can be quite cunning, can't they?"

Jack nodded. "It wasn't until Bon began sawing at the yardarm that I realized they were in port to do more than just restock supplies and pick up fresh girls or whatever macabre they found themselves—she was there for me."

My heart slapped against the inside of my chest. As much as I hated this story, now I wanted—no, *needed*—Jack to continue.

"The men kept coming, and the girls kept taking them out. Each one of them topless, like their flag. Quite the distraction down below, I'm sure."

Angel-Arse Hazel.

"Bon was sawing away. I was excited at first, until I heard it. The crack from the gibbet arm when it cracked was like nothing I'd ever heard before. Praise God Almighty that Bon knew what she was doing when she began her enterprise down below. Had I fallen the other way, toward the land, our story would have had a very different outcome." Jack offered me a wink. "But Irish Bon always has a trick, or a card, damn her, up her sleeve. Before I knew it, I was falling, falling, through the nighttime darkness in a metal coffin. That feeling was terror, close as I've ever felt. When I hit, I hit the sea. Hard."

I closed my eyes, but it did nothing to block out Jack's vivid description of his jailbreak. Trying to put myself in Jack's place, to live through this horror with him, was too much for me. I shook the thoughts away.

"I sucked in a deep breath before I hit but had no idea how long I'd have to hold it. Figured I might drown in that metal frame before Bon could figure out how to fish me out. But if I was going to go down, I was going to fight to the last breath, literally." Jack shrugged off the recent memory as though the hellish experience had only been a story, meant to be told to entertain and then go on your way.

"Anyway, someone grabbed a hold of the rope that had held me aloft and they started to reel me in. Like a fish." He smiled that bright, handsome smile that erased the years and made my heart flutter. "I didn't learn who it was until I got on deck and out of the irons."

I tried not to let the smile dampen.

Angel Arse Hazel. No doubt.

"When I finally stood up, I was on the deck of *The Molly Maiden* and we'd already set out to sea. You can imagine my surprise when I saw a man's face hovering about."

"A man?" My brows knitted across my brow. "I'd never figured Bon to take a man aboard."

"Me neither." Jack peered intently into my face. "His name was Captain Daniel Johnstone. Does that sound familiar to you?"

I thought for a moment. "Actually yes. That does sound familiar. Who is he?"

"He was the fiancé of Monica Joan." Jack's face softened. "The letter that was addressed to him, Bon promised to post it."

"I remember!"

Jack nodded. "She kept her word. Which isn't surprising, especially since she made the promise to you."

I dared a peek at Jack through my watery eyes, searching

his face for any sign of sarcasm, or jealousy. Of course, I found none. "The letter reached him. And it was he who reeled me in like an anchor."

I clapped my hands over my mouth and made no attempt to hide the surge of emotion. I couldn't have hidden it even if I had tried. "Oh Jacky."

Jack stroked the side of my face with his thumb. "He found Bon and came aboard. He offered to join up with *The Black Otter* fleet. In Monica Joan's honor."

A veil of tears blurred my vision.

"She wrote about you. Daniel said, '*I must meet this Redella*'."

Sentiment knotted my tongue. "Bon?" I sniffed back tears. "How is she?"

Jack's eyes were soft. "I figured you'd ask after her, just like she asked after you."

I studied my husband's face and listened to his words. There was no jealousy there, anywhere.

"*All for Redella*, Bon told me as I lay sputtering on her deck. But she didn't stop there. *She loves you*, she said, *and anyone Back from the Dead Red loves doesn't deserve to hang like a dog*."

A strange emotion weighted my happiness. Nostalgia, perhaps?

Jack continued. "I got a bit emotional myself. I grabbed Irish Bon up, once she busted me out of my metal coffin. I twirled her around the whole of the deck." He chuckled to himself. "Half figured her to stab me in the back, but she didn't. Thankfully."

I shook my head. The image of Jack twirling Irish Bon anywhere was a laughable one. "I bet she gave you a cussing."

"Even better." Jack touched his hat. "Said she plucked this hat off a dead man's head and had to make sure I got it back. Then—"

Jack flipped back his coat. Slowly, he drew his jewel-handled cutlass.

"Gave me this back, as well. And a griping to go with it."

I let go a belly laugh as tears streamed down my cheeks. Only these tears weren't borne of sadness. They were borne of happiness. "I can only imagine. What'd she say?"

Jack screwed up his face in jest. "Russian Jack Rackham," he mocked in a bad imitation of Irish Bon. "If that damned sword wasn't so flashy, people wouldn't be wantin' to steal it. Do you realize half my life I've spent recovering your damnedable blade?"

I couldn't help myself. A fit of laughter doubled me over. I let go a whoop. "That sounds like Irish Bon all right!" My face ached from the smile that pushed my lips wide.

Jack continued when I finally stopped laughing. "By the time the pomp died down about my daring escape from the grips of death and it was safe to come back to shore, the first thing I did was come to find you."

Cold stones fell in my gut. *You came to find me and you found me. At the altar, about to wed another man.*

"I heard about your impending wedding. Lucky for me, you chose to marry up with the richest man in Wales. News like that travels fast, even over the sea."

I sucked in a breath and held it. *Oh Jacky—*

Jack ignored me. "And that's how I came to see you now. At your wedding. To another man."

I sobered at the twinge of hurt that colored his words. "Oh Jacky."

I dared a look into my husband's eyes. They twinkled.

"If you want to stay and marry the landlubber Red—you have my blessing."

I cocked my head and stared at him as my hint of a smile faded. *Could it be Jack doesn't want me anymore?*

"You'd have a respectable life," Jack explained. "More money than God. No sad memories. Perhaps even children, someday."

Loreena Jacqueline. My empty arms ached with the memory of the night I became both a mother and a mourner. I squeezed my eyes shut and shook my head. "Please, Jack."

His voice was soft. "God knows you deserve a better life than what I gave you." His arms were around me in a moment. Cradling. Comforting. I melted into them at once.

Jack's breath was warm in my hair. "I love you Redella. My only wish is that your life is a happy one."

Chapter Sixteen

Aboard The Black Otter on the high seas

Where's Cap?" Solo's voice sounded oddly hopeful, though he had to have watched Rusty and me row back to *The Black Otter* from the shore. Solo stood in the middle of the deck and, in the tall black boots, he looked the part of a ship's captain as he handed me Jack's hand-me-down sword.

Tommy sat on the crates along the side, trimming his fingernails with his knife. Poison Lightning descended the ratlines and jumped to the deck. Red Legs stood close to Rusty, who still wore the cloak she'd worn on shore.

We stood there on the newly blackened deck as the blood red sails Rusty had expertly sewn fluttered in the breeze. Anchor was dropped, but the way the waves lapped at the side of the ship, it seemed even *The Black Otter* herself was ready to be on her way.

"There was a trap—" I began.

I glanced back toward shore. Thankfully, I could see nothing. The thought of Jack hanging in the gibbet caused an almost tangible pain in my gut.

"They laid a trap for me. At the base of the gibbet. Where he's hung."

Solo dipped his head. "Is there hope? If I—if we—go to try and bust him out?"

Rusty shook her head. "They said they were purposefully keeping Jack alive in hopes Red would try and rescue him."

Her quiet voice sounded even more meek than usual. "If you tried to rescue him, you'd all hang for piracy. Those of you who survived, would anyway."

"There were so many of them," I said. "Intent on bloodshed. With Jack as the sacrificial lamb."

Solo's lips tightened. "There must be something?"

"There is." I sucked in a breath. "Are the prisoners still locked below decks?"

Tommy piped up from the crates on the side of the deck. "They is, Miss Red, they is."

"Good." I nodded. "Bring me Dark Water and Charles Swan."

The sun was low on the horizon when Dark Water and Charles were brought on deck.

"What do you want with us, Witch," Dark water seethed.

Despite having saved his life in battle, Charles looked at me with hot hate in his eyes.

I ignored the both of them. "Is that how you address your Captain?"

"Captain," Dark Water scoffed. "She's no captain. She's a witch who birthed a monster and killed her husband."

I tried not to let the hurt of his words show on my face. Not now, not ever. The time for sentiment was over. "Dark Water, you sailed with the infamous Captain Kidd, did you not?"

He stared at me, laughter behind his eyes and a sadistic smile on his lips.

"So you should know this well. Aboard Captain Kidd's ship, those who tried to mutiny were punished, were they not?"

The smile faded from Dark Water's face.

"Well, were they?"

Still, Dark Water remained silent.

From the corner of my vision, Red Legs yanked the rope that was tied to Dark Waters' neck, and he yanked hard. Something popped in the tall African. "Answer your captain," he barked.

"She not my captain," Dark Water seethed. He spat in the general direction of Red Legs. "And neither are you."

I cocked an eyebrow. "Captain Kidd had a special punishment for mutineers," I started. I paced before the pair of misfits like a lion I'd seen once in a menagerie. Back and forth. Back and forth. Pacing, staring. Never taking my eyes off my prey. Or my victims. Finally, I stopped in front of Dark Water, so close my breath had to be hot on his face. "He keelhauled them."

Dark Water looked away.

"You already knew that, yet you tried anyway, didn't you?" The red ring came to my vision and every ounce of anger I'd pushed down; losing Jack to losing my daughter; to almost losing my life, came to flaming fruition. "So it's only right that we honor his legacy."

Dark Water's eyes widened and his jaw went slack.

"Red Legs? It's time we keelhauled Dark Water William."

"Yes, Captain." Red Legs didn't change expression as he trussed up the tall African and prepared him for the horrific death that awaited him.

Dark Water, however, did. His coffee eyes bulged and a strange sound strangled in his throat. "No, Miss Red. You can't kill me. You don't have it in you."

I ignored his pleas. "Witches kill all the time, wouldn't you agree Swan?"

Charles Swan ignored me.

Poison Lightning stepped up and looked me squarely in the eye. "Poison Lightning help Red."

He has been waiting a long time for this.

I nodded. "Nail Swan to the deck, feet only. Long nails. He can listen while we keelhaul his lover."

Red Legs dragged Dark Water to the side of the boat. He fought and kicked, but it was no use. In a succession of quick knots, the condemned was tied to the rope that was looped beneath *The Black Otter*. Behind us, Poison Lightning carried out his task to the tune of glass-shattering shrieks from Charles Swan.

"What's keelhaul?" Rusty appeared at my elbow. Her face was

screwed up in horrific planes. "What's going to happen to him?"

I couldn't look at her. Not yet. "That rope that runs under *The Black Otter* there, it is what we use when we dock. Someone has to go down and clean off the barnacles and such. Barnacles are very, very sharp. But today, it's going to bring death to Mr. William."

"Miss Red, please—" Dark Water's pleading words were such that I knew he would say anything to spare his life. "You are not a killer. Or a witch."

I unsheathed my sword and pointed it at his chest. "You tried to kill me when Blackbeard attacked. You were going to kill me if you had the chance when you and Swan tried to mutiny. And what's worse—"

Red tinged my vision again and the words slid over my teeth in a hiss.

"You were going to leave Jack to *hang like a dog*."

I ignored his tears that fell as I approached him. Red Legs stepped back when the last knot attaching Dark Water to the keelhaul rope was tied. I tossed my sword to Solo.

"You're a coward, Dark Water. Die a coward's death." I drew back my arms and shoved him hard. Dark Water William, arms and legs bound and tied to the keelhaul rope, fell into the water with a blubbering shriek.

I spit where he fell then turned my attention to Red Legs. "Much obliged." I held out my hand for the rope. "But I'll carry out his punishment. You don't have to."

Red Legs nodded and surrendered the rope.

I walked the side of the ship to the bow, pulling Dark Water against the ship beneath me.

He was going to kill me.

I continued to the other side and pushed the thoughts of how long it had been since the submerged portion of *The Black Otter* had been cleaned out of my mind.

He and Swan were going to rape Monica Joan.

I tried not to think of how sharp the barnacles must be.

He was going to leave Jack to hang.

He was right. I'm no monster. I took pity on the African and began to run.

"You're merciful to gift him a quick death, you are," Tommy said. "But dead he still is, he is."

In a mere pass or two across the deck of the ship, there was no more resistance against the rope. Dark Water William was dead.

I dropped the rope and, huffing for breath, turned to Charles. Blood pooled around his feet and he stood, awkwardly on our blacker than black deck. "Your britches are soaked through, Charles. I see that you've wet yourself."

I didn't wait for an answer. "Solo, keep watch to make sure we weren't followed." I pointed my blade at Charles Swan. "And you. Planned on leaving Jack to hang. The man who told me that *you* were of the most loyal on the sea. You deserve a fate *worse* than death."

The fleeting thought of beating him to death as he stood, immobile, flashed in my mind. I'd heard of it being done before in Oriental waters, by a madame turned pirate queen.

"You had good in you, remember when I tossed you my steel to save your life when Blackbeard attacked? I was at your mercy and we both knew it—"The red ring was back. "You could have chosen a better way. Instead, here you are. Breathing your last."

Charles whimpered. What hair was left on his head was hanging in his face. Nobody moved to help him tidy it.

"Cannonballs attached to the legs before being tossed overboard, like China Joe had done to me, or being made to walk the plank."

The burst of anger I'd felt before fizzled into numbness. Jack was hanging in a gibbet and I was set to sleep alone. Until the pirate hunters caught up to me, too.

I looked at Red Legs. "I just wanted to be done."

He dipped his head in a knowing nod. "Shall I?"

"No. I will." I cupped my hands around my mouth. "Solo, my sword!"

Solo jogged back from where he'd been standing watch. "Here you are, Cap." He tossed it to me easily.

Without Charles Swan nor I speaking another word, I put the mousey mutineer out of his misery.

Tommy's voice rang out. "Shall I sink them? I can do it well, I can. Cannonball tied to each will sink them both quite fine, it will."

The moon hung, bright and silver, over the distant horizon. Moonbeams reflected off the gentle North Atlantic waves. Any other night, Jack and I would be at the helm, holding each other, in the cool of the evening before retreating below decks to get lost in each other's embrace. Tonight, I was alone. And I was a killer.

Nothing was tranquil anymore.

"Yes, Tommy. Throw the traitors overboard. But don't waste a cannonball on them. Let them float."

I heard Tommy gasp. By not sinking the dead, I was condemning them to an afterlife where they would find no peace. No rest. Everyone killed at sea, no matter how bad they were, received the blessing of being sunk. Like Catholics, receiving the Last Rites.

But I wasn't a priest and I wasn't going to extend any kindness to mutineers, not to Charles and not to Dark Water. They would receive no sympathy from me in this life nor the one to come.

"Solo," I called. "Can I see you for a moment? In the wheelhouse." I didn't look at Tommy, who stood open-mouthed, as I stomped by.

I reached the wheelhouse first. Solo stepped in behind me. "What can I—"

My mouth was a hard line as I began fidgeting with my belt.

"Red, what are you—" Solo sputtered, looked away, and immediately stepped back out.

Typical man.

I ignored his hesitance and yanked off my belt and blade. "Here, Solo."

A look of astonishment replaced his nervous façade. "Red, I don't understand."

I tried to smile, but it was futile. "I'm not running this outfit without Jack." I held my belt and blade out to him. "So I'm turning it over to you."

Solo accepted my sword and turned it over in his hands. He sucked in a deep breath and pursed his lips before he dared look at me. "Was there any way to bust him out, Red?"

The silence grew louder and filled the space between us in the cramped wheelhouse. I shook my head. "I don't know. But I know I have to try. I couldn't try anything on shore, because I couldn't risk Rusty getting captured."

Solo nodded. "Was there really a trap?"

"Yes. And so many men guarding the gibbet. I can't figure a way to get to Jack, but I'll have plenty of time to figure if out—" I glanced at my friend. "If you'll be so kind as to lend me the rowboat tonight. If I go to shore under the cover of darkness, maybe there's a chance."

"It goes without saying, Red. But someone should come with you."

I shook my head. "Whoever comes with me is likely to hang. As am I, if I'm caught."

"Doesn't matter. I can't send you into almost certain—" Solo cut himself off. "I can't send you into a dangerous situation alone. I'll come with you myself." His bright eyes sparkled and his eyebrows arched skyward.

"Is it your princely background that makes you think you're right?"

Solo shrugged, a small smile finally gracing his lips. "Perhaps."

Best to appease him. I nodded. "It's a deal. But none of the crew can know."

"Agreed, then." He held my blade back out to me and winked. "Better hold onto this little beauty though. You know, just in case you might need it."

Almost as soon as I closed the door to my sadly empty bunk,

fully clothed and waiting for the ship to go to sleep, the unthinkable happened. Howling wind whistled outside the portholes and shrieked through the blackwashed boards. Patters of rain dotted the windows as I pushed myself to my feet. Much too nervous to even sit still, I paced the bunk I shared with my late husband.

All jittery, I pulled one of Jack's shirts and a pair of his britches over my own clothes. I rummaged in the trunk until I found his long, black coat and donned it, too. By the time I closed the door to my bunk and made the climb upstairs to the deck, the wind was howling and the rain pounded down in sheets. Solo was there.

"Poison Lightning's on watch." He had to yell to be heard over the gale-force wind. "But judging by this weather, I think we'd be better advised to wait and go tomorrow night."

My breath came quicker. "How long can he live in the gibbet?" It felt strange to scream the words into the wet wind.

"About three days."

I glanced overboard at the rowboat that pitched against the side of the ship. The lights of shore flickered through the squall. "At least this rain will give him something to drink." Thinking of Jack's dry, parched throat made me physically hurt. I looked back at Solo. "You're probably right about going in the morning."

He patted my shoulder. "Get some sleep, Red. We'll take care of Jack, don't worry." His bright smile shone from under his hood. "You have my word."

I nodded and returned his smile. "Thank you, Solo. For everything."

I watched as my faithful cohort trotted off across the deck, back to where he would climb down into his warm, dry bunk. Once he was safely out of sight, I sprinted back toward the room I'd shared with Jack. Instead of climbing down the stairs, I unhooked my belt and saber and stashed it on the stairs to the captain's quarters. Steeling my reserve, I pulled the door shut and dashed back across the deck to the rope ladder that lay, unused, in an innocent coil.

I flung it over the side.

I'm coming Jacky.

I threw one leg over the side, then the other, before daring a glance up to the eagle's nest. Though the sheets of rain had turned white and opaque, I could make out The Poison Lightning's hand as it waved to me in wide waves.

Did you cause this storm, my unlikely friend? For me? For Jack?

I threw him a salute before climbing down the rope ladder, toward the rowboat. The wind whipped me this way and that, sometimes beating me against the ship like a human hammer. My fingers smashed with each fling as I tried to adjust my grip on the rope.

I only made the mistake of looking down once. The scourging waves, whitecapped and frothy, looked angry. Hungry. I squeezed my eyes shut and tried not to think about what sea creatures lay in wait below. White-knuckled, I gripped the ladder and felt for each sopping rung.

Just a little more. Surely you're almost there, Red.

Raindrops felt like needles as I forced myself down, down, down, toward the tempestuous sea. I was powerless to look down, even if I wanted to, for fear I'd be blinded if I opened my eyes.

Then, I heard it. Like thunder, but lower. Angrier. Wetter. The rogue wave built up speed and sounded like one of those new, impossibly loud steam pumps that miners used to pump water out of flooded mines. I braced myself and gripped the ladder with all my strength before the devil of a wave met the side of *The Black Otter* and like the hand of God.

I was made helpless by the wrath of the wave. It tore me easily from my ladder.

A scream, lost to the wind, tore from my throat as my fingers reached for something, anything, as I fell. Jack's face flashed to the forefront of my mind, followed by the ghastly gibbet.

Please—don't let me die like this. Not until I have a chance to at least try and save Jack. So he knows I didn't abandon him.

My back arched as I hit the bottom of the rowboat.

Thank you, God.

I ignored the throbbing in my battered body and unhooked the rowboat's rope from *The Black Otter* and with shaky hands. I fumbled for the oars with aching arms. The wind screamed in my ears, like a siren calling sailors to their deaths, as I pulled hard against the swell.

"There's nothing standing between me and Jack now," I called to nobody. "Only a stormy sea, a rocky coast, and a mob of angry killers." My voice dropped with the more things I named, but something deep down made my arms work harder against the wind, the rain, and the white-capped waves.

Not long after I started rowing, I began to think that Solo was right in his desire to wait until morning.

I shook the thought off at once. If I had waited, then Solo would have tried to accompany me to shore. I could not risk Solo getting caught by the bloodthirsty lot of pirate hunters.

Caught and hung.

I forced a swallow and tried not to think about what a scratchy rope around my neck would feel like. Sheets of torrential rain came in unending undulation and erased everything from my sight. Eyes closed fast against the driving rain, I was effectively blinded. Incessant waves slapped me from first this way, then from that. I dared a peek at the world around me though it did no good.

Am I even going toward the shoreline? There were no more lights to guide me and it felt as though I'd been turned a thousand different ways by the storm.

Am I even rowing?

A huge wave washed over me and my tiny boat and ripped one of the oars from my hands. I scrambled to grab it, but missed. It disappeared into the bubbling sea.

The first oar was lost to the wave. The second, to my stupidity in grabbing for the first one.

Oh no. Not only is Jack going to lose his life, but you're going to lose yours, too, Red.

I ducked my head into Jack's large jacket and fought my way into the bottom of the boat. I jammed myself beneath the little seat and curled up as tight as I could. The waves threatened to pitch me out into the churning, angry sea, but in a stroke of luck, I held on and my tiny boat didn't capsize.

I would like to think I didn't cry, but I'm fairly certain I did. It was no matter though, since any screams of mine could not be heard over the shrieking winds.

The sickening crack from the side of my little rowboat woke me from a nightmarish sleep.

What the—

Thwack!

I dared a peek at my surroundings. Jagged rocks rose up all around me.

Smack!

I'm being beaten against the rocky coast.

Crunch!

Oh Lord, it's really happening.

Wham!

I skimmed the shore, but there were no lights, only rocks for as far as I could see. Which wasn't far.

This doesn't look right. Where am I?

Crack!

An angry wave pulled me back and smacked me hard into a sharp rock.

That's the one that is going to seal my fate, right there.

I was correct. My tiny boat split in two and with a frothy surge, icy storm water rushed in. I grabbed for the craggy rocks, my fingertips digging for any kind of hold. I pressed all my weight against the rock and started to climb as the water yanked at my heavy legs.

Just a little more—

Before I could swing my numb leg onto the rock, my fingers slipped and I slid into the ocean. I ignored the slicing pain as the water-sharpened rocks slit my palms. I planted my feet and tried again, feeling with my feet for anything to use as leverage. The tip of my boot caught the remnants of *The Black Otter's* rowboat, as the boat succumbed to the violent waves.

I clung to the unforgiving rocks like the little gray cat-creature, the ring-tailed lemur, had clung to the Queen of Madagascar's shoulder.

The image of Jack hanging in the gibbet flashed into my mind with white-hot precision. I pushed it away and tried to focus only on climbing the rock, even as the sharp edges bit into my palms and knees. Exhaustion gripped my arms and legs, threatening to send me sprawling back into the sea.

To my death. And Jack's.

Lightning flashed around and illuminated the hopeless scene. Angry, white-capped swells lunged at the rocks and tried to wash me away. Thunder boomed and drowned out everything except for the infernal roar of the sea. I closed my eyes and forced my muscles to pull my weary frame up the rocks—or be dashed against them.

When I awoke, the world was quiet.

Am I dead? Is this heaven?

The storm was over, the bed was soft, and a kind-faced woman leaned over me.

"Where am I?" My voice was a whisper over my dry, cracked lips.

"Why, you're in hospital. In Wales." She smiled and held a spoon of broth to my lips. "Welcome back from the dead, madam."

Chapter Seventeen

Swansea, Wales

Charles Hoolihan fidgeted with his blade. A few of the wedding guests had trickled out when the snippets of conversation that wafted in through the open windows from the balcony turned bloody. Others sat more attentive, backs straight in their pews, not daring to whisper for fear they might miss the next exchange between the woman who was almost Mrs. Charles Hoolihan and her notorious pirate husband who was rumored to be dead, but so clearly was not.

Everything about what should have been the happiest day of his life was already destined to be Swansea gossip for years to come. He dug in first one hairy ear with his finger, then the other.

The harpist rose from her stool with a huff. "Mr. Hoolihan, if I may," she began. The room silenced. "I suggest you either go get your bride or leave with what dignity you have left."

Voices muttered their agreement from the pews.

"They needed time to catch up is all." Charles wiped his finger on his vest. "Drucilla will come back in when she's ready. It isn't as though she'll clamber down the balcony with that notorious pirate, now is it?" Charles chuckled to himself, but nobody joined him. He stood there at the wedding altar, smiling, but he was chuckling alone.

The harpist shifted her weight and squeaked. "Her name is Back from the Dead Red, Charles, didn't you hear her? By her own admission. She is a murdering pirate, just like Russian Jack. Didn't you see the scar on her face?"

Charles hung his head like a whipped pup.

He didn't lift his feet as he shuffled toward the balcony. With a halfhearted glance over his shoulder that bespoke defeat more than desire, Charles flung open the door. He peeked outside, then boldly stuck his head over the threshold. "Oh my."

"Well, Charles?" The harpist's voice clanged out like a cracked church bell. "What is it?"

Charles didn't answer. He only quickened his lumbering steps and disappeared onto the balcony. It was empty.

The veil he'd insisted on buying for his young bride fluttered like a wounded bird on the stone floor. The muggy breeze brought it to life only for a moment. When the breeze passed, the veil, like a brief afterthought of the marriage that almost was, lay dead again.

Charles flexed his swollen fingers, put his plump hand to his brow, and scanned the distance. There was nothing at all out of the ordinary. The waves curled over the rocky shore. Seabirds swooped and called. There was a black dot far, far out on the sea. It sort of looked like a ship, sailing in fair winds, toward the horizon—or perhaps into a distant fog.

I pulled myself up the rope ladder. Muscles, tight and forgotten, sprang to life with the familiar movements I'd missed so much. Moments after leaving the rowboat that took us from the mainland to the side of *The Black Otter*, that bobbed, waiting, around a rocky outcropping, I caught up to my husband. I tapped the bottom of his boot to hurry him along.

"Somebody has missed climbing ratlines and ladders, I see." I didn't need to see Jack's handsome face to know that he was smiling.

Jack pulled himself onto the deck and turned to offer me his hand. Ever playful and grateful to be home, I stared into his eyes and finished the climb myself. A wave of emotion rolled over me as I pushed up onto the black boards of the ship I so dearly loved and missed more with each memory that came rushing back.

The smell of the boards, like an old seaside library on a rainy day. Their achy creaks as they swayed with the ever-present ebb and flow of the tide. My heart quickened to a gallop, just as it had when I pulled myself up this ladder behind Russian Jack for the first time, so long ago.

Sully's face flashed to mind without warning. His smug smile as he sat behind the wheel of *The Scarlet Rose*, as he carried with him to the islands a lost, hopeless bride and a boat loaded full of dirty secrets. Russian Jack and *The Black Otter Fleet* saved me from the hell that might have been.

Sully's memories elicited no emotion from me other than gratitude to Jack, but seeing the side of *The Black Otter* certainly did. My nail marks in the wood, where I struggled to stay aboard after having cannon balls attached to my legs, were still there. Painted over black, but still there. I ran my finger over them and shuddered.

"This might help with those *less* than idyllic memories." Jack held out my sword—*his* sword—and belt. "Solo found these stashed in our cabin stairs. Why did you choose not to bring them when you left on the row boat?"

"I dared not risk losing them. That sword is much too precious."

Jack covered my hand in his. Still, I felt the marks from my fingernails. "My darling girl, you are what's precious."

I smiled up at him, but a tremble shook me.

"Red?"

"The fear, when China Joe—" My voice refused to rise above a whisper. Still, the words strangled in my throat. "I don't know how to explain it, Jack."

Jack simply nodded. He seemed to follow my reminiscent train of thought. "He was a bad one, wasn't he?"

I nodded and closed my eyes. "Because of him, Monica Joan never reached her love."

Emotions I hadn't anticipated washed over me like a rogue wave. Tears sprang to my eyes and my throat clenched tight. "Oh Jack, Monica Joan."

"I know, my love. I know." He took me in his arms. "If not for her beloved, I would be resting at the bottom of the sea right now."

"Speaking of Monica Joan—" A man's voice I didn't recognize came from somewhere. I looked around.

"Jack, who—"

A tall man in an even taller black hat stepped forward. He was dressed as though he'd just stepped freshly off a London street, or right out of Buckingham Palace. "Thank you for being such a true friend to her."

He extended his hand.

"You must be Captain Daniel Johnstone." I grabbed his hand and pulled him into a hug. "Thank you for saving my husband, Captain."

"Thank you, my dear girl. For loving Monica Joan when she needed someone most." He hugged me back, with quivering arms. "You were her angel, you know."

An angel.

Captain Johnstone released me from our embrace. When he stepped back, he had tears on his salt-and-pepper bearded cheek. It was enchanting to look into the face that Monica Joan loved. His face showed no expression apart from the tears as he disappeared into the throng of our crewmates.

"Our daughter." The tears ran freely down my cheeks as I whispered to my husband. My insides ached with a righteous, empty ache. A *mourning* ache. An ache that would never, could never be filled, ever again, even if I had a thousand more children. "She's not here."

Jack cupped my face and slid his thumb along the blade scar on my cheek. "And her absence is sorely felt. By all."

"She was an angel, Jack." Destined to be ever empty, my arms yearned for my beautiful baby girl. "*Our* angel."

"We'll see her again, Red." The tone of sincerity in Jack's voice made me believe that would be true.

Someday.

"In the meantime, somebody else can't wait to see you."

Rusty, big with child, waved. Her wide, bright smile was colored in relief.

"Rusty!" With her auburn hair flowing and her face glowing, she had never looked prettier. "I have so much to catch up on!"

"Red Legs married me!" She grasped her little baby bump and beamed. "It was *killing* me to not be able to tell you."

I sniffled and opened my arms wide. "Pregnancy agrees with you, Rusty."

She rushed into my arms. "Mama," she whispered into my shoulder. "Thank God you're home. I could *not* have this baby without you."

"Yes you could." I gave her a squeeze. She made no move to let me go. "You can do anything."

Her sweet voice, one I thought I'd never hear again, was quiet so that only I could hear. "I prayed that you'd come back. Every night and all the day. Sometimes, Red Legs even prayed with me."

I gave her shoulders a final squeeze and held her at arm's length. Her hazel eyes matched the color of the Welsh sea. "Tell me something. Is Red Legs treating you well?"

"Yes, he is." She wiped her nose across the back of her hand. "Sorry Mama, I just get so emotional."

"Never apologize, Rusty. You've done nothing wrong."

She wrapped me in a hug again. "Thank God you're home."

Red Legs joined us. For the first time since I'd come to know him, he was smiling. "Welcome home, Back from the Dead Red."

Rusty grabbed his hand.

"Such a difference in this girl," I said.

Rusty blushed as I sang her praises. "When she came aboard *The Black Otter,* she was a scared captive. I never dreamed she'd beg to stay aboard as mine and Jack's daughter. Only to become wife to the most unlikely pirate."

Like his wife, Red Legs flushed as red as Rusty's hair.

"Thank you, Red Legs."

He is smile widened.

Behind Rusty and Red Legs, Solo and Poison Lightning's movements caught my eye. "Hey," I began, "what are they—"

I cut off my thought and slapped my hands over my eyes. "Lord above!"

Poison Lightning pretended to nail Solo's feet to the deck with an imaginary hammer. Solo flailed his arms and cried, just as Charles Swan had the night I truly took control of *The Black Otter*. In tandem, both Solo and Poison Lightning stopped and looked at me with mischievous grins.

"Why, it's a reenactment, just for you. Of your bloodiest moment." Jack spoke from beside me. "When they retire from pirating, I believe the two of them could make a go of it in a theatre troupe."

I shook my head and howled. "I can't—" Tears, this time of a different sort, streamed down my face as I watched Solo and Poison Lightning go back to their nailing.

"Over here, over here," Tommy cried from beside the rope that, that fateful night, doubled as the keelhaul rope for Dark Water William. He jumped up and down, and his paunchy belly bounced over his britches. "Tie me up and push me over!"

I buried my face in Jack's shoulder as a rabid flush burned in my neck and face. "Seeing everything you missed, Jack, from your brutal killer of a wife?"

"I've heard about and these things and more, my love."

I pushed back from Jack. "Oh I cannot even imagine what you have—"

My words died on my tongue as Bon's face appeared over Jack's shoulder. Of course, her garb was mannish and ragged and heavy with salt. Her brown hair stuck out this way and that, as wild and untamed as the waves themselves. The dagger on her belt gleamed as she reached out toward me.

"No downcast faces when Irish Bon is about." I could hear

the smile in Jack's voice. "Say hello to the woman who saved your husband's life."

"That she did, too many times to count!" With a belly laugh, I took Bon's outstretched hand.

"Look who's alive after all!" Bon turned me a circle, as though we were on a dance floor back in London. We swept across the deck to a song only we knew, laughing and smiling. Her arms tightened around me as we made our way back round to where Jack stood, clapping and smiling along with everyone else.

"Welcome home." The words were a whisper on her lips as Bon dipped me low. She pressed her mouth to mine in a kiss that raised catcalls from the crew. Passionate. Lasting. Like a promise that would be kept even if I didn't keep mine.

Russian Jack smiled and held out his hand as our dance ended. I took it but watched my precious friend.

Irish Bon stepped backward into the throng of crew. Something in her eyes dimmed as Jack wrapped me in his arms. My own smile took on a hint of sadness.

"My precious friend." I kissed my fingers and held them out to her. She kissed her fingers, too. Before she could hold them out to me, I saw a tear slide down her cheek.

Jack's voice was warm in my ear. His breath on my skin sent excited sparks down my neck. Other muscles ached with anticipation of what the night held in store for my husband and me. "Welcome home, Back from the Dead Red," he whispered, "to what is already yours."

This book was inspired by the lives of historical women who just happened to be pirates. But where there are women, there are also men. Below you will find a list of the actual pirates, who lived their lives and sailed the seas and in doing so, inspired this book.

Edward Low—1690–1724. Edward, or Ned, was an English pirate during the Golden Age of Piracy. He was markedly cruel and even earned the titles of bloodthirsty and wicked. It was said by those who served upon on his ships, that Low murdered out of "passion and resentment." Ned inspired Charles Swan.

Red Legs Greaves—abt. 1649–1700. Red Legs was a Scottish man born into slavery in Barbados. He became a sailor then a pirate, though he was called even then "the gentleman pirate". He was captured and tried for piracy and sentenced to death. A freak earthquake that demolished the prison which held him gave him the chance to escape. He earned a royal pardon and retired from piracy and became a philanthropist. He inspired Red Legs Roberts.

Mary Read—1690–1721. An English pirate also known as her late brother's name, Mark. Her mother raised her as a boy and she continued to dress as a man the remainder of her life.

She came to work on Calico Jack Rackham's ship where Anne Bonney was also on board. The two were fast friends and may have been lovers. When Rackham's ship was overrun, everyone aboard was tried for piracy and sentenced to death. Mary and Anne, found to be pregnant, weren't executed with the others but Mary died of fever while in prison. There was no record of her child being born. Mary inspired Redella and Irish Bon.

Anne Bonney—1700–1782. Anne was an Irish pirate whose father dressed her as a boy and called her Andy. She was said to be a red head with a temper to match. She supposedly married Calico Jack Rackham, but was probably in a relationship with Mary Read, too. There is no record of her dying or being executed after she and Read "pled the belly" at their trial for piracy. She inspired Redella and Irish Bon.

Thomas Tew—abt. 1640–1695. English sailor-turned-pirate. He is rumored to be the father of Ratsimilaho, who created a kingdom in Madagascar. Tew may have created a pirate colony called Libertatia, which may or may not be real. Captain William Kidd, before he was a pirate, was commissioned by King William III to hunt down Thomas Tew. He inspired Tommy Tew.

John "Calico Jack" Rackham—12/26/1682–11/18/1720. Calico Jack was an English pirate who was known for wearing calico clothing. He, along with Anne Bonney and Mary Read, operated during the Golden Age of Piracy and his first mate, Karl Starling, designed the Jolly Roger flag. He was hung for piracy and has a cay named for him in Jamaica, where he was executed. It is said that his wife, Anne Bonney, told him upon their capture that, "Had you fought like a man, you need not been hang'd like a dog". He inspired Russian Jack.

Ching Shih—1775—1844. Ching was a Chinese prostitute who turned to piracy when her brothel was captured, and she married the pirate captain. Known for her brutality and her code which favored women's fair treatment, Ching grew to be the most successful pirate in history, even after her husband died. Her strict code, or articles, were adapted as the articles in this book. She was pardoned for her piratical acts later in life and opened a gambling house. She inspired Redella.

Grace O'Malley—1530–06/18/1603. Irish pirate who spoke Gaelic and Latin, but no English. She met with Queen Elizabeth of England and refused to bow and was even carrying a dagger, though she swore she meant Elizabeth no harm. Though married, she rescued a shipwrecked man fifteen-years her junior and he became her lover. When he was killed, she turned revolutionary. She is still a popular Irish folk figure. Grace inspired the women in this book.

Anne Dieu-Le-Veut—08/28/1661–01/11/1710. She was a French pirate. Her husband was killed in a barfight by pirate Laurens de Graff. He insulted her, as well. To avenge her husband, she challenged de Graff to a duel. De Graff was so taken aback, he proposed to her instead. She accepted. Anne inspired Redella.

Christina Anna Skytte—November 9, 1643–January 21, 1677. Christina Anna was a Swedish baroness and a pirate who was an active participant in brutal pirate activities alongside her husband. Christina inspired the women in this book.

Jacquotte Delahaye—A French-Haitian whose best days came around 1656. She was a female buccaneer who faked her own death and assumed a male identity. When she revealed herself later, she was known as Back from the Dead Red, on account of her red hair. Jacquotte inspired the title of this book, and the main character.

Racheal Wall—1760–October 8, 1789. Racheal was attacked by a group of girls on a dock, only to be rescued by George Wall, a small-time pirate. They married and began their life of thievery and pirating. After storms, Racheal would stand on their deck and scream for help. Any who came to their aid was murdered and their vessels, looted. After George and his crew washed out to sea, Racheal attempted to steal a girl's bonnet and rip out her tongue. She was sentenced to die by hanging and was the first American woman to become a pirate, and the last woman to be hung. Racheal inspired the women in this book.

Black Caesar—born in west Africa and was hanged for piracy in Williamsburg, Virginia in 1718. He sailed with Blackbeard and was an African who would never be a slave. Big, strong, and smart, he was able to outwit the slave traders every time. Rumors of his buried treasure have never come to fruition. He kept a harem on a rocky island named for him, but left them no food or water, so many died. Dark Water William is based on this legendary pirate.

Charles Swan—A reluctant and arrogant pirate who wound up speared in the water in 1690. Charles was inspired by this pirate of the same name.

Some of the prostitutes aboard The Molly Maiden were also taken from colorful wenches of the day.

Mary Carleton, or orphaned **Princess von Wolway of Cologne**—January 11, 1642–January 22, 1673. Mary took on many false identities and defrauded countless men, many of which were too embarrassed by their having been taken to report her. She was tried for bigamy when she was found to be married to two men at the same time. She was banished from Europe to Jamaica, but when she was discovered to have come back to England an assumed identity, she was sentenced to death and hanged.

Salt-Beef Peg of Port Royal—An infamous Port Royal prostitute; it cost 500 pieces-of-eight just to see her naked.

Unconscionable Nan and **Buttocks-de-Clink Jenny**—Port Royal prostitutes who worked alongside Salt-Beef Peg. To spend the night with one of these drinking, swearing, promiscuous ladies-of-the-evening would cost a pirate 2-3,000 pieces-of-eight per night.

But what are pieces-of-eight?

Pieces-of-eight were silver Spanish coins that were worth eight Spanish reales, which were the currency at the time. However, pieces-of-eight became popular and were used as currency all over the world from the Americas to the Orient—and especially by the pirate faction.

The funeral for Loreena followed the traditional pirate funeral and burial at sea traditions as outlined in *A General History of the Pyrates*.

About the Author

Sara Harris is the author of more than fifteen books in a variety of genres for both children and adults. She lives with her family—including a number of rescue pets—in a small town west of Houston, Texas, where the sunsets are gorgeous, the ice cream is perfection, and the ocean is close enough to visit each weekend.

Sara has her Bachelor of Arts degree in History and is currently enrolled in nursing school.

Visit Sara online at

https://saraharrisbooks.com/

Also Available From

WordCrafts Press

Fiery Red Hair, Emerald Green Eyes, and a Vicious Irish Temper
Ralph E. Jarrells

Demimonde
James E. Cressler

A Pale Horse
Michelle A. Sullivan

Saturday and the Witch Woman
Thomas O. Ott

www.wordcrafts.net